THE MURDERER'S GIRL

THE MURDERER'S GIRL

A
DETECTIVE
CALLIE FORDE
MYSTERY

K.L. MURPHY

For those we miss. May they always be with us.

Chapter One

Now

Gordon Little knew chicken wings. He'd prepared thousands of them and eaten almost as many. There was something rewarding about standing over a hot grill and flipping wing after wing, watching for the char marks and adding exactly the right amount of sauce to caramelize the skin without drowning the thing. Just the smell of charcoal and wood chips made him happier, bringing back memories of his grandfather and, by extension, his brother.

Max learned to grill first. Gordon remembered how proud his brother had been the first time he'd grilled a burger that lived up to their grandfather's standards, how the family had talked endlessly about that burger, the way the cheese had melted just enough to become gooey without losing its shape. Even now, Gordon avoided grilling burgers. Those belonged to Max and always would. Wings were Gordon's specialty.

For a brief time, Gordon had considered opening his own barbecue and wing joint, but that took money, something he'd never had much of. Initially, he'd sought backers—starting at home—but his track record kept getting in the way.

"You're a college dropout," his uncle had said, wiping his sauce-covered lips with a napkin. "Why would I give you money?"

Gordon had eyed the man's empty plate, cocking his head toward the grill.

"Okay, okay. So, your wings are good." He'd pointed a finger at his young nephew as he spoke. "And you've got guts. I'll give you that." Gordon's heart had beaten a hair faster, and he'd sucked in his breath. "But what do you know about running a business, kid?" He'd pushed his plate of gnawed bones away. "No can do."

His parents hadn't been much better. "How does that square with the money we've already shelled out for school? Money we'll never see again." He'd stopped listening before they got to his lack of a diploma or began comparisons to Max.

Even his sister had turned him down. "Gordon, I love you, but you're the kid who goes from one obsession to another. Remember how you were going to be a golf course designer and then it was extreme sports, and what was it before that?" she'd asked as she tapped a finger against her lower lip. "Oh, yes, you were going to make movies." Her voice had softened when she looked at him, one light eyebrow arched. "How much have you raised so far?"

"A thousand from Nana."

She hadn't said anything for a moment. "Do mom and dad know she gave you money?"

"I'm not sure."

"Which means no. Geez, Gord." Creases had appeared between her brows. "Just don't waste it, okay?"

He hadn't, or at least he didn't think he had, even if making a true crime podcast was a far cry from running a wing joint. He'd paid Nana back, or mostly anyway.

Gordon stared down at the chicken wing in his hand now, examining it for a full minute before dropping it back in the paper-lined basket. Although starred on the Hampstead Tavern menu, he suspected the sauce on the Asian-style wings was more ketchup and soy sauce than teriyaki and ginger. But if the tasteless wings left something to be desired, at least the beer was cold, the barstools next to him empty, and the pretzels salty and crunchy.

The bartender, a burly man with a white beard that extended to his chest, nodded toward the half-eaten wing. "Somethin' wrong?"

"Nope," Gordon lied. "Just wasn't as hungry as I thought." He picked up his mug. "Am thirsty though. One more?"

"Sure. It's a bar, ain't it?"

The big man refilled the mug, setting it back down with a thump. He glanced around the mostly empty tavern and lowered his voice. "You the reporter I heard been askin' questions?"

Gordon drank, savoring the hoppy flavor before wiping the foam from his mouth with the back of his hand. "I'm not really a reporter, more of a podcaster." The man blinked. "You listen to it on an app or download it."

"Oh yeah, I've heard of that. Don't listen to them myself. I got satellite radio, though." He wiped his own hands on the stained apron tied around his thick waist. "Gotta name?"

"Gordon Little."

"Buck Miller." He thrust out a meaty hand before resting his forearms on the scarred wooden bar. "See that pair over there?" he asked, nodding his head toward the corner. "Cops."

The podcaster, recognizing the two local detectives, let out a soft groan. Since he started making true crime podcasts, he ran into two types of people. The first tended to be overly helpful, eager to be a part of whatever mystery he was trying to solve. He was grateful, of course, but the eager ones weren't usually the ones with any answers. The second kind held back. They were short on words and long on suspicion. In Gordon's experience—limited though it was—the police fell into the second group. Not that he blamed them. No cop wanted to be told that a snot-nosed twenty-nine-year-old college dropout could show up and clear cases that had been sitting on the books for a decade or more. Well, one case if he were being honest, the Hamilton Hayes case, the one that put him on the podcasting map. Even he didn't know where he'd gotten the gumption to do it, but now here he was, sitting in a dark tavern in a small Virginia town, digging around a new case.

Aloud, Gordon said, "We met today. Henderson and Chang."

"Oh, yeah? How'd that go?"

"Welcomed me with open arms," Gordon said. "Thrilled to have me here trampling all over one of their cases."

The bartender chuckled and shook his head. "Yeah, I'll bet they were."

Gordon lifted a hand in the direction of the detectives. Neither returned his greeting. The older one, Henderson, had a friendly enough face, but the other one, Chang, looked as though he'd sucked on an entire bag of lemons. Gordon figured he'd be wise to steer clear of Chang whenever possible. Besides, he still hoped to meet with the captain, and he didn't need any bad words before he got an interview—*if* he got an interview. Sighing, he swung back around on his stool.

Buck eyed a man at the end of the bar nursing a whiskey but stayed where he was. "Guess the news about the Lawson thing brought you here, huh? That's what your podcast is about?"

The younger man didn't answer right away. It was true the headlines had been part of the reason he'd come to Hampstead, but not the only one. He wasn't like the rest of the media hounds. They chased whatever story was the flavor of the day, landing just long enough to shine their lights and point their microphones before taking off to report the next big thing. Scandals ruled, the juicier the better. As scandals went, this one ranked high enough, but a small-town murder was just that—small town—maybe good for a *Dateline* episode on a slow night. Gordon could hear the narrator's voice in his head now. "Who really killed Lisa Lawson, a loving wife and devoted mother, along with her best friend, Tina Cox? And how exactly did the police get this so-oo wrong?" The cheese factor would be high.

But the police did get it wrong. Lisa Lawson and Tina Cox had been dead for more than fifteen years, and for most of that time, Lisa's husband had been serving time for their murders. Harry Lawson insisted he was innocent, although he didn't seem to have too many supporters. After the trial, he'd fought his conviction but fell short of getting an appeal. He was dead now, too, falling over in his cell one morning, his heart giving out after a long illness. But that wasn't what made the case interesting. A long-buried video had surfaced after Harry's death showing he was in D.C. the day of the murders, exactly as he'd claimed. Half the country had seen it by now. Harry Lawson had turned out to be every police department and prosecuting attorney's nightmare, an *actual* innocent man.

The media had descended as they do, but it wasn't long before another headline drew them away. Without any new evidence or a new suspect, there wasn't much to chew on. Of course, they didn't have the one thing Gordon had and the real reason he'd come to this small town: Lynnleigh Lawson, Lisa and Harry's only surviving child.

Gordon set his beer mug back on the bar. "Do you know much about what happened?" he asked Buck now.

"Not a lot, but hell, you'll have no shortage of opinions around here if you're lookin' for 'em," the bartender said. "Harry Lawson didn't have too many friends 'fore his wife got killed and probably none after he went away. Now they're saying he was wrongfully convicted. That ain't sittin' too well with some folks."

"The evidence says he was innocent." Gordon saw no need to argue further. Enough had already been reported to bother.

The big man lifted his wide shoulders. "I ain't sayin' he wasn't. Only that the evidence said he was guilty fifteen years ago. What about that evidence?"

"It was wrong."

"See? There you go. If it was wrong then, maybe it's wrong now." The bartender wiped up a spill from the bar. "Harry Lawson was a strange guy. Not the kind of strange that means it's obvious you're gonna go off one day and kill your wife and her best friend, but strange. He served, you know. A veteran, so I'm not blaming him, but he could get a little paranoid, if you know what I mean. Anyway, people didn't have that tough a time believing it."

Gordon leaned in, lowering his voice. "Had he been in any trouble?"

"Some. He'd had some problems at his shop. Got robbed a couple times. Kids mostly. Word is he planned to put in a mess of cameras but those cost money. If he had his way, he'd have locked it down tight, like some kind of Army ground operation."

"Do you mean The Hampstead Market?"

"Yep. Family sold it after. Heard the brother used what little money it got to put the daughter through school." This Gordon already knew.

A couple came through the doors then, the woman's hair rising with the gust of hot summer air that blew in with them. The pair nodded at Buck, who returned the greeting. "Well," he said, "Where was I?"

"Harry Lawson's brother."

"Right. Ned raised the daughter. She went off to school and was gone for a while, but she came back last year."

"Do you see her around much?"

"Not to speak of. She's been in a couple of times is all."

"Does she come in alone?" Gordon did his best to keep his voice casual. "With anyone else?"

"Alone."

"So, not many friends?" The bartender shrugged. "How've people been around her?"

"You mean before or after the news came out?"

"Both, I guess. According to the articles I've seen, she's been pretty vocal about her dad's innocence for a long time."

Buck scratched at his chin, his long beard bobbing up and down with the motion. "Yeah, she has. I think most people chalked it up to denial. Ain't too many kids who want to believe one of their parents killed the other one. Especially not the way Lisa Lawson…" his mouth closed, any words he'd been about to say dying on his tongue.

Gordon didn't comment. Lisa's murder had been the kind that made a person know it was personal. In comparison, the friend's murder had seemed quick, clean even. It was one of the many reasons the police had homed in on Harry Lawson. "And after?"

"Can't really say for sure. I'm sure Lynnleigh's got her supporters. She's got family here—Ned and his wife, a couple of cousins—but a lot of folks ain't buying it. Can't say I really blame 'em."

Gordon thought maybe he should be surprised, but he wasn't. Small towns had a way of staying the same, being resistant to change and upheaval. He ought to know. He'd spent the first eighteen years of his life in an Indiana town not much different than this one.

"Why's that?" he asked now.

The man's jaw tightened, and his face flushed. "Because if it's true Harry Lawson didn't kill his wife and Tina Cox, that would mean someone else did. Someone else who gets up and goes to work every day like you and me. Someone who maybe has kids. Comes in for a beer after work." He paused, and Gordon waited. "Someone else in Hampstead who could do that to a woman." He shook his head again. "If you lived here, would you want to think that?"

Chapter Two

Fifteen Years Earlier

All Callie Forde wanted was an easy summer, the kind where she spent her days soaking up the sun and her evenings dishing up burgers and beer at the local grill. She wanted to read books from a lounge chair and admire the cute lifeguard from behind dark sunglasses. She wanted to take a few road trips and go shopping with friends. After all, she figured it was her last easy summer. According to the counselors at school, she needed an internship next summer, the last before her senior year. Besides, once she got her business degree and landed in an office, pool lounging would be limited to two weeks a year. Three if she was lucky.

What Callie hadn't planned on that summer was the oppressive heat, the kind that melted the makeup from her face, crowded the pool, and worst of all, fueled tempers. She couldn't have foreseen the way the town would turn on itself, suspicious and accusing. She couldn't have known there would be no business degree or cushy office job. No one could have.

On the third night of the heatwave, she woke to the sound of the front door clicking shut. Blinking in the darkness, she rolled onto her side. It was late, but her father often came home late. As a detective with the Hampstead police, he sometimes had to work long hours. If he minded, he never said, and she doubted he ever would. John Forde wasn't the kind of man who complained. She rolled back toward the wall and yawned, her eyes drifting closed once more. It was the sound of her mother's voice, wobbly and desperate, that made her open them again.

"Is it true, John? Please tell me it's not."

"Depends on what you think is true."

"Lisa and Tina. May called me. She said it was bad…" Her mother's voice broke, fading away.

Fully awake now, Callie sat up on her elbows. Maura worked three twelve-hour shifts a week at the hospital on the pediatric wing. It wasn't like her to be awake this late the night before she was due in to work. But it was more than that that made her throw off her covers and pad toward the door. Her mother was upset, near tears. She strained to hear, but the words faded in and out. Either Maura had stopped talking or she was speaking too quietly to hear. Opening her door, Callie stuck out her head before tiptoeing down the hall.

"I can't tell you much," her father was saying, "because we don't know much."

"But it's true? They're gone."

"Yes."

A gasp and a muffled sob. And then, "Is it true they were murdered?"

"Yes."

Callie's mouth fell open in the dark hallway. Murdered. Not one but two people. Who had her mother said again? Lisa and Tina. Lisa Halloway? No, she was a few years older than Callie and had moved to Australia. That wouldn't make sense. She thought about the way her mother had said the names. No last names. People she knew fairly well then. Callie had met many of her parents' friends, but like most teenagers, she didn't pay much attention unless they were her own friends' parents, like the Billings and the Jensens. They were like second parents to her. Lisa and Tina. She said the names over and over in her mind until she thought she remembered. Bridge club. No, movie club. One of those, but even then, she wasn't sure she could put faces to the names.

Maura was talking again. "May said there was a lot of blood."

"May shouldn't be talking," her father said. "I might need to have a word with Terrence."

"Oh, don't, John. She only called me because Terrence was crying. A mess, according to her." Her voice trembled. "She didn't know what to do. I think she was scared. He kept saying he'd never seen anything like it."

"No, he wouldn't have. It was…bad." There was that word again. Footsteps sounded then. "Is the whiskey bottle in the cabinet?"

Callie drew in a breath. Her father allowed himself a single cocktail before dinner, two for a special occasion like holidays or their anniversary. She'd never seen him the way she saw some of the regulars down at the grill, slurry and stumbling.

"Pour me one, too," her mother said.

In spite of the heat, Callie shivered against the wall. *He'd never seen anything like it,* her mother had said. She knew Terrence. He wasn't a detective like her father, but he'd been a police officer for as long as anyone could remember. *It was bad.*

"What about Harry and Barton? Are…" There was a pause before Maura continued, "Are they okay?"

A kitchen cabinet banged shut, followed by the sound of liquid sloshing into two glasses. Callie inched further down the hall.

"I think so. It's not my case, but both were at the station until two. Weston and Jackson caught the case. I saw some of their interviews. Neither had much to add, so they had to let them go."

"What do you mean? You don't think one of them…" Her words drifted away as if the idea was so horrible she couldn't speak it out loud.

"I don't think anything, Mo. No one does. It's procedure. You know that."

"I know. It's just unimaginable. We know Barton and Harry, and…" Again, her mother paused, and the young woman could imagine her shaking her head as she spoke. "They wouldn't. It had to be someone else."

John didn't offer an opinion, and although Callie found herself mildly disappointed, she wasn't surprised. "Jackson and Weston will be back at the house first thing. I'm going to meet them there."

"What about Lynnleigh?"

"At a friend's. I don't think she knows yet."

"Jesus, John, she's going to be devastated. They were so close. I used to see her and Lisa shopping sometimes, and she talked about Lynnleigh all the time." A heavy breath. "No child should have to go through this."

"No," John agreed. Another stretch of silence followed. Callie pictured her father sipping his whiskey, his eyes closing against what must have been a brutal day. Her mother would be gripping her glass with both hands, curled into her father.

Standing with her back pressed against the wall, it occurred to Callie that while she knew what her father did was important, she'd never considered the horror. Or danger. More than once, she heard the way people spoke about him, and she was proud, except for those early years of high school when she wished she could forget. Being the cop's kid came with a different kind of handcuffs. Breaking the rules had been harder for her, as she was often reminded. That hadn't stopped her brother, though.

Callie had been to the station, of course, had met the other detectives and their families at the annual cookouts, and even shadowed her father one "Bring Your Daughter to Work Day." By the age of twelve, she'd decided her father's job sounded way cooler than it actually was. Boring. Until that night. *It was bad.*

"What's going to happen?" Maura asked.

"An autopsy. Full investigation."

"But it's not your case? You won't be a part of it?"

"Not directly, but I'll have to help where I'm needed. We all will, until whoever did this is found." His glass slammed against the table then. "Goddammit."

Callie flinched in the semi-darkness.

"John." Maura's voice was gentle.

"Mo, nothing like this has ever happened before. Not in Hampstead. The only thing that even comes close is that time Winnie Marlowe put anti-freeze in Dennis's dinner 'cause she thought he was seeing Kristy Hunt behind her back. Turned out he wasn't, but it also turned out Winnie hadn't been right in the head for a long time."

"I remember."

Seconds ticked by, and she sensed rather than heard movement.

"Are you okay?"

"No," he said, finally. "But I will be. I didn't really know them like you did. I'm so sorry, Mo."

"Me, too." Another pause. "We hadn't seen each other as much lately. Tina was too busy, and Lisa had a lot on her plate. I wish…" Her voice broke, her words falling away.

"Come here."

Her mother's quiet sobs were the only sound for a few minutes. "It doesn't feel real," she said through tears.

"I know what you mean." In her mind, Callie could see her father stroking her mother's hair the way he had when she'd lost her mother the year before or her sister five years before that. Alone in the hall, Callie wrapped her arms around her own body.

John's voice softened. "You should get to bed."

"I will. Are you coming?"

"In a few minutes. But Mo, you need to talk to May. Tell her not to share with anyone else." Her mother promised to call the woman first thing in the morning. "Good. It's going to be tough enough without the kind of speculation this kind of thing invites. We need to wait for the facts."

Callie let out a breath. Her father sounded like himself again, sure and solid. But even as the muscles in her shoulders loosened and her hands unclenched, her father's next words made her blood run cold again.

"Terrence was right." His tone, so controlled a moment earlier, sounded shaky to her ears. "It was bad. Really bad."

Chapter Three

Now

Captain Fred Jackson spilled the half-full pot of coffee. He watched it splash across the counter in a pool before cascading onto the floor in a dark waterfall. By the time he jumped back, dark spots already dotted the hem of his crisply pressed pants.

"Cheese and crackers." He reached for the roll of paper towels. Actual curse words flowed now.

Callie, walking by, halted in the doorway. "Captain?"

"I'm fine, Forde," he said without looking up. "Just clumsier than usual."

Callie knew better. Jackson hadn't been fine for weeks. Hell, the whole office knew it. The Lawson case—the video in particular—had bled into the way he started the day's meetings, the way his sentences dropped off, the way he stared into space for minutes at a time. It didn't matter that the story was weeks old. The Lawson and Cox case now fell into the unsolved category—not officially—but that reclassification was only a matter of time. Like it or not, a case like that left a black mark on any cop's reputation, a very public black mark. Jackson wore his like a scarlet letter.

Fifteen years earlier, he'd been partnered with Mark Weston when they'd caught the case. Weston had long since retired to Florida and lived in memory care now. That left Jackson to face the scrutiny. She felt bad for the man, not only because no cop wants to believe they made a mistake, but also because Jackson cared. The idea that an innocent man had gone to prison probably kept him up at night, aggravating his already aggravated ulcer. Even worse, the Lawson case opened up questions about all his convictions. From her perspective, he didn't deserve that, but it wouldn't be her call.

"Is there anything I can do for you, Captain? Anything I can help with?"

He dropped the dirty paper towels into the trash and lifted his head. New hollows darkened his cheeks. The skin around his mouth and jowls drooped. He looked every day of his sixty years, and it took all of Callie's self-control not to show her surprise. It wasn't that she hadn't seen Jackson tired. That came with the job, but this was something deeper. Along with the exhaustion she would have expected, she saw pain and doubt.

Jackson couldn't hold her gaze. "They're gonna make it official." He licked his lips, and his hands fell back to his side. In spite of his six-foot-two frame, he appeared shrunken, physically diminished under the strain. "Clear Harry Lawson. Posthumously, of course. And reopen the case." He gave a small shake of his head as though he still couldn't quite believe it. "He was the only real suspect we had. Every scrap of evidence is fifteen years old. There's no crime scene. Nothing."

Most of this she already knew. "Cold cases get solved every day," she said.

The captain stared at the drying spot on the floor.

"Captain?" Jackson either didn't hear her or didn't have anything more to say. She stepped closer, tried again. "Captain?"

"Lisa Lawson and Tina Cox deserved justice," he said finally in a half-whisper before raising his eyes to hers. "And they didn't get it. I didn't give it to them."

"Captain. You followed the evidence. You thought you'd gotten the right man."

"Thought I'd gotten the right man," he repeated, his tone bitter. "Did you know he claimed he was innocent? I know, I know. They all claim they're innocent. He swore he wasn't even in Hampstead that day, but he didn't have any proof, and we had witnesses who might have seen him in town that morning." That faraway look returned. "Or thought they had. And I had a witness who swore he'd come into the Stop 'n Gas just outside town at two p.m. Remember that place?"

Callie did. The Stop 'n Gas had been replaced a few years earlier by a chain gas station with a sandwich counter. "Sure."

"Lawson bought a candy bar and a Coke there, so he couldn't be in DC like he claimed." The captain paused, his words coming faster. "The ID at the gas station. That should have bothered me more than it did. No one else saw Harry that afternoon. A candy bar and a Coke, but no gas. Cash transaction. Cameras broken. All I had was this guy's word. Why didn't I question him more? I should have questioned him more..." his words trailed away.

"You had no reason to suspect your witness got it wrong, Captain." Callie recognized that no matter how tight an investigation appeared, there would always be room to second-guess a decision, a question, a search. In a lot of people's minds, the legal system had been built on that very premise. Still, detectives did the best they could, and she had no doubt about Jackson's dedication to the Lawson case. If he pursued and arrested Harry Lawson, it was because he believed he had the right man.

Jackson waved a hand in the air. "It doesn't matter. I should have questioned it anyway."

Before she could bite back the words, she asked, "Who was the witness?"

He didn't answer for a moment, but when he did, she understood the depth of his remorse a little better. "Anthony Battle."

Chapter Four

Now

Gordon sat at the plastic table and chairs he'd installed in his double room at the Hampstead Inn, laptop open in front of him. The room wasn't much, and the table took up most of the floor space, but he needed the extra workspace. He'd asked for a room at the back of the hotel, as far away from the other guests as possible. That was another thing he'd learned from the Hamilton Hayes investigation. Too many late-night guests would keep him up all night. For days, Gordon and his producer Jeremy Thomas had worn bags under their eyes so dark, they'd looked like they'd been drawn on by an enthusiastic football coach.

Gordon glanced over at his oldest friend now. "Hey, do we have any beer left?"

"Two. One each. Think we should get more?"

"Later." Gordon crossed the room to the mini-fridge and grabbed the beers. Tossing one to Jeremy, he took a long slug from his bottle. Wiping his mouth, he searched through the tabs on his computer and recited what they knew.

"Lisa Lawson and Tina Cox were found at four-thirty in the afternoon by a friend who'd come by to drop off some homemade bread. Harry Lawson shows up at five-thirty to find police all over his house."

Jeremy flopped down on one of the beds. "Which is when he tells police he just drove back from DC, and he's been gone all day."

"Right. They take him in for questioning, but he's all upset, and they don't get much. They don't have any evidence at first, nothing concrete anyway, so they have to let him go but tell him he can't go home. Needs to stay in town, blah, blah, blah. He goes to stay with his best friend, Barton Cox, Tina's husband."

"Who is also upset."

"Right. Both men have been at the police station all night and have dead wives."

"What about the friend that found them?"

"Close to eighty and uses a walker. Plus, her husband was waiting in the car. No opportunity or motive."

"Got it." Jeremy rolled onto his side and propped his head up with one elbow, his bottle in his other hand. "And where's Lynnleigh during all this?"

Gordon didn't need to consult his notes. He knew most of the story by heart. "It was a Saturday. She left her house at one with a friend and the friend's mom. They went to a mall in Richmond, then a movie, then came back. Lynnleigh spent the night with the friend."

"So, Lisa Lawson was killed sometime between one and four-thirty."

"No," Gordon said. "Tina Cox had a hair appointment at twelve-thirty, and according to her hairdresser, she didn't leave until almost two. Counting in the drive time from the hairdresser to Lisa's house, that would put the murders between two-fifteen and four-thirty."

"Do we have the hairdresser lined up?"

"I've reached out."

Jeremy didn't respond right away. Both young men knew that could go either way. The podcast would be better the more on-air witnesses they had, but to be on the podcast, a person had to talk. Not everyone was willing to do that. The young producer scratched his head, going back to the timeline. "How do you know Lisa wasn't killed at one-fifteen and the killer waited and killed Tina later?"

"Good question. Lisa Lawson made a call at one-fifty to her mother. They spoke for a little more than fifteen minutes. The phone records verify this."

"Is this stuff in the trial transcript?" Gordon told him it was. "Okay. So,

Lisa gets off the phone a little after two, and a few minutes later, Tina Cox shows up."

"Right. The murder had to be sometime between then and when they were found at four-thirty."

The two young men sat silent for another few minutes, each thinking about what had happened during those couple of hours.

"Good stuff, Gordo," Jeremy said, sitting up and swinging his legs around. He drank another swallow of beer. "Are you thinking reenactment? We could do that in the second episode, maybe."

Gordon angled his head toward his shoulder as he considered. After a moment, he shook his head. "I don't think so. That's too *America's Most Wanted*, and we didn't take that route on the Hayes case. What I really want to do is load up on interviews like the hairdresser. Captain Jackson is unlikely, but we'll try. Barton Cox. Harry's brother. Any other friends and family. And Lynnleigh. If we can get her to do it, so much the better."

Jeremy's head bobbed up and down. "Cool. The whole grieving daughter trying to get to the truth thing. That'll get people listening."

"It will. But like I said, that's *if* we can get her to agree."

"What do you mean? She's the whole reason we're here, isn't she?"

Jeremy knew about the emails Lynnleigh had sent, the ones asking—no, begging—Gordon to investigate.

"Yes, but she's worried about being the focus." Lynnleigh Lawson didn't just want her dad's name cleared. She wanted to know who had killed her mother and Tina Cox. She wanted justice. But she'd made it clear she did not want the show to be about her, even if it was only incidental.

Her voice had cracked across the phone line. "I'll help you in any way I can. Introduce you to people, get you pictures, letters, anything you need. But talking on air is not something I'm comfortable with."

"I can't leave you out of it completely, but we can save it for later," he'd said.

Her sigh was so heavy, he could feel her breath through the phone. "Fine, but only because I trust you."

Those words rang in his ears now. *I trust you.* They weren't words he'd heard many times in his life, and he didn't want to let her down. Still, this podcast wouldn't work without her, perhaps more of her than she might be willing to give. His kind of podcast came with sponsors, and he had an investor this time, a real one.

"Let's start without her," Gordon said to Jeremy. "Build up to her. It will be more effective that way."

His friend shrugged and drained the last of his bottle. "You're the boss." He sat forward. "Listen, I've been editing the opening. You ready to check it out?"

Gordon put down his pen. He wasn't sure he was, but he figured it couldn't hurt. Might even help keep his energy up. He settled back in his chair, his hand closing around his warming beer. "Sure. Why not?"

"Hang on. Let me queue the start." Jeremy pushed some buttons on his laptop and fiddled with the volume. "Here goes."

The theme song they'd selected played over the speakers. It had a driving drumbeat and steady intensity. Gordon's skin tingled as he listened. His own voice followed.

"Welcome to *Catch a Criminal* podcast. I'm your host Gordon Little, and we're happy to be back with season two. If you haven't had a chance, check out season one where we helped authorities find the evidence to arrest and prosecute Congressman Hamilton Hayes." He went into a short recap of the case, careful not to take all the credit, although he felt sure the damn thing would never have been solved without him.

"Hubris," his girlfriend had said after a cable network contacted him to dramatize the events. "Show some humility, Gordon, for once in your life. Don't act like a jackass."

But he had—acted like a jackass—and the network had decided he wasn't worth the effort. They'd bailed. Same as his girlfriend. That's why this season was so important. He needed to prove he wasn't a one-shot wonder, that he could carry a show. He just wasn't sure who exactly he was proving that to.

"We're doing something different this season," his voice said from the laptop. "We'll have weekly episodes, of course, but because we want this to be as interactive as possible, we'll be adding shorter episodes as things happen. And there will be live episodes—at least one—so you'll want to subscribe to get notifications as soon as possible. So, what are we investigating, you ask? Let me tell you."

The background music filled the time it took for him to take a breath. "This season, we're taking a trip to a small town in Virginia. Hampstead. Home to Hampstead College, a dozen farms, and a packaged materials processing plant. Population less than twenty-five thousand. Why we're here is no mystery. By now, most of the country knows that Harry Lawson was an innocent man, wrongly convicted in the double murder of his wife and her best friend." His voice went on to describe the release of the video footage. "WCVC in Washington found unreleased video taken at a grocery industry conference the day of the murders. Independent forensic analysis has verified the video is credible and unaltered. At exactly three thirty-nine, the same time Lisa Lawson and Tina Cox were being brutally murdered, Harry Lawson can be seen walking past a row of exhibits at the conference. He's alone, his head low until he's about to round the corner. It's then that he stops and looks around. When he catches sight of the camera, which has been panning the hall, he takes off, almost as though he doesn't want to be seen." There's a pause where Jeremy had added a pounding electronic track in the background. Although low, the volume went up a notch. Gordon looked over at his friend and nodded.

"Why would a man who is supposedly a hundred and twenty-five miles away murdering his wife want to avoid the very camera that is clearly his alibi?" There's a second pause. "Well, that, my friends, is just one of many questions we'll try to answer on this season of the *Catch a Criminal* podcast. Stick with us. We'll be right back."

Jeremy punched a key, stopping the recording. "What do you think so far?"

"I like it," Gordon said, and he did. "You don't think I sound like one of those newsmagazine hacks, do you?"

"Not at all. Those guys talk like they've got to take breaths after every sentence. You sound normal. Like you're talking to me."

Although Gordon wasn't sure that was true, that Jeremy wasn't just saying what he knew Gordon wanted to hear, he decided it didn't matter. He had a test audience lined up to help him work out the opening. After that, most of what would be recorded would be off script, and the interviews, along with the editing, would shape the story.

He picked up his beer bottle and brought it to his lips. This case wasn't like the first one. He'd picked that case at random, the same way he'd picked the idea of being a podcaster. Gordon had taken the money he'd been planning to use to start his wing business, and he was off. He'd waded in with no real investigative experience beyond working on his high school paper, but he was good at making waves. Good enough to make the Boston police pay attention and get his name in the paper. Good enough to stumble his way to the truth. Gordon set his bottle down. The first time had been luck. If he wanted to find the killer this time, he'd need more than luck. He'd need to be good.

Chapter Five

Now

Callie sat across from the captain, her hands clasped in her lap, her right leg bouncing lightly. Behind her, the blinds rattled as Jackson let them fall over the glass. Circling back to his desk, his gaze halted on the large family portrait that hung next to a pair of service awards. Chin dipping, he sank into his chair, his movements slow and sluggish. Callie swallowed the lump in her throat. She'd never seen the captain like this, and she struggled to find the right words, anything to bring back the man she knew.

"You'll solve this, Captain. I know you will."

His head swung back and forth in a robotic motion. "Won't be me. Chief's orders."

Callie took this in. The defeated expression made more sense now. It was one thing to have made a mistake that sent an innocent man to jail, but not to be given the opportunity to make amends, to find the real killer was something else. She wondered at the reasons. Chief Waters wasn't a bad man. Nor was he a particularly good man in her opinion. Chief Waters liked Chief Waters. "Why not?"

"Laundry list of reasons. Conflict of interest. Fresh eyes. All kinds of bullshit." There was no flash of fire in Jackson's eye, no resentment in the way he spat out the words. Only resignation. The job came with that sometimes. A cop got worn down, the things you saw, the things you couldn't unsee.

Sadness. Heartbreak. Defeat. Even her father, when he was on the job, couldn't always hide the emotional toll. But Captain Jackson had always seemed like the exception, the division's own Pollyanna and cheerleader all rolled into one. He let out a long breath, lifted one hand, and let it drop again. "Not my case anymore."

Callie wanted to shake him. "So, tell him he's wrong. There's no one better to work this case than you, Captain. You know the players. You know the evidence. You'll have the benefit of knowledge when you look at it through a new lens."

One corner of his mouth turned up but stopped short of a smile. "I appreciate the vote of confidence, but maybe Waters is right." He held up his hand at her protest. "Hear me out." Callie pressed her lips together. "I was never the detective your father was. I never liked that expression to think outside the box. I'm more comfortable with facts and discipline." He leaned forward, his elbows on his desk. "The thing is, I like rules and regulations and the letter of the law. Maybe that's why I became a cop. Follow the evidence. I did that in the Lawson case. Everything pointed to Harry." He paused, sadness tinging his words. "Your dad wasn't like me. He would have asked himself if it felt right, would have considered other suspects."

She wanted to argue with him, but she bit back the words. Every detective wanted to solve investigations, and every detective had their own way of doing it, their own style. Some were full of bluster on the outside, quietly tallying up the evidence on the inside. Some were instinctive. Some were plodding. Some were better than others. Jackson's record hadn't been remarkable, but it had been solid. Until now.

"They'll probably take a look at all the cases I closed." His gaze landed on Callie. "Did a few of those with your dad, although not many."

She nodded. Her father gave up his badge several years earlier, having been paralyzed from the waist down after a shooting in a sting operation. That case had cost him his career, but more than that, for a while, it had cost him his desire to take part in life. He'd shut himself in, effectively shutting everyone else out. He was better now—they all were—but some days were still harder than others.

"You were a good detective, Captain. You still are."

That almost smile appeared again, and he nodded. "There's a podcaster that's been nosing around."

"I heard. Hendo and Chang told him to get lost."

"I would've liked to have seen that."

"Me, too."

He tapped a pencil against the corner of the desk. "I hear he's the Hamilton Hayes guy, the one that got it reopened." A tic pulsed at the corner of his eye. "Led them to the evidence."

Callie knew the case. It didn't matter that she hadn't heard the podcast. She'd heard of Hamilton Hayes. A congressman who gets indicted for the murder of one of his fellow politicians tends to make headlines across the country. "He got lucky. That's all."

Jackson snorted. "I'm sure he did, but even so, I don't want him getting lucky around here. This is Hampstead police business."

"Damn right," Callie said, although she wondered if the town's population outside the department would feel the same. Fifteen minutes of fame, a moment in the spotlight, had an added allure in today's world—like a viral siren. She steered the conversation away from the podcaster. "What's going to happen now?" she asked.

He pulled back, the pencil falling from his hand and landing on the desk. "The case is being reassigned. Chief Waters will keep me out of it as much as he can." He grimaced as though he'd been physically wounded. "I'm a liability."

Again, Callie struggled to hold her tongue. If she wasn't a fan of Chief Waters before, she was less so now. Seeing the captain like this hit a little close to home, too reminiscent of her father's physical and mental battles.

"Waters will oversee the team leading the investigation," Jackson said. "I don't have to tell you he'd like to see this solved sooner rather than later."

A low groan rose from Callie's throat. Another point against the Chief. He wasn't a detective, having started in operations and rising through the ranks as an administrator.

Jackson kept talking. "Waters wanted to take the case outside, bring in the FBI or some other heavy hitters, but I managed to talk him out of it. Lisa Lawson and Tina Cox were Hampstead residents." His long fingers curled into a fist, and he thumped it against the desk. "Giving them justice is our responsibility."

Callie understood what he was really saying. Giving the women justice was *his* responsibility. Now that his chance had been taken from him—at the very least—he'd keep it in house.

The captain pinched the skin between his brows with long fingers. "While I can't be involved in the investigation, Waters is allowing me to choose the team that works the case." He stared hard at her, his eyes searching. "I've recommended you and Zeleniak take lead."

She shifted on the chair, her hands falling to her knees. "What about the break-in out near the college?"

"Hendo and Chang can take over. You can bring them up to speed."

Her breath caught in her throat. To take on this kind of case, a double murder with no new evidence in fifteen years outside of the video, would be difficult, and that was before you considered the media coverage or the upcoming podcast. Still, she told herself, she came to the case without preconceived notions or theories, with limited knowledge. That gave her a fresh perspective. That also meant she wasn't at the crime scene. She'd never spoken to a witness or testified about evidence. She knew little more than the viewer halfway across the country who saw the story on the news. How many friends and family still lived in Hampstead? How many would be willing to talk? Callie's head told her this mountain promised to be a steep climb, and yet, as she turned it over in her mind, the hairs on the back of her neck prickled with anticipation.

"Captain, I don't see how you can't be involved. You wrote the reports, interviewed the witnesses. Whoever takes on this case will need you."

"When necessary, I will be available. But I'll have no access to the new investigation's notes or theories." His gaze drifted a moment before he straightened, lifting his chin. "You'll report to Waters."

"Captain, I—"

"Non-negotiable, Forde." Whatever wallowing the man had allowed himself was over. He was all business now. Coming around the desk, he indicated she should follow him.

She stood, looking up at him. "Where are we going?"

"To pull the evidence." He looked down at his watch, tapping it with one long finger. "You start now."

Chapter Six

Fifteen Years Earlier

Callie strode across the lawn that separated the high school from the middle school, her boots sinking in the muddy grass. She glanced up at the gray sky, her steps quickening. Two days of rain and dreary weather had settled over Hampstead, dampening her mood along with everything else. Her mother called it seasonal affective disorder or something like that, but Callie didn't care what it was called. For days and weeks since the murders, a dark cloud had settled over the town and her house. She understood the town after the murders, but not what was going on with her parents. She'd never seen them fight—at least not the way they had been. Lately, there'd been less fighting though, as if one of them had called a truce. But if the hard words she'd overheard through the walls at night had faded, they'd been replaced by something that worried her more. Silence.

Once inside the school, she hurried down the hall to the study room off the library, not wanting to be late for her tutoring session. It wasn't that she thought the students would mind, but she didn't want to let Mrs. Holcomb down. Every Wednesday, she helped out, working with students on their essays and papers.

"Writing is a talent, but it's also a skill," Mrs. Holcomb always said. "An essential one, and you were one of my best students." Callie drank in those words, the same as she had in high school. She hadn't excelled at creative fiction the way her friend Jilly Jensen had, but she'd aced every book report and essay. She liked the structure of writing, the rules, and the grammar. Those things she could memorize and understand. Mrs. Holcomb called her the baker of writing and Jilly the cook. "Two different species," she said. "Both important." Callie hadn't hesitated when Mrs. Holcomb had asked her to help out with the summer school students.

The study room was only half-full when Callie came through the door, but that wasn't unusual. The reasons each student enrolled in summer sessions varied. There were always a few who were in danger of failing and needed help to pass. Others struggled with a specific assignment. All of those were somehow easier than the ones who'd landed there for repeated behavioral problems. The last time she'd come in, a boy who'd been caught passing around porn pictures he'd printed off the internet had stared at her in a way that made her wish she had a parka to cover her tank top and shorts. She let out a sigh of relief that he wasn't in his seat on that day. She recognized most of the other kids as repeats, all except one, a small girl who sat alone, her shoulders slumped. Callie paused. There was something familiar about the girl, but maybe it was the way she'd folded in on herself as though she could disappear if no one noticed her.

"Oh, good, Callie. You're here." Mrs. Holcomb waved her over. She shifted away from the students, speaking in a low voice. "I'd like you to help Lynnleigh today."

"Who's Lynnleigh?" she asked even as she guessed the answer.

Mrs. Holcomb nodded her head toward the girl sunk low in her chair. "Do you know who she is?"

"Should I?"

"Lynnleigh Lawson."

The name made Callie take a step back. She'd heard the name, of course, but she'd never met the girl. Her gaze landed on Lynnleigh now. That's why she seemed familiar. Her long, brown hair appeared half-combed and hung in a greasy sheet over pale, hollowed cheeks. The oversized sweatshirt that hid her shape was too heavy for the summer, but Callie guessed that was the point. Lynnleigh Lawson didn't want to be noticed or seen at all. Callie couldn't blame her.

"Her uncle is worried about her. She's supposed to start high school in the fall, and she missed her exams at the end of the last semester after…well, you know." The teacher handed Callie a folder. "We're going to let her make them up, but she needs to review the material." She paused. "I've tried talking to her myself, but she won't say anything. She just sits there, mute." Her creased brow wrinkled further. "I don't blame her. I mean, who would? But maybe you could get through to her."

Callie's mind reeled. This was too much. Lynnleigh's parents were the reason things had gone sour in her house. Her father was doing what he always did—working—and her mother had grown snappy one minute and vague the next. Callie would go back to school in a month. She didn't want to leave them this way, but in truth, she wasn't convinced they'd even notice she'd gone. The Lawson case had taken over their thoughts and their moods. In that moment, the sight of the girl made her angry, and she had to shove down her resentment. Lynnleigh hadn't done anything wrong, and yet every part of her rebelled against Mrs. Holcomb's suggestion.

"I don't know if I'm the right person," she managed to say.

"You are." Mrs. Holcomb's head nodded along with the words. "I've given it a lot of thought. You're my best tutor, but you're also strong. She needs to see that. She needs to learn how to be strong."

Callie's mouth dropped open. She wasn't sure if it was because Mrs. Holcomb thought she was strong or because she expected her to teach the girl strength. That was hardly in the curriculum or the folder she held now.

The teacher touched Callie lightly on the arm. "Just be yourself. Be kind. Chances are, she won't even talk to you today. Maybe not tomorrow or the next day either. But we have to try." She followed Mrs. Holcomb's gaze back to the girl. "None of this is her fault. Not what happened or what people are saying. And the trial hasn't even started yet."

Again, Callie knew all this. She understood how things worked better than most. More than once, her father had lectured both Callie and her brother on the justice system. Sometimes she actually listened. She had another thought.

"She might not want to talk to me, because of who my dad is."

Mrs. Holcomb sighed. "You may be right, but…" Her words faded as she lifted her palms. "I'd like you to try." Before Callie could say anything more, Mrs. Holcomb's head swung toward the rest of the students and the chatter going on behind them. "Alright, everyone, we're going to get started." Most of the kids stopped talking long enough to glance up. "Lucy should be here any minute, and we'll divide into two groups."

Callie's eyes went back to Mrs. Holcomb, but the teacher had already moved away from her toward the students. Folder in hand, Callie looked back at the girl hunched behind the desk.

Taking a deep breath, Callie squared her shoulders. "Well, here goes nothing."

Chapter Seven

Now

Jeremy pushed his empty plate to the middle of the table. Sunlight streamed through the diner window, spotlighting the toast crumbs that dotted the table and the front of his shirt. "I called Barton Cox at home and at his business, but he wasn't there. Same as when you tried. I left messages about what we're after."

Gordon sat back. He didn't know if he was disappointed or not. Barton Cox, the grieving husband of Tina, was at the center of the story. He'd let Lawson into his home the night their wives had been found. They'd been best friends then, according to all the reports. And Gordon had to hand it to Barton. Even after his friend had been arrested and convicted, he somehow managed to avoid the press. Gordon had combed through every site he could find and had yet to find a single usable quote from Barton Cox. The most he'd learned was that Cox attended every day of the trial and that he'd helped Harry's brother broker the sale of Harry's market. And when it was all over, when the noise had died down, he'd quietly picked up the pieces and moved on. He had a new wife and a couple of kids. He had friends. He had a successful business. A normal life—until the video. Almost instantly, the network news and big papers had all come looking for a comment from the surviving family members, Lynnleigh Lawson and Barton Cox. Only one of them had been willing to speak.

Even the prosecutor had gotten little out of Barton Cox at trial. His testimony had been mostly limited to establishing his alibi, something the defendant lacked.

Avery: "Mr. Cox, you claim you were at your mother's house during the time of the murders."

Cox: "I was. My mother has Parkinson's, and on Saturdays, I spend the day with her."

Avery: "What time did you arrive?"

Cox: "I can't remember exactly, but usually around ten. That way I can make sure she's taken all her pills, clean up, and start making her lunch."

Avery: "And how long do you stay?"

Cox: "Until six, so I can give her dinner before the night nurse comes in."

The trial transcript included three witnesses, all neighbors, who verified seeing Barton's car in his mother's driveway from a little after ten until sundown.

"It doesn't matter," Gordon said now. "We'll keep at him. The first couple of episodes are more about laying the foundation."

"Sure, but what if he still won't talk to us?" Jeremy brushed the rest of the crumbs from his mouth.

"He will, and if he doesn't, people might start wondering what he's hiding."

A grin stretched over Jeremy's wide face. "You son of a bitch. You playing hardball now?"

Gordon returned his friend's smile with one of his own. "I'd rather not, but this podcast doesn't work if the only people we talk to are randos who don't know more than what hair dye Tina used or what time Lisa went to work or God knows what other trivial stuff. Fifteen years is a long time." He didn't miss the way Jeremy's eyebrow lifted and knew the reason. Lynnleigh again. But Gordon wasn't prepared to explain his reluctance to push Lynnleigh, at least not yet. "Listen," he said. "A couple of things. I'd like you to get some video and still shots of the house. Maybe the old market building, too, and the salon. Also, I want to have a timeline that shows the movements of both women hour by hour. We can use those on the website for promotion. The audio trailer should tie in."

"Is the copy ready?"

Gordon had a draft. He'd been working on it for two weeks, but something was missing, something he hoped to find now that he'd arrived in Hampstead. "Almost."

"I thought the sponsors wanted the trailer yesterday."

Gordon shrugged. "I got an extension."

Jeremy gave an appreciative whistle. "You should have been in sales, bro."

"Probably make my dad happier than this gig."

Jeremy's lips puckered. Gordon didn't take offense. Not many of their friends liked Gordon's father. Overbearing. Rigid. Harsh. All words he'd heard applied to his old man. Some days, Gordon thought maybe those words were kinder than his dad deserved. More than once, he'd wondered if things would have been different if his brother had lived. Gordon wasn't Max, no matter how he tried. Before Jeremy could comment, Gordon got back to the podcast.

"I'm going over to the VFW this morning, and then I'm seeing the hairdresser. She agreed to be interviewed. I think I can get some good sound clips out of those."

Jeremy gave a nod of approval. "The hairdresser's good. The last known person to have seen Tina Cox alive, right?"

"Yep. I want her in the early episodes." He pulled out a pen and drew a line across a paper napkin. "We need to do a timeline of the day, but also the days leading up to the murder and through the trial." He wrote a handful of dates along the line. "These are the ones I've got mapped out in my head so far. The idea is to establish state of mind for each of the players. We'll talk to friends and neighbors. Co-workers. Anyone who's willing."

Again, Jeremy nodded. Both men understood that while it could be challenging to find people willing to talk, it would be more challenging to find information worth learning.

Gordon pushed the napkin aside. "I don't expect much from the VFW, but it should be good as background. According to the articles and the trial transcript, Lawson was paranoid, maybe delusional. PTSD stuff."

"You should get a doctor to talk about that shit."

"Already on it." He slid out of the booth, grabbed his backpack, and pulled one strap over his shoulder. "Meet you back at the Tavern later?"

Jeremy nodded. "Your turn to buy."

***

Karen Huddleston touched a hand to her hair, smoothing it under the headphones. Gordon ducked his head, hiding his smile. No matter how many times he explained his podcast was an audio production only—unlike some of the others out there—people still wanted to look their best. Karen was no exception.

She eyed the microphone. "Do I talk into that?"

"Just talk normally. You don't have to lean in or anything." The microphone—all the equipment, really—was a big upgrade from the bargain basement equipment he'd used in the first season. Limited to Nana's investment money the first time around, the only thing he'd remotely splurged on was the microphone. This season, even that had been upgraded. He had a bigger budget now, and he'd chosen one with built-in boost and multiple sound signatures. Although it came with a foam windscreen, he preferred the pop filter—particularly since he recorded in so many different locations. Along with the mic, the headphones were better, too. About the only thing that hadn't changed was the free software Jeremy used, although he'd been known to play around with different options from time to time.

"Are you comfortable?" he asked Karen now.

"Ready," she said, her voice breathy.

While the small space wasn't as soundproofed as he would like, he'd closed the doors leading out to the hallway, minimizing any chance of outside noise. He wasn't worried, though. Jeremy would mix the sound later. He adjusted his own headphones and pressed the record button.

"Karen Huddleston is a hairdresser in Hampstead, Virginia." Gordon recapped how long she'd lived in the town, where she worked, and her relationship to Tina Cox. "So, on the day of the murders, Tina had an appointment with you at twelve-thirty."

"That's right. She was a few minutes late, but I expected that. Tina was always late."

Gordon sat forward. "How late?"

Karen didn't think long. "Ten minutes. Not long. She was always running from one thing to another."

Although he didn't know if he'd use the full interview or not, he couldn't pass up the opportunity to bring Tina to life. "Tell me about that. What Tina was like."

"Late for one thing," she said with a short laugh. "She was always running late. Classes. Dances. Even graduation. Not sure how Barton put up with it, but he did."

"They were high school sweethearts, right?"

"Oh, yeah. Barton and Tina started up our junior year. Same year as Lisa and Harry."

Gordon snuck a look at his laptop to make sure the recording was working. Jeremy would kill him if he knew Gordon forgot to run a quick test first. Once, during the Hamilton Hayes podcast, he'd lost an entire interview when there was nothing to play back. When Hamilton's stepsister realized she'd been given a reprieve, she blocked Gordon's calls and messages. She even went so far as to have him removed from her building. It didn't matter in the end. Her stepbrother went to prison anyway, and the gravy train that was Hamilton Hayes came to a screeching halt.

"I didn't really know what she saw in Barton at the time. Tina was head cheerleader. She was funny and pretty. Barton was kind of a nerd. I think he managed the basketball team or something."

"Barton is smart, right? Maybe that's what she liked," Gordon suggested. Barton Cox had attended college on an academic scholarship with a plan to double major in accounting and economics. But he didn't last a year away from home, returning to Hampstead's local college and Tina instead.

"He is that. I guess she knew it even back then, knew he'd make something of himself. Worked and put himself through Hampstead, got a CPA. Has his own tax company now. Not just in Hampstead. He has an office in Richmond and one down in Raleigh. To tell you the truth, I think he'd rather be in North Carolina, but Cindy won't have any part of it. That's his new wife. Her momma's here for one thing. Not to mention, I think Cindy knows Raleigh's too big for her. She'd disappear in a city like that."

Gordon nodded but didn't comment. Instead, he brought the conversation back to Tina's high school days and the couple's early marriage.

"Tina and Barton married pretty young, didn't they?" The couple had married soon after Barton had returned to Hampstead.

For the first time, Karen seemed to hesitate. "I didn't understand what the rush was at the time, but who can explain love? They seemed happy, except for…" Her words fell away. Although Gordon had an idea where Karen was headed, he decided to save it for later.

"Tina worked up at the college?"

"Right. She worked as an assistant for Dean Marks, the senior one." She crossed one leg over the other. "Tina loved working for that man. He was like a father to her. Her own daddy died when she was still in middle school."

Gordon gave her an encouraging smile. "A plane accident."

"Yeah. He loved flying, you know. It was his hobby. I remember him taking us out to the airport once. He had this prop plane he would fly whenever he could. Tina's mom didn't like it much. She refused to get on the plane with him, and she forbade him from taking Tina or her brother Tim. He used to laugh about it. He laughed a lot actually. It was one of the things everybody liked about him." She paused and let out a long breath. "Anyway, I guess Tina's mom was right about him taking chances. Probably had no business flying that day with the storm coming and all." Her shoulders gave a small shudder. "Hard to survive a crash like that."

He allowed a couple of seconds of silence before he spoke again, the better for the audience to take in the tragic death of the young family man. If it was too long, Jeremy could cut the dead air. "I'm sure that was hard on the family. And Tina."

"Oh, it was. Tina cried so much I thought she was gonna shrivel up like a prune. Then we started high school that fall, and things got better after a while. But she never stopped missing him. I'm sure of that."

Gordon nodded at Karen. The hairdresser was a natural. She didn't talk too fast or slow. Her words were clear and rang true, the emotion just right.

He wished all his interview subjects were like Karen.

"Let's go back to the day of the murders. What her last hours were like."

Karen visibly flinched, as though she'd been thrown back in time to the actual day, and her words were harder to hear.

"Okay. Sure."

Pushing his hair out of his eyes, he pondered the next question. Since he'd arrived in town, he'd been met with more than a little skepticism, followed by curiosity. But he was good at blending in, and some of the time, they forgot he was there. At the Diner and the Grill and especially the Tavern, he'd overheard funny stories, sad memories, and more than a bit of gossip. It was this last that was on his mind now. Turning the words over in his mind, he leaned in and took a deep breath.

"Karen, there's something that's come up about Tina that I wanted to ask you about."

Chapter Eight

Now

"This is everything." Captain Jackson gestured toward the two boxes on the conference room table. "All my reports. Copies of forensics. Interviews. Everything you need to get started."

Callie eyed the boxes. They weren't small, but nor were they large.

"What is it?" he asked.

She hesitated, not wanting to appear critical or rub salt in the wound, especially since he seemed to be putting all his trust in her. "I thought there'd be more," she said finally.

To Jackson's credit, he didn't react. Not much, anyway. Still, she saw the way his fingers pressed into the back of the chair. "At the time, the prosecutors were satisfied with the case we presented. And as you know, the jury took less than two hours to come back with a guilty verdict."

She nodded, making what she hoped sounded like approval noises.

Slipping back into the past, his grip loosened. "The courthouse was packed. You could hardly move in there. It was one of those Indian summer weeks—you know the kind—where the leaves are turning, but it's hot as Hades outside." His voice softened with the memory. "They had to switch on the air conditioning; it was so damn hot, but it didn't matter. By the time I got called to testify, my shirt was stuck to my skin." Jackson took a step forward as though he were climbing up into the witness box. "Brock Avery was the county prosecutor."

Callie didn't know Avery well—he'd retired before she made detective—so she said nothing, letting the captain talk.

"Avery was a hardass back then. I heard somewhere he kept a whiteboard with a tally count of all his cases. How many wins and losses? How many pleas? He didn't like to lose. Probably still doesn't, although now the only people he's putting away are his golf partners." He forced a chuckle, his dark eyes finding Callie's. "That's how he was about Lawson. He wanted the man locked up for life." He drew in a breath. "We had the evidence, and Lawson was paranoid. His behavior had been erratic. There'd been some calls about the store. There were…other problems." Jackson lifted a hand and dropped it again. "You know how these things go, Cal. We always look to the spouse first, and in this case, everything added up. I thought…" Callie waited to see if there was more, but Jackson fell silent.

She ran a hand over the boxes. "I'll get started on these," she said.

Whatever memories were swimming around the captain's head seemed to evaporate. He straightened. "I'll leave you to it then. Don't forget to keep Waters updated." He started toward his office and stopped. "Find him, Cal." Without another word, he walked away, disappearing behind the heavy door.

She sat down at the table, pulling open the first box. Before she could start reading, her cellphone buzzed. Her partner, Detective Todd Zeleniak.

Heard we picked up the Lawson case. Headed back now.

Callie's fingers flew over the tiny keyboard.

No rush. Catching up on the reports. Going to need to hand off the robbery.

She watched as dots hovered over the text window.

I'll bring Chang and Hendo up to speed when I get there. On my way.

Biting her lip, Callie thought about the break-in they'd caught less than two weeks earlier, although it wasn't entirely clear when the robbery occurred. The owners had been away for close to a month, visiting family. They'd come home to find a broken back window and holes in their walls. A list of missing items proved shorter than expected: a laptop, jewelry, AirPods, and a vase the wife said she bought at Target.

"I don't think it was worth fifty dollars," the woman had said. "Who would bother?"

All of the stolen items were easily transportable and could be pawned for quick cash. As of that moment, none of the stolen items had surfaced in any of the nearby pawn shops. Callie didn't like handing off the case, but everything about Jackson's demeanor told her he needed her on this. She only hoped she wouldn't let him down.

Returning her attention to the box, she spread the folders across the table. Over the next several minutes, she sorted the folders into piles. Statements. Interviews. Forensics. Photos. Evidence. She frowned at the short stacks.

With no real plan in mind, she started with the autopsy reports. Halfway through Tina's, she stopped, blinking. She read the findings a second time and a third. There was no mistake. She thought she'd known most of the story, the basic facts, but she'd been wrong. These test results hadn't been reported on the news or anywhere else. There'd been rumors, but that's all. Had it come up at trial? Had Harry known? She thought back to what Jackson had said earlier that morning.

"The county psychiatrist claimed Lawson was competent to stand trial, but I was never sure about that."

"Did his lawyer try to claim not guilty by reason of insanity?" she'd asked.

"No." The lines above Jackson's brows had furrowed. "He never budged from saying he didn't do it. That he wasn't here that day."

"But you had Battle's testimony that he was."

"Yeah. And a whole lot of reports that jived with what we found at the crime scene." He'd paused, rubbing a hand across his chin. "Medical examiner used the word frenzied when he described Lisa's wounds. There were so many knife wounds, she was probably dead long before her killer was finished." He'd paused again. "It was bad, but you'll see that for yourself."

"What about Tina Cox?"

"Two wounds. A nick on her abdomen, and another, deeper one at the heart. That was the fatal one. Very precise, not like Lisa at all."

Just two wounds. *Not like Lisa at all.* Perhaps that was why the results of Tina's blood test hadn't been brought out at trial. According to the psychiatrist's interpretation of the autopsy reports, she wasn't the primary target of the killer. For the doctor and the detectives, the knife wounds, the number and manner, told a very specific story. What they couldn't know was whether the murder was premeditated or what had set the killer off. Until a few weeks ago, the presumption had been PTSD induced paranoia, a shaky marriage, money problems. Any one of those or all of them. That menu of motives—for what it was worth—was gone now.

She pulled the folder of photos toward her and flipped through the pictures until she found what she was looking for. There were eighteen photos in all from eighteen different angles. Six of Lisa Lawson, six of Tina Cox, and six of both of the women, lying side by side in twin beds. Callie picked up a photo of Lisa and held it up toward the light. Her hands and feet were tied to the bedposts, same as Tina. But that's where the similarities ended. Every inch of Lisa's body appeared to be covered in blood. Stab wounds, some deeper than others, could be seen on her arms and legs and torso.

She understood the M.E.'s comment now, although she considered frenzied to be an understatement. Dropping the picture as though it burned, Callie sat back and closed her eyes, her chest tightening. Lisa Lawson wasn't stabbed to death. She was butchered.

Chapter Nine

Now

"I heard the rumors," the hairdresser said, staring down at the table between them, "but that's all they were. If it was true, that just makes everything worse, doesn't it?" Her voice dropped to a whisper, and she lifted her head again. "I mean, the year before, Tina thought she was pregnant—was sure of it—but that turned out to be a false positive. She was devastated, let me tell you. She and Barton had been trying for years and nothing. Then to think finally…well, that must have been the worst. Tina tried to hide it, but a woman knows. I did my best not to talk about my kids or anything around her. I didn't want to be insensitive, but Tina always asked. Even after. Just that kind of friend, you know. Anyway, I think the pressure to have a baby was getting to her."

"So, not pregnant?"

"Well, I couldn't swear to it, but I don't think so."

Gordon thought about the way the woman hadn't looked him in the eye but knew better than to jump to conclusions. Maybe she didn't know. Or maybe she wasn't as close to Tina as she pretended. He'd keep an open mind. For now, he decided it was best to move on.

"Can you tell me if she seemed worried or bothered about anything else besides that?"

"Well, not so you could tell. Talked a mile a minute like always. Well, until I asked about Lisa. Clammed up quick."

Gordon's pulse jackrabbited. This was unexpected. All the articles had described the women as lifelong best friends, and there'd been nothing to dispute that in the trial transcript. Keeping his voice even, he asked, "Had their relationship been strained?"

"For sure, although they were still together more than they weren't. But there was something different between them, I could tell. Like if Tina went to movie night, Lisa couldn't make it, and vice versa. They were both at that fundraiser up at the college, though." Her head tipped to one shoulder. "Do you want to hear about all this?"

"I want to hear whatever you want to tell me. Do you know why they weren't getting along?"

"It probably had something to do with Harry. He wasn't quite right, although you'd never know it by Lisa. Even when he got in that fight down at the Tavern and near knocked out Jerry Morgan's teeth, Lisa wouldn't say nothin' bad about him."

Gordon made a mental note to follow up with Jerry Morgan. "And this bothered Tina?"

"A little, maybe. She loved Harry, of course. They'd all been friends for years, but I think he scared her." She swung her leg under the table. "Barton was big on loyalty; I know that. In spite of everything Harry did, Barton stayed loyal. He never said anything. Not at the trial. Not to reporters." She clucked her tongue as she shook her head. "Even after losing his own wife."

Since it turned out that Harry hadn't actually committed the crime, Gordon opted to steer Karen back to Lisa. "Did Tina tell you she was going over to Lisa's after her appointment?"

"Yeah, but she didn't seem that happy about it. She always picked at her fingernails when she was upset, and her fingernails were nubs that day."

"Did you ever tell anyone about that?"

She shrugged, and he had to gesture at her to give an oral answer.

"Oh, right. Um, no one asked me, but really, I don't know why it matters. Friends get mad at each other all the time. You ignore texts and walk the other way on the street, you know. You don't stab each other. Anyway, knowing Lisa and Tina, they would have been over whatever it was by the next week. That's how they were, you know."

"Right, okay."

Gordon swallowed his disappointment even as he filed the question away for another day, for another interview. Conflict—no matter how innocuous it seemed—made for content, the kind listeners lapped up. Switching gears, he pivoted back to the day and the sequence of events leading to the murders.

"You had finished doing her hair, and then what? Did anything unusual happen when Tina was leaving that day?"

"Unusual? I don't know if I'd say unusual. Like I said, Tina had a lot on her mind, I think." She tapped one neon pink nail on the table before snapping her fingers. "Wait, I do remember one thing. When I was drying Tina's hair, a group of women came in from the college, wives of professors and deans—we used to call them the stiffies 'cause of the way they stuck their noses in the air and the way their heads never moved on their necks." She snorted. "Like being married to a smarty-pants made you one by default. I mean, most of the folks at the college are nice, but back then, some could be downright snotty, if you know what I mean."

"Sure," Gordon said. He didn't know how this was relevant, but he let her talk anyway.

"The ladies coming in wasn't all that unusual, and Tina didn't normally pay them any mind except to go a little quiet. She was a townie and an employee. She knew her place. Anyway, there were four or five of them up front, waiting for manicures and chatting away when Tina jumped out of her chair with wet hair, saying she had to go right then, and out the back door she went."

"Out the back door?" he asked, repeating her words.

"Yeah. So, that was unusual. Guess she didn't want to go past the stiffies that day, not that I could blame her. There was one that really had a burr up her butt when she came in. We used to draw straws to see who had to do her hair."

"Who was that?"

"Amanda Marks. The old dean's daughter-in-law. She was married to Byron—or at least she was then. I think they got divorced soon after they moved away but that could be completely wrong. It was a long time ago." She waved a hand. "Listen to me rambling, but honestly, more than once I've wondered what might have happened if those stiffies hadn't come in that day. Tina might have let me finish drying her hair for one thing, and then she would have been late to Lisa's, and she might have been the one who found Lisa, and who knows, you might be asking Tina questions today instead of me. If anyone knew whether or not Lisa Lawson had an enemy, it would have been Tina Cox." She gave a shake of her head. "To this day, I don't know why anyone would want to kill Lisa Lawson. I mean, she could be tough sometimes—she was never short on opinions, I can tell you—but still, it makes a person wonder, doesn't it?"

She looked at him expectantly. "Right," Gordon said, just to say something. "You're right." Somewhere along the line, he'd lost control of the interview. Determined to take it back, he pressed his hands together. "Let me see if I understand. You're thinking someone went to Lisa's house to kill her, and Tina just happened to be there?"

"Exactly," she said, nearly jumping out of her seat. "Although I have a theory on that. I think it was someone who was fried out of their minds, like a Charles Manson kind of thing. But no matter who it was, if Tina hadn't gone over there when she did, she would be alive today." The hairdresser sat back, spent now, tears threatening. "Think about it. I mean, talk about being in the wrong place at the wrong time. What could be sadder?"

Chapter Ten

Now

"I need to get out of here," Callie said to Zel. "Get some air. Do you want me to bring you a sandwich?"

"The usual would be great. With extra—"

"Pickles. I know, I know." She threw him a smile. "You're hopeless." It was a running joke between them. He asked for the same turkey sandwich with mustard and extra pickles every day. Where Zel was a creature of habit, Callie liked to experiment. Pastrami one day. A salad the next. Soup. Tuna fish. Zel liked routine. He liked sameness.

"Boring," Callie told him after the first few months they'd partnered together. "Must drive Marcie crazy."

"One of us has to be boring," he'd counter. "I'm the sliced turkey to your spicy fried chicken."

"What? That doesn't even make sense."

He'd laughed and agreed, but his order never changed. When the long hours on a case meant it was fast food they needed, he was consistent there, too. Plain burger with mustard and extra pickles. And double fries. Even Zel had some vices.

Callie headed down the street toward the Hampstead Diner, but halfway there, detoured toward the park instead. She found an empty bench facing the playground and sat, lifting her face toward the sun. She let the warmth seep into her bones, draining some of the tension. Cold cases presented challenges fresh cases didn't. Sometimes witnesses died or disappeared. Evidence trails dried up. Reports went missing or were incomplete. Every town and city had a backlog of cases like this, and Hampstead was no exception. They might only be a small college town, but nonetheless, the ones they missed haunted them. There wasn't a day that went by that she didn't think about the pictures still thumbtacked to the large board behind her desk and none more than the photo of Emma Nicholls, the missing teen who'd been gone more than five years now. That one kept a lot of them up at night.

Over her head, a songbird chirped, the sound bright and alive. On the playground, a young mother pushed her toddler on the swing. A college student sat under a tree, his back pressed to the thick trunk, a textbook on his lap. Normal life. Lisa Lawson and Tina Cox would never look up at the sun or push a child on a swing again. They were taken from their families and their friends. That wasn't what made this cold case different or harder in Callie's mind. Everyone would be watching. The chief. The captain. The media. Worst of all, the families. Reopening the case tore the scabs off old wounds, made them bleed again. It stole the closure and any sense of peace these families might have attained. They'd expect answers. Answers she didn't know if she could give.

Callie knew Lynnleigh Lawson. The few times she'd attempted to tutor the girl that long-ago summer hadn't been particularly successful. Lynnleigh had said little, forcing Callie to do all the talking. By the time the girl had taken her makeup exams, Callie had gone back to school, her failed attempt at tutoring forgotten in the rush of new classes and favorite friends.

Lynnleigh, too, had left, but Callie knew she'd moved back not long ago. Callie had even spotted her a couple of times, sometimes by herself, sometimes with a friend, although they hadn't spoken or even acknowledged the other. While not unusual for someone to return to their hometown, Lynnleigh's homecoming was anything but normal. For most of her life, she'd been both an object of pity and derision. Callie certainly believed only a cold-hearted monster wouldn't have sympathy for a young girl who'd lost both parents in a single night, one to murder and one to prison, but there were many whose sympathy had waned, had been replaced by scorn when Lynnleigh continued to trumpet her father's innocence long after his conviction. Callie hadn't needed to question Harry's guilt to understand a child's desire to believe in her parent unconditionally. Her relationship with her own father had been a rollercoaster of emotions in recent years. It was better now, but far from easy.

Now, Callie let her gaze wander over the storefronts that made up the center of town. Behind the buildings, in the near distance, she spotted the gleaming dome of the Hampstead College library. Further to the west, the road stretched out toward the plant, where hundreds of Hampstead residents worked. Lisa Lawson and Tina Cox had been dead fifteen years, but life had moved on for the people of Hampstead. Even for Barton Cox. But the town would be watching now, their loyalties divided. She'd heard the mutterings around the newly surfaced evidence.

"You know they can do things with video, right? Make it look like someone is on it. Doctor it up. How do we know it's real?"

She understood. No one wanted to believe the police had gotten it wrong, that a killer might still be among them. Hell, she didn't want to believe it either. And yet, the killer had gone dormant, hadn't they? There'd been no other crimes exactly like the murders of Lisa and Tina before or after. The image of Lisa Lawson's body on the bed pushed itself to the forefront of her mind. Maybe all murders were personal, but there was no denying that anger or hatred or both had a part in Lisa's slaying. Tina had been luckier in that respect. Her murder seemed tame, impersonal. If there was such a thing.

Callie rubbed her hands across her legs, remembering the words she'd read in the transcript. Harry hadn't helped himself, insisting on taking the stand.

Avery: "Isn't it true you chased after the Holton boys with a rifle, Mr. Lawson?"

Lawson: "I told them to get off my property."

Avery: "With a rifle?"

Lawson: "What of it? I didn't shoot anyone."

Avery: "The Holton twins were fourteen at the time, Mr. Lawson. Did you know that?"

Lawson: "There ain't no age limit on bad. Those boys are rotten at the core. Always have been."

In spite of herself, Callie had found herself nodding as she read Harry's words. Derek and Dwayne Holton had looked like grown men by the time they were fourteen and acted like it, too. They were drinking, doing drugs. Dwayne was expelled from Hampstead High, and Derek was sentenced to five years for assault before his twenty-first birthday. It wasn't a stretch to picture them causing trouble at Harry Lawson's store.

Avery: "And you're the judge of that, are you, Mr. Lawson?"

Lawson: "They were stealing from me, knocking over displays, harassing my customers."

Avery: "Did you call the police?"

Lawson: "You already know the answer to that. They did shit."

Judge: "Please watch your language in my courtroom, Mr. Lawson."

Avery: "Let's go back to earlier this year, then, to the second weekend of May. You were working late that Friday, weren't you?"

Lawson: "I always work late on Fridays."

Avery: "And do you remember Derek Holton coming into the store to buy some milk for his mother that night?"

Lawson: "That's what he said after."

Avery: "His mother confirms she sent Derek to buy milk."

There were objections about hearsay, but Lawson expounded on his earlier answer anyway.

Lawson: "He didn't bring any milk to the counter. Only beer. Maybe that's the kind of milk his mother wanted."

Avery: "There's no need to get ugly, Mr. Lawson."

The judge warned the defendant to keep his comments confined to the questions and the cross-examination had resumed.

Avery: "Derek claims you refused to serve him. Is that true?"

Lawson: "I refused to let him have the beer."

Avery: "And when he began to protest, you pulled a knife from under the counter, didn't you? To scare Mr. Holton?"

Lawson: "He misunderstood. I took it out to clean it. That's all."

Avery moved on to the questions Callie assumed he'd been building to all along.

Avery: "And where did you get the knife, Mr. Lawson?"

Callie could imagine the prosecutor doing his best to remain calm as he began this part of the questioning. The Holton boys had been an appetizer, setting the table, but the knife and its uniqueness had always been the entree. In the end, the judge had suspended testimony for the day.

Sitting on the bench, Callie thought about Harry's volatile testimony. Brock Avery had succeeded in showing Harry for the hothead he was. A better defense lawyer might have been able to offer objections, but it wouldn't have mattered anyway. Harry's conviction had been inevitable. For the jury, it was only a hop, skip, and a jump to make the leap from volatile to cold-blooded killer to a verdict. Guilty.

Chapter Eleven

Now

During the trial, Harry Lawson's military record had been a source of inquiry for both the prosecution and the defense, each side quick to paint the details in whichever light suited them best. Gordon knew the basics. Twelve years enlisted in the Army, assigned as infantry. A tour in Afghanistan. For the young man, the whole thing sounded like every other PTSD story he'd heard. He didn't doubt the truth of Lawson's diagnosis, nor did he consider it extraordinary. At the trial, the defense dug up a couple of old Army buddies to talk about his courage under difficult circumstances, cementing Lawson's good-guy veteran status. The prosecution found its own witness who testified to Lawson's volatile nature prior to the difficulties he faced in Afghanistan. Only two facts were not disputed. Lawson signed up willingly and, after twelve years, was honorably discharged. Everything in between seemed to be a matter of opinion. Gordon and Jeremy decided to take a Switzerland approach.

"The best thing to do is give the facts only. Dates he enlisted. Tours. Discharge date," Jeremy said.

"What about his expertise with weaponry? Do we mention that?" Gordon asked, sipping a glass of orange juice. His mouth puckered as he drank. He didn't really like orange juice, but his diet since he'd been in Hampstead had consisted of too much greasy take-out. He needed to find other places to go, ones that didn't feature the word fried in every special.

Jeremy considered Gordon's question as he scooped a forkful of home fries into his mouth. "Honestly, I'm not sure it matters. Does it take expertise to stab a woman? Couldn't anybody do that?"

Gordon thought Jeremy had a point, and yet, he thought maybe it did matter. "I think I'm going to add it in. He had that knife, the one he brought home from the Army."

"The L something, right?"

Pushing his plate away, Gordon said, "The Gerber LHR Knife. They don't make it anymore. Pretty scary looking actually." He wiped his napkin over his mouth. "The blade alone is seven inches long, and it's got a serrated area near the tip. According to what I read, the thing was designed to be used in hand-to-hand combat, to kill when necessary. It's definitely not a small knife."

Jeremy shrugged. "Still doesn't take expertise."

"It does actually. According to the testimony from the kid in Lawson's store, it was in some kind of holder before Lawson waved it in his face. It's got a special quick-release sheath system and safety lock so your enemy can't just reach in and grab it."

Jeremy put his fork down. "Correct me if I'm wrong, but that sounds a whole lot like you're saying that whoever killed those ladies knew how to use that specific knife."

"Not necessarily, but possibly."

"And as far as we know, the only person around here who knew how to use it was Harry. I thought we were here to peg someone other than Harry as the killer. Doesn't that contradict what we're trying to do here? To clear Harry Lawson?"

It was a good question, but Gordon had an answer. "We're not here to clear Lawson. The video already does that. We're here to find out who really killed Lisa and Tina."

Confusion clouded his friend's eyes. "But the stuff you said sounds like it was him. How do you explain that?"

Again, Jeremy's question was logical, and again, Gordon had an answer. "The murder weapon was never found."

This had been discounted by the prosecution. "There are hundreds of ways to dispose of a knife," Avery had proclaimed at trial. "Drop it in a river, a garbage truck, or bury it in the woods. So, yes, we do not have the murder weapon in our possession at this time. But we know exactly which weapon was used to mutilate—yes, mutilate—Lisa Lawson and stab Tina Cox. And only one man in Hampstead had such a weapon."

More than once, Gordon wished there was video of the trial. He would have loved to see Avery in action. He planned to call on the former prosecutor soon.

"The fact is, there's no proof that Harry's knife killed Lisa and Tina." He saw the look on Jeremy's face and rushed to explain. "I know, I know. The description of the wounds matches that particular type of knife." He'd read over the pages on the knife three times. The testimony on the dozens of cuts and slashes to Lisa's body had taken an entire morning. While the transcript he received didn't include the photos, he knew that the pictures of Lisa's body had been front and center for the jury. The attorney for the defense did her best to argue that another knife, a similar one, could have been used in the slayings. But the pathologist refused to budge. She allowed that it might not have been Harry's knife, but the type was the same. In the end, that was enough for the jury. "And don't forget, Harry said his knife had been stolen."

"What else is he gonna say, bro?"

Gordon gave a quick nod of approval. One of Jeremy's special talents was to play devil's advocate. In truth, he could have asked half the town to play that role, but Jeremy was a little friendlier. The missing knife presented more than its share of questions. Lynnleigh insisted that her father's postmortem innocence was evidence that he'd told the truth on the stand. However, to be fair, Gordon needed to consider all possibilities.

"Let's assume you're right. He lied about the knife being stolen. The police searched every inch of his property, his car, his store. They used dogs to try and find it. Nothing."

"That only means he didn't have it after the murders."

"True. But knives don't vanish into thin air on their own. What else could have happened to it?"

The waitress chose that moment to fill Jeremy's cup and drop off the check. "Y'all let me know if you need anything else." She lingered a moment. "Or if you have any questions or anything. Y'all are doing that podcast, right?"

Gordon studied her for the first time that morning, reading her nametag. Shelley. She wore jeans and a whitish t-shirt that bunched at the roll of flesh just above a dark apron. He took in the plain wedding band and the hair swept back into a ponytail, secured with a barrette. If asked, he'd say she was pretty, but she had the tired air of a woman who left work at the diner for more work at home. He guessed there were kids to go with the husband. Maybe aging parents.

The crinkles when she smiled told him she was older than they were, maybe ten years, maybe fifteen. If he was right, she might have been in Hampstead at the time of the murders.

"That's us," Gordon said.

"We had a lot of reporters here right after the news broke, you know." She pointed out the front window toward the town hall and police station. "Had microphones and cameras set up over there. Shawna, one of the waitresses here, even made it on TV." She smiled at the young men. "They've been gone a few weeks now, and to tell you the truth, people around here are kind of relieved."

Gordon suspected she was right, but there were others who enjoyed the attention the case brought.

"Hampstead's a quiet town. A good town. I hope you won't go making up stories just to get listeners."

Blood rushed to his face. This was the second time he'd been suspected of creating a false narrative. First, the Hampstead police, and now, a local waitress. "I'm just trying to find the truth, uh…" His words floated away. "Shelley. We don't make up stories. We look for facts."

"Please." She stopped short of rolling her eyes, but the look she gave him had the same effect. "Facts are subjective these days, aren't they? You interview someone, and they tell you their story, how they remember things, or how they saw them. From their viewpoint. You put it on your podcast or post it on your page, and it's out there for anyone to see, copy, or share. Get enough views and add a headline, it becomes accepted as fact. Never mind that the viewpoint might be biased or flat out wrong."

He started to object, but she cut him off.

"I know how it works, Mr. Little. At least when I was a kid, we knew the stuff written in certain magazines was fake. Nowadays, nobody knows what's real and what isn't. Just because it's on some website doesn't make it true. The internet is one big tabloid if you ask me."

Jeremy couldn't stifle a laugh, and Gordon sat back, throwing up his hands. "Really?"

"She has a point, Gordo."

"I'll climb off my soapbox," she said, taking a step back. "I'm just saying," she said with a nod toward the other tables, "these are real people in this town with real families. Some of them are going to believe everything you tell them on your podcast."

"What's wrong with that?"

"Maybe nothing," she admitted. "Maybe a lot. Depends on if you really want to find the truth or if you just want publicity for yourself and your podcast. Maybe it's about money or a way to attract a bunch of girls." She brushed a loose strand of hair from her face. "But let's say you really do want to find the truth, how likely is it you'll give two shakes about who you might hurt along the way to get it?"

"That's not fair."

"You're right. It's not. None of this is fair, but for a lot of folks, fair stopped mattering a long time ago," she said. "All I'm asking is that you think about it."

Chapter Twelve

Fifteen Years Ago

Callie rolled onto her side, blinking in the dark. Her father's voice, soft at first, got louder as the conversation grew more heated. Something in his tone drew her from her bed again, and she tiptoed down the hall.

"Harry isn't all bad—I know that—but things don't look good. The press is breathing down our necks. The phones won't stop ringing with people scared there's going to be another attack. And Harry doesn't help. Blowing up one minute, sobbing the next."

"He's lost his wife, John."

"This whole thing smells bad." She heard a rustling sound, a bump. "That's all I have to say."

"And yet, you're investigating him."

"I'm not investigating him. I'm not on the case."

"You might as well be. You're involved."

"Everyone is involved. You know how this works, Maura."

"Lisa would be rolling over in her grave, and you know it. She protected him."

"Harry Lawson doesn't need protecting."

"You don't know that, John. Harry might look strong, but that doesn't make him strong. Lisa worried about his obsession with keeping them safe, his paranoia. That's only my opinion, mind you, but I know I'm right. Lisa was a pretty private person. She didn't talk much about Harry other than the good things, but I sensed she was holding back." Maura's hands rose and fell with her words. "I remember Patty asking her about that barfight, you know, the one with Jerry Morgan, but Lisa brushed it off. She said it wasn't Harry's fault, that there were things he couldn't control, and she swore he was trying." A short silence followed. When her mother spoke again, it was reluctance Callie heard. "The Army prescribed some antidepressants, but there were side effects, and he shut it down. He stopped taking them a few months ago. She made me promise not to tell anyone, and I never did, but you should know they were working together on his issues. Together, John."

"If that's true, Mo, he almost knocked out that man's teeth while on the meds. That was before this. Maybe he should have stayed on them."

"Oh, please. Weren't you the one who told me Jerry Morgan made pushing buttons a sport, that he'd been in more bar fights than anyone in this town?"

Callie heard the concession in her father's voice. "Yeah. Morgan's an ass, but he took a beating that night. If Buck hadn't stepped in, Harry might have killed him."

Several seconds passed before her mother spoke again. Callie leaned forward to hear better.

"What button did Jerry push, John? It was about Lisa, right? Wanting to…to be with her and saying suggestive things." Callie smiled at the way her mother had phrased what was most likely vulgar and sexist behavior. Unfortunately, she and most of her friends knew the kind. Most women did.

"That's no excuse, Mo." Her father, true to form, held to the letter of the law. "Harry threw the first punch. It doesn't matter if Morgan said he'd slept with Harry's mother. It's assault, no matter how you look at it."

"But the charges were reduced."

"Only because Avery didn't want to prosecute a Vet unnecessarily, and Morgan is who he is."

"It would have been a miscarriage of justice for Harry to go to jail."

Her father grunted. "Maybe, but his temper is going to get him in trouble one day. Maybe it already has."

"You can't believe he's guilty, John. You can't."

It wasn't the first time Maura had pushed her husband on this. Callie waited now, but it was a long moment before her father spoke again.

"It doesn't matter what I believe."

"It does to me. I don't think I'm wrong when I say that protecting Lisa and Lynnleigh is the only thing Harry Lawson has ever cared about. He would have done anything to make sure no one hurt them. Ever. And now someone has."

"His issues go deeper than Lisa and Lynnleigh, and you know it. Lisa should have—"

"Enough. You weren't in her shoes, John." She paused, her breath coming faster. "Look, I'm sorry, but Lisa was doing everything she could. She'd even gotten him to agree to see a new psychiatrist at the hospital. Had even made him an appointment. They were both hopeful."

"You never told me that."

"I'm telling you now."

Neither said anything for a few seconds, each lost in their thoughts.

"I should tell Jackson," her father said at last, but his voice lacked conviction.

"About an appointment that never happened?" Maura rose to her feet. "And what would that accomplish, John? Are you trying to help build a case against him?"

Callie saw her father flinch, but he didn't deny it either.

"I'm going to bed," her mother said finally.

Callie scrambled back down the hall, sliding under the covers. Lying in the dark, she thought about the Lawsons, about their daughter. Unsurprisingly, Callie had made little progress with the girl, barely getting her to acknowledge the papers spread out before her. At their second tutoring session, Callie had stopped talking and waited, but Lynnleigh didn't seem to notice that either.

Lying in the darkness, Callie stared up at the ceiling, a tear slipping from the corner of her eye. The girl had lost her mother, and now it looked like her father was going to be arrested for that same murder. Lynnleigh must be overwhelmed with grief and terror at the same time—with no place to get away or hide. How could she not be? No one in town was talking about anything else. Even inside Callie's house, this case consumed her parents, driving a wedge between them like a wrecking ball. She didn't fully know why, but she was suddenly glad her father wasn't on this case. He was right. It smelled. Bad.

Chapter Thirteen

Now

Callie had never liked digging into the lives of victims, poring through their belongings, interviewing their family and friends, exposing long forgotten ills as though death had stolen not just their life but also their right to privacy. This case was no different. Maybe worse. Time had a way of dimming memory for some and sharpening tongues for others. She sighed as she took a stack of photos from a folder. Walking over to the whiteboard she'd rolled into the makeshift war room, Callie hung the first picture on the left side. Using a marker, she wrote Lisa Lawson underneath. On the right, she did the same with Tina's photo and name. Over the next half hour, she drew the spokes that made up the wheel of connections between the women and their friends and families. She added names and relationships. Aunt. Daughter. Co-worker. Some were deceased now or had moved away, but they would have had families and friends who might remember. She added more names and photos.

Under Harry's picture, she hesitated before adding the last spoke. Not a friend, but he mattered. Anthony Battle. Cloaked in a dark hoodie, his face, florid after years of heavy drinking, looked older than it should. In the photo, his chin tilted upward and his lower lip jutted forward in an expression that made her think of a petulant teenager. Shoulders sinking, she knew that was only the tip of the iceberg with a man like Anthony Battle.

From Tina's folder, she pulled a contact list, comparing it one more time to her whiteboard. Albie Anders. Check. Alice Brown. Check. Connie Bynes. Check. On and on it went. She slowed at the last name Marks. There were two. Dean Robert Marks, she'd expected. But there was also his son, Byron. She knew the name. He was the dean of the hospital now, but he wouldn't have been then. She searched through the file but found nothing more about him. Tapping her pen against the pages, she considered the already growing list. After a minute, she sighed, adding the name under his father's anyway.

Zel came through the door, food bags in each hand. He held them up in the air. "Bagels or biscuits. Take your pick."

"What kind of bagels?"

"Plain. I don't want to suffer the wrath of Callie Forde if the everything bagel brushes up against the cinnamon bagel."

Her nose wrinkled. "You know how wrong it is when that happens. And what do you mean by wrath? You make me sound like a witch. I was annoyed, that's all."

"Huh. I guess one person's annoyance looks a whole lot like another's wrath."

She folded her arms across her chest.

"Just kidding," he said with a grin, "but I'm sticking to plain from now on."

"You're an ass," she told him, before poking him in the ribs.

He laughed. "Watch what you say, witch."

The easy camaraderie between the two detectives settled Callie's nerves, and she looked at the board again, at the dozens of spokes and names.

"A lot of people in this town knew Lisa Lawson and Tina Cox, and if they didn't, they know someone who did. We're going to have to talk to all of them again, especially the ones who saw them in the last days leading up to the murders."

Zel grunted through mouthfuls of biscuit. "It's been a long time, Cal."

"We have their original statements. We can use those to refresh memories if we need to. But maybe we can find someone who didn't come forward before, someone who thought what they had to say didn't matter. I don't know."

"Okay. How do we want to do this?"

"We start with the Bradys, Lisa's parents. Talk to her brother. Tina's mother. And keep going from there."

"What about those guys?" He pointed at the two names she'd written at the bottom of the board. Neither lived in Hampstead then or now. One was a drifter who'd picked up odd jobs, and the other, a traveling salesman who came through town from time to time. Both had been questioned during the original investigation. Neither had alibis. Or apparent motive.

"I've got a line on the salesman, but still searching for the other one."

"Okay. What about the daughter? Lynnleigh? I hear she's called the Chief, wanting to know what's being done."

Lynnleigh Lawson. Callie had lain awake half the night thinking about the girl she'd met the summer of the murders. That young and frightened girl would have given anything for one of Harry Potter's invisibility capes. This one—the grown-up version—stood tall and wasn't afraid to use her voice. Callie had seen her on the news. Any teenaged gawkiness had long since gone, although Callie guessed the anger and suspicion remained.

"Did you know this case was the reason I became a cop?"

Zel stopped chewing. "Why am I just now hearing about this?" he asked through the last of his biscuit.

She waved a hand in the air. "Probably because it's the first time I've said it. At least I think it is."

"Wait, is this some kind of epiphany?"

"No, nothing like that. I mean, I've always known, but not in a conscious way. That summer was hard. People were on edge. My dad was gone all the time, even though it wasn't his case. There were more fights that summer, more need for the police. Every tourist was a suspect of something until they arrested Harry. Even then, it took a long time for things to go back to normal. You remember, right?"

"Yeah. I was a beat cop. Worked more overtime than I ever had before or after." He balled up a paper wrapper and tossed it in the trash. "It wasn't a fun time around here, I can tell you that. Why would all of that make you want to chuck a cushy office job with AC and real raises?"

Callie looked over at the whiteboard, the images of the two women staring back at her. Once upon a time, she'd taken notes on debits and credits from whiteboards. She'd deciphered balance sheets and created slide presentations. All of that seemed a long time ago now.

"It wasn't the case exactly. When I was little, I was a daddy's girl."

His eyebrows shot up. "When you were little?"

"Okay. Maybe I've always been a daddy's girl. I looked up to my dad."

"You had good reason."

"Yeah. Anyway, for a while, he could do no wrong. Then I went through a time when I thought what he did was boring. And when I was in high school, his job wasn't cool, you know."

"Only too well," he said. Callie nodded, remembering Zel's daughter, whose own rebellion had resulted in her leaving home on her eighteenth birthday.

"But deep down, I never stopped admiring him and by extension, his job. The truth is, I didn't think I could live up to that or to his expectations. And so, a career in business seemed like a good choice."

"But?"

"But that summer, I saw that what made him so good was more about his humanity than being stronger or smarter than everyone else. I mean, I still thought he was those things, but he had compassion and empathy, and to him, it wasn't always about winning." *Like Avery*, she thought, but left the words unsaid. "He said once it didn't matter if a man fumbled his way to the truth as long as he got there, that each investigation was like a maze with wrong turns and dead ends, but if you kept at it, a man would find his way out." She paused, her face soft with memory. "And he said more than once that no detective was infallible, but I'd always thought it was just words until this case. He wavered. He had doubts. But it wasn't his case, and he respected the process."

"He was right to doubt."

"Sure, but he didn't know that then, and I don't think he could have named his doubts at the time. It's easy in hindsight. My point is that I realized I wanted to do what he did, too—even the boring stuff. I felt it in my gut in a way I never had in business school. I wanted the maze, the puzzle. And in a way, he'd given me permission because now I didn't have to be perfect to do that. I could help people instead of spending my days crunching numbers on an endless stream of spreadsheets."

"Not that there's anything wrong with that," he said with a wide smile.

"Right," she said, smiling back at him. "Not that there's anything wrong with that. But the moment I made the decision, I knew it was the right one. Being a detective here matters to the people of this town. It matters to me."

Zel nodded again and jerked his chin toward the whiteboard. "It matters to Lynnleigh, too."

She followed his gaze to the picture she'd tacked under Lisa's.

"Should I reach out?" he asked.

Callie studied the photo, the same that had been used by the papers. Lynnleigh looked right into the camera, no hint of amusement, no smile. Instead, there was only sadness and loss. She deserved better than she'd gotten. "Not yet," she said. "We'll talk to her, but I'd rather wait. I'd like to have something to say first. And right now…" her words faded as she waved a hand toward the board. "We don't have a thing."

Chapter Fourteen

Now

The man watched the podcaster cross the street and enter the squat office building. It wasn't hard to figure out where he was going. The building only had three floors. The Hampstead Credit Union occupied the first floor, and while bank records might be relevant to any murder investigation, that wasn't why the kid had gone inside. He pictured the young man riding the elevator to the third floor, stepping off, and stopping in front of the door at the end of the hall. McKay's Insurance. Randy McKay sold an assortment of products: car insurance, property insurance, and life insurance. It was that last kind that was likely to have caught Gordon's attention, or more specifically, the life insurance policy that Harry had insisted the couple take out on Lisa shortly before her death. Two hundred and fifty thousand dollars. Not lifetime money in the grand scheme of things, but enough to raise plenty of eyebrows. The man figured the premium had probably been a stretch for the couple, but Harry was nothing if not prepared. Unfortunately for him, his Boy Scout ways had come back to bite him in the ass.

Raising a hand to shade his eyes, the man looked up at the building, imagining the questions the kid would ask. It was doubtful he'd learn anything new. The insurance had always been a red herring, although you wouldn't know it by the way Avery had framed it at trial. A master class really. He remembered the bulldog of a prosecutor now.

Brock Avery took a sip of water before crossing the floor of the courtroom, his gait more amble than stride. With his jacket pushed back and hands tucked into his pockets, he nodded once at the jury before approaching Harry on the stand.

In the audience, a woman with a steno pad in her lap clucked her tongue and shook her head. "Good Lord, Harry Lawson doesn't stand a chance."

Another voice whispered back, higher-pitched. "How do you know?"

"Are you kidding? I've been covering Avery for years. When Avery goes all casual like that, he's going in for the kill. Lawson is as good as convicted."

Lawson waited on the stand, his face stony, bordering on antagonistic. For a man like Lawson, a man who'd fought hard for most of his life, it was the only way he knew. The best defense is a good offense. Other than his rigid posture, he appeared calm. His eyes didn't flit around the courtroom. There were no telltale beads of sweat. No doubt he believed his innocence would protect him. That same naivete probably drove him to insist on testifying, an action any seasoned defense lawyer might have vetoed, not that it would have mattered. Harry would have his day in court. He was tough. No one would ever dispute that. Smart was another thing.

Avery stopped short, halfway to Lawson, allowing the jurors a clear view of the defendant. It was a show of confidence, an impressive strategic move.

"I've been wondering somethin' these last few days, Mr. Lawson," Avery said. He kept his pitch low and soft, with just a hint of twang—the kind that said he was just a regular guy. "You loved your wife, your family. Married to your high school sweetheart. A daughter to raise. A man that loves his family feels that responsibility." Avery didn't look at the defendant, his sharp eyes now locked on the jury. Every head turned away from him toward the defendant.

For his part, Lawson nodded along. "Yes, sir."

"Family is a wonderful thing. A thing to be treasured. That responsibility can be a thankless task for some." Avery approached the jury. "We've all had tough times, tough days. Layoffs, sick kids, broken down cars. Any number of things can add up to stress when trying to take care of your family. We all know how that feels." He allowed a small shake of his head. "It's a mighty burden to carry."

Lawson's lawyer jumped to her feet. "Is there a question in there, Judge?"

"Gotta say I agree with Ms. Thompkins. Can you get to the point, Mr. Avery?"

The prosecutor glanced over his shoulder and offered a small smile. "I'm getting there, Judge," he said and faced the jury again. "A man who feels a responsibility to his family works hard. Maybe he buys a house. Maybe he takes a second job. Maybe he takes out life insurance." Avery paused, swinging back toward the defendant. "Did you purchase a life insurance policy, Mr. Lawson?"

"I did."

"As any loving husband would." He shoved his hands deeper into his pockets. "And how much are you insured for?"

The audience leaned forward, all intent on an answer that didn't come. The Judge shifted to look down at the defendant, his thin lips pursed. No one moved or spoke, the quiet louder than any words.

"Mr. Lawson," the Judge said. "Please answer the question."

"I'm not insured."

Avery didn't miss a beat. "But you just told us you purchased life insurance. Did you lie to the courtroom, Mr.Lawson?" His voice rose an octave.

"I didn't lie. I wouldn't. I did buy life insurance, but the policy was for my wife."

"You took out an insurance policy on your wife?" A collective gasp sounded in the courtroom. Two of the women blanched at the admission, and three men openly scowled.

"Yes."

"I'm going to confess I find that a curious thing, Mr. Lawson." Avery took one step closer to the stand, a perplexed frown on his face. "Why would a man take out an insurance policy on his wife and not on himself? You were the breadwinner in the family, weren't you?

Lawson's chin shot up. "Lisa worked."

"Part-time, as I understand it. And how much was this life insurance worth?"

No one breathed in the long seconds before Lawson answered. "Two hundred and fifty thousand."

Avery's whistle echoed in the rafters. "Two hundred and fifty thousand dollars. A quarter of a million. That's a lot of money." He took another step. "Let's see. Your wife worked ten hours a week at the local preschool, isn't that right?"

"Yes, Sir."

"By my calculation, it would take her more than thirty years to earn the money

you took out on her."

"I guess. I didn't think of it like that."

"How did you think of it then?"

"I wanted to be sure Lynnleigh was taken care of."

Avery shifted back toward the men and women of the jury. "In case something happened to her mother?"

"That's right.

Lawson's lawyer's shoulders sank like a leaky ship as she fell back in her chair.

"But no policy for you. I suppose it didn't occur to you that something could happen to you." Before Lawson could answer, Avery pressed on, pulling his hands from his pocket and straightening to his full height. "Which leads me to the assumption that your concern, your only concern, was that something would happen to Lisa, your wife." His tone hardened along with his stance. "You purchased a life insurance policy worth two hundred and fifty thousand dollars." He pointed his finger up in the air. "Two hundred and fifty. Not in case something happened to your wife, but when something happened to your wife, Mr. Lawson. When. You knew your wife was going to die."

Although red-faced, the man on the stand didn't flinch. "Sure. I knew."

Lawson's lawyer slid lower in her seat. Murmurs of indignation among the audience grew louder until the judge banged his gavel, ordering quiet.

Avery moved back toward the jury. "As you heard, Mr. Lawson knew his wife was going to die." He spun around. "That's what you said, isn't it, Mr. Lawson?"

"I didn't mean it the way you're saying it. We're all going—"

"He admits it." Cutting off the defendant mid-sentence, Avery's voice boomed. Again, the judge banged his gavel, and again, a hush fell over the courtroom. Avery, of course, wasn't finished. "You bought an insurance policy on your wife six months before her death. Two hundred and fifty thousand dollars. Only. Six. Months. Earlier. Because you knew your wife was going to die."

The man's lips twitched now at the memory. A flurry of objections had followed, but it didn't matter. Lawson's lawyer had been too young and inexperienced to do more than sputter, and Lawson's anger at Avery's accusations only made him look more guilty. The damage had been done. The man remembered the articles that ran the next day. If there had been anyone left in town who believed in Harry Lawson, they hadn't after that.

Now, the man looked up at the glittering glass windows. How much did the insurance salesman know, and how much would he say? As the man recalled, McKay had been quite forthcoming at Lawson's trial.

Avery paced the floor in front of McKay. "Did you ask him if he might want insurance on himself?" Avery asked.

"I did, but he said he didn't need it." The insurance agent shot an apologetic glance at the defendant. "He was very clear that only his wife's life needed to be insured and as soon as possible." As before, a couple of the jurors recoiled. McKay saw the shift, too, and began to explain. "But the thing is—"

Avery spoke over him. "I was wondering, how long did the process take?"

"The process?"

"Yes. How long from the time Mr. Lawson came in until the policy was effective?"

The small man in the witness box hesitated. "Not long, I guess. We had to go through the usual steps. We got a physical and mental evaluation of the insured. We went over the cost and different options."

"Options? Can you tell us about those?"

McKay droned on for a few minutes, nearly losing the jurors, before Avery brought him back to what was surely the point all along.

"And what were the terms of the policy Mr. Lawson settled on?"

"Well, he chose a sliding policy that gave the largest sum of money to the beneficiary in the first ten years. The amount dropped significantly after that."

"Is that unusual?"

"Not unusual exactly, but not common either."

"Not common." Avery repeated those last words with yet another shake of his head. "A sliding policy with the biggest payout if death comes sooner rather than later." He introduced a copy of the policy as evidence then, giving another summary of the contents as he did. McKay slumped on the stand the longer the prosecutor talked. "One last question, Mr. McKay. How did Mrs. Lawson seem to react to her husband's request—or rather insistence—that she have this large life insurance policy?"

"She didn't seem pleased. I specifically remember her saying they couldn't afford the premiums on top of the insurance on the store, the house, and the cars."

Avery's thick brows drew together as though he were hearing this for the first time. Unable to pass up an opportunity to characterize Lawson as single-minded and determined to ensure his wife, Avery gave his own testimony. "I do believe a certain kind of man will go to extreme lengths when money is involved, and I do believe Mr. Lawson's store was bleeding cash of late. Clearly, that is the case here, Ladies and Gentlemen."

The judge saved the defense the trouble of objecting. "Save it for summation, Counselor."

"Of course," the prosecutor said with a slight bow. "Let me rephrase." Focusing on McKay again, he asked, "Isn't it true that Mr. Lawson desperately needed a cash infusion for his store and a sliding policy on his wife could serve as the perfect solution?"

Lawson's attorney did object this time, but the jury squirmed even as the judge ruled in favor of the defense.

"Withdrawn." Avery took it all in stride. "Let's focus on Lisa Lawson. Is it fair to say, Mr. McKay, that Mr. Lawson wanted the policy more than Mrs. Lawson?"

"I guess."

"And less than six months after you sold a two hundred and fifty thousand dollar sliding life insurance policy on Lisa Lawson—six months almost to the day—Lisa was murdered in a most brutal way. Seems quite the coincidence, doesn't it?"

The tired and overworked defense attorney objected once more, and again the judge sustained, reminding Avery to save his comments for summation, but his ruling meant little. The damage had been done. Every juror had made up his or her mind about that policy.

The man's thoughts returned to McKay and the podcaster. He couldn't know whether McKay was willing to talk or what he even had to say after all this time. Fifteen years is a long time to remember. Chances were, the podcaster's visit to McKay would be a waste of time, but the man knew better than to rely on chance. He'd keep his eyes and ears open, make sure the kid never got too close to the truth.

Stepping out of the shadows, he walked down the street toward the park and the bustle of shops. He lifted a hand in greeting to a woman he recognized but couldn't name, smiling broadly as he passed her. The smile faded, falling away as quickly as it had appeared. Everything would be fine. It had to be.

Chapter Fifteen

Now

Callie made checkmarks, working her way through that morning's list. The six women she'd spoken with so far had little to offer in the way of new information.

"Lisa was a natural-born teacher," one woman told her. "So good with kids. Tina and Lisa were like sisters, you know. I remember them back in high school, the way they wore the same color headbands or dressed as twins on spirit days. Such a shame."

Most of what Callie heard was the same. She checked the next address and waved it in front of her partner. "Next stop: Tarrant Road. Patty Handler."

"Handler as in the bed and breakfast."

"One and the same." Callie knew Patty Handler. She'd worked at the hotel near campus until she inherited her mother's house on the edge of downtown. Over the years, she'd converted it into a busy bed and breakfast with front porch swings and a colorful garden. It was especially popular with the college parents who wanted something different from the sameness of a hotel for graduation or parents' weekend.

"Another high school friend?"

"Yep."

Zel pulled into the circular drive that led to a two-story white colonial with sunny yellow shutters. Additional parking had been set up on the side of the house, but the small lot for guests was empty on that day.

Patty greeted them at the door with a wide smile. They followed her into a large dining room with seating for twelve. Callie could imagine the table filled with guests and the sideboard loaded with eggs, bacon, and toast. Now, a tray sat at one end of the table. It held a pitcher of tea with floating lemons, three glasses, a bowl of sugar cubes, and another with more lemon. Waving a hand at the chairs, Patty said, "I haven't seen you in ages, Callie. How're your parents? I hear they're getting out more. Really, that's the best medicine, isn't it? I'm sure your dad will be back to his old self soon."

Zel elbowed Callie in the ribs. It was a running argument between them. Callie loved Hampstead, the small-town feel, the sense of community, but along with that came everyone knowing about your family and your friends and even your relationships. A by-product of familiarity was a never-ending supply of opinions. She'd certainly learned that the hard way.

Zel diverted Patty from saying more by pointing at the pitcher. "Sure would love some tea in this heat," he said. Winking at Callie, he added, "Haven't had a thing to drink all day, and that looks delicious." As expected, Patty beamed.

Pulling out her notebook, Callie sat down, too. "Thanks for taking the time to talk to us, Patty. We won't take up too much of your time."

"Oh, I'm not busy today. No guests until the weekend this time of year. Besides, anything for Lisa and Tina. I still miss them, you know." She poured three glasses of tea and passed around the other items, setting the pitcher back on the tray. "We had a movie club. We'd drive into Richmond to one of those big movie theaters and then go out to dinner. I mean, the theater in town is fine, but it's usually movies for kids."

"How often did you do that?"

"Oh, once a month, sometimes longer in between. Lisa always drove, because she didn't really drink. Tina, though, she could put away some wine." She looked from Callie to Zel. "I don't mean that the way it sounded. Not all the time. Just sometimes."

"It's okay," Callie said.

"Of course, she wasn't drinking at all before she died, you know, because..." her words fell away.

Callie exchanged a glance with Zel. "We're aware of the rumors."

Patty ducked her head. "I'm not one for gossip, and I've never said a word, but I've always suspected it was more than rumor."

"Oh?"

"Well, no wine for one. And I heard her getting sick a couple of times. And she seemed tired." Her mouth drooped. "I'd like to think I'm wrong. It's too terrible otherwise."

Callie sat forward. "Did you tell anyone else what you suspected?"

Pink crawled up Patty's face. "One person, but I'm sure she didn't tell anyone else. She wouldn't."

"And who was that?"

The woman looked down at the table before facing Callie again. "Your mother."

Callie felt her own face grow hot. Why hadn't her mother said something all those years ago? Or maybe she had. Still, it seemed like something Callie would remember.

"Huh," Zel said. He knew better than to confirm Patty's suspicion. They'd both read the autopsy report. Nine weeks pregnant at the time of her murder. Tina Cox's fetus wasn't saved. Even if it were possible, no one knew to try. Except Barton, and he'd been in shock.

Because Barton insisted that Harry had no idea Tina was pregnant, Harry was never charged with the murder of the unborn baby. Avery had wanted to include it, but Barton had begged him to leave it out. He insisted he didn't want the added attention after losing his wife. They'd already suffered through years of difficulties getting pregnant. The judge agreed, ruling the fact of the pregnancy would not be admitted on the basis that it could be prejudicial, particularly since there wasn't a shred of proof that Tina had shared news of the pregnancy with Harry. In fact, in spite of the rumors, the only people who knew about the pregnancy at all were Tina and Barton. As far as Callie knew, Patty Handler was the first friend who admitted to suspecting the pregnancy. And now her mother.

"Lisa knew," Patty said now, surprising Callie yet again. "They were arguing about it. At least I think they were. It could have been something else, but I don't think so."

Digesting the new information, Callie's head tipped to one shoulder. "Why would they be arguing?"

"It's been a long time," the woman said. "I might not remember this exactly right. I mean, no one really asked me about it before."

"It's okay," Zel said. "Whatever you can remember."

"We were at this fundraiser they had up at the college, and Tina and Lisa were down this hallway near the restroom, arguing. I didn't want to interrupt, so I backed away. I don't think they saw me, but I could still hear some of what they said."

"And what was that?"

"Tina said something about it being too soon to say anything. She didn't know if it was safe yet." Patty looked at Callie. "You don't have kids, but a lot of moms don't like to say anything until they're through the first trimester. Miscarriages, you know."

"That makes sense."

"Yeah, but Lisa wasn't having it. She said something like 'He should know he might be a father.' Lisa seemed mad that Tina hadn't told Barton yet. That wasn't like Lisa at all, but I could see her side. I mean, I know Jeb Handler would not want me to keep something as important as having a baby from him. Even to protect him. But I could understand Tina's side, too. She and Barton had been trying so long. What if she lost the baby? He'd be heartbroken."

"What happened after that?" Callie asked.

Patty's shoulders rose and fell. "Not much. Tina made a comment about how she was sorry she'd told her. I don't know what Lisa said after that because Tina started to cry."

Callie's hand went still. "Tina was crying?"

"Only for a minute. Lisa told her to pull herself together." Her lips trembled as she spoke. "Lisa had a way of taking control of every situation. Probably the teacher in her. Anyway, she told her to get it together. I'm not sure exactly what she said next, but I do remember Tina nodding her head and saying she'd tell him. Right after the fundraiser."

"Okay," Callie said as she scratched out a few notes. If Tina followed through on her promise, she would have told Barton that same evening. "Is there anything else?"

"Not that I can think of." Her fingers tapped the edge of the table. "No, wait. There is one thing. When they came back into the dining room, Tina went off to check on things with the fundraiser. Lisa went back to the table and sat with Barton for most of the night. I remember thinking that was odd."

"Odd, why?"

"Because Lisa usually didn't sit still for long. By then, she'd learned to do most social functions alone. Not that we normally got invited to things like college fundraisers—that was Tina's doing. But backyard barbecues or darts down at the Hampstead Tavern, those are where you'd usually find us. Even there, Lisa could work a room. Maybe it was because she talked to three-year-olds all day, I don't know. Maybe it was because Harry was the way he was. I mean, Lord knows he didn't have the temperament for social occasions. And definitely not fundraisers with deans and professors."

"Harry wasn't there," Callie said. She'd read this already but knew it couldn't hurt to have further confirmation.

"Oh, no. He didn't go to things like that. To be honest, I don't know if Lisa would have wanted him there anyway. He could be like a loose cannon, you know. Don't get me wrong, Harry could be a good guy, but he was…unpredictable. Anyway, like I said, Lisa loved a party. I would have expected to see her hobnobbing with the best of them. Lisa never met a stranger." She paused a moment, remembering. "But that night, she spent most of the evening sitting with Barton. Tina, what with her duties running the fundraiser for the dean, was barely at the table at all. So, Lisa sort of stood in for her, almost like she was Barton's wife."

"And this was the Saturday night before they died?"

"That's right."

"Can you tell me anyone else who was there that night?"

"Some, I guess." She rattled off a short list of names, and Callie wrote them down. "I know a few more people now, since I have the bed and breakfast, and we work with the college for special events sometimes. But I didn't know many that night." Her words slowed, and her face flushed. "It was a big night for Tina, and she invited the whole movie club and their spouses. Free food and drinks, she said. We didn't really fit in. My husband wore his best suit, but it wasn't a tux. Tina put us at a table near the front, although I don't know why. We stuck out like a sore thumb." She paused again. "Well, maybe not Barton and definitely not Tina. She kind of floated around the room, since she knew a lot of staff already." Patty's shoulders rose and fell, and she gave a short laugh. "Dean Marks stopped by our table. I heard he has a few memory issues now. Seems ironic for such a smart man to start forgetting things, doesn't it? Anyway, he came around to say hello. He was looking for Tina, I think, but he took the time to speak to each of us. Everyone kind of perked up then. Except Lisa. She was even quieter than usual."

Zel set his glass on the table. "Why do you think that was?"

"Probably the fight with Tina. She was a take-charge kind of lady—could get things done—but that didn't mean she liked confrontation. We talked about it once after Harry had that fight in the bar."

"What did she say?" he asked.

"Just that any kind of fighting made her sad. She did it plenty when she had to, but it took a lot out of her. She probably felt bad about raising her voice and making Tina cry." Lines creased her forehead. "It wasn't like them to fight."

Callie spoke again. "When you all left the fundraiser, were Lisa and Tina fine, or did things seem awkward?"

"Fine, I guess. Tina and Barton had to stay longer since Tina had to take care of a few things. The thing about Lisa and Tina was, they were more like sisters than friends—even best friends. They loved each other that much, you know. Through thick and thin and all that."

Callie said nothing, but she knew from experience that sibling relationships didn't automatically translate into love or compatibility even when you tried. And Lisa and Tina weren't blood. Their friendship had been born in childhood, nurtured through their teens and jobs and marriage. Yet even the family you chose could disappoint you. Was the relationship between

Lisa and Tina more fractured than their friends knew?

Patty's voice softened, and she looked down at her hands. "That was the last time I saw them together."

"I'm sorry," Callie said.

After a moment, Zel cleared his throat, and Patty lifted her head. "Did you ever tell anyone about the fight in the hall?"

Her answer didn't take long. "Besides your mother, only my husband, but that was later."

"Not the police?"

"No reason to, and they didn't ask. Most of the focus was on Lisa and Harry. I always felt sorry for Tina about that. And Barton. He was absolutely heartbroken."

Closing her notebook, Callie stood up. "Thank you. If there's anything else you can think of, would you give me a call?"

The legs of Patty's chair scraped the floor when she stood. "Well, there is one thing." She flushed again. "That podcaster, the young one, called yesterday." Her gaze went from one detective to the other. "I didn't talk to him. My husband was here, but I expect he'll call back. I've heard he's trying to find the truth about what happened to Lisa and Tina. Just like you."

Zel snorted. "Probably best if you don't speak to him, Ms. Handler. We're trying to—" His words faded when Callie held up her hand.

"While I mostly agree with my partner, Patty, it's your right to talk to him if you choose. I only ask that you don't reveal anything my partner or I said or asked."

"So, I can't mention the fight?"

"You can, just not as a result of telling him what we were or weren't interested in."

It took a moment before the woman seemed to grasp what Callie meant. "I think I understand."

"Good. Thank you again," she said as they were shown out the door.

They weren't two feet outside the house, summer sun beating down on them, before Zel's head whipped around. "What do you mean by telling her she could talk to that podcaster?"

"We can't stop her," Callie said, slipping on a pair of sunglasses. "It's not illegal."

"But she wouldn't if we told her not to. We don't need that kid nosing around our investigation, Callie. Have you heard him? Acting like no one did their job the first time."

Callie couldn't disagree. The tone of the first episode had rubbed her the wrong way, but she also recognized something she hadn't expected. The kid wasn't half bad. And she thought it was possible he had instincts. As they climbed in the car, she explained her thinking.

Zel's thumbs played a tune against the steering wheel. "I kind of get what you're saying, Cal, but it's like climbing in bed with the enemy. Why would we want to do that?"

"Come on, I'm not suggesting that. But if I was, you know the expression about keeping your enemies close, right?"

"Is that what this is?"

"I don't know, Zel. I can't even pretend to know what his motives really are but—"

"Ratings, money, and sponsors," her partner said, interrupting.

"Yes, that, but at the end of the day, he gets more of all of those by solving the case, right?"

"But in trying to solve it, he muddies our waters. What if his investigation— if we can even call it that—causes us to lose key evidence or makes something inadmissible? He's no different than any other civilian sticking his nose in police business."

"True, but this time is different. I think we might be able to use this civilian to our advantage."

Zel's head swiveled a second time. "Say what?"

"Look, Patty Handler kept what she suspected a secret for fifteen years. She's clearly not the gossipy type, and even she was intrigued by the idea of speaking to this podcaster. So, how many folks around here are be willing to talk to him, to get themselves on a podcast that's heard nationwide, but won't give us the time of day?"

Zel wasn't convinced. "First, not everyone cares about being on a podcast, and second, how do we know the ones who do aren't making shit up?"

"You're right, but to ignore his interviews is foolish. I'm not proposing we partner with him, but I do think we can use what he gets as a way of saving time. It's been fifteen years, Zel. That's a lot of ground to cover."

Zel's mouth opened and closed. "Are you seriously saying we should encourage people to talk to this guy?"

"I'm not saying we should do anything specific. I'm saying we let things play out unless it's a problem. Besides, I think we can learn more by being friendly than adversarial."

"Friendly, huh? Is this the honey catches more flies thing?"

"Exactly."

Zel ran his hand through his hair and clucked his tongue. "Just when you think you've heard it all." He shifted toward her. "I hate to ask, but where's Chief Waters on this?"

She stiffened. "Updating the Chief on what we learn doesn't mean he has to know how we learned it."

He wagged a finger. "You're walking a dangerous line, Forde."

"Maybe." She latched her seatbelt with a click.

"Alright, Partner. If that's how you want to play it, but I still don't like it."

"Neither do I," she admitted, looking over at him. "But I'm all for trying anything that helps us find who killed Lisa and Tina."

He switched on the ignition. "Yeah. I get that. Where to next?"

She didn't hesitate. "The Hampstead Inn. Let's find out a little more about our traveling salesman."

Chapter Sixteen

Now

Captain Jackson raised a hand toward Callie and Zel, his fingers in a beckoning motion. "Can you two join us in my office?"

The detectives exchanged a glance before following. They found Hendo and Chang already seated, eyes on an enlarged map of the houses surrounding the campus. One of the houses was circled in black. As Callie sat down, Jackson picked up a marker and drew a second circle.

"Another house?" Zel asked.

Chang answered. "Yep. Got hit last night." He lifted his coffee cup in the air. "That makes two."

Callie looked from Chang back to the map. Both of the houses were in the same neighborhood, but not on the same block. "What was taken?"

"Not much. A couple of necklaces, a laptop, a wallet with less than a hundred dollars, and a couple of credit cards." Seeing the question in Zel's eyes, Chang answered again. "No suspicious activity. We found the wallet thrown in a yard a couple of houses away, the money and cards gone."

"Any prints on the wallet?" Callie asked. "Or in the house?"

"None. Or at least nothing that hit the system."

"Sounds like the same kids," Zel said. This had been his feeling when the case had belonged to them, when there was only one house.

"I'd agree," Hendo said, "if it weren't for the holes in the walls."

Callie sat up straighter. The first house had been vandalized as well as robbed. "How many?"

"That's just it. There weren't any."

"None?"

"Nope. No vandalism at all."

Zel said what Callie was thinking. "Maybe it's not the same kids."

Jackson spoke up then. "That's why we called you in. Wanted to get another opinion on whether we're looking at one set of thieves or two." He pointed at the map. "Same neighborhood and in both cases, there's nothing missing but trinkets, some electronics, and a little cash."

"How'd they get in?" Callie asked. In the first house, a window had been smashed, and the back door unlocked.

"A window into the basement was open."

Callie's leg bounced up and down. Similar, yes, but not the same. "I don't know," she said. "If it's kids, why rip up walls in one house and do nothing in the other?"

"Maybe they got scared," Chang said. "Something spooked 'em."

"Could be," Zel said with a nod.

"Can I see the pictures from the first robbery?" Callie asked.

Chang handed over the folder. Inside were the photos taken from both houses. She flipped over to the house that had been vandalized. The holes ranged in size from a silver dollar to a small painting. "See these," she said, pointing at the smaller holes. The group leaned in. "They look like someone banged a hammer against the wall, right?"

"Could be," Jackson said.

"These are different, especially this one." She held the photo up higher, turning it up and down and on its side. "Where is this?"

"Dining room," Hendo said.

She shuffled through the stack again, pulling two more photos from different angles. The whole thing struck Callie as odd. Why put a few holes in some walls? What was the point?

Captain Jackson shifted his attention from the images to Callie and Zel. "What do you make of it?"

"Could be an M.O.," Zel said. "Weird one, but so is breaking in to steal cheap jewelry and small amounts of cash. There are plenty of neighborhoods with bigger houses and better hauls."

"So, we've established this thief—or thieves—can't tell the expensive stuff outside of laptops from the fake. A plastic vase and costume jewelry," Jackson said.

"Is there anything connecting these houses?" Callie asked. "Are the owners friends? Do they have kids in high school together?"

"Not that we've found," Hendo said.

"All the owners were out. That's what they have in common," Chang said.

Hendo leaned in. "Think we should keep digging at a connection?"

"It couldn't hurt. Why these specific houses?"

Jackson addressed the pair. "So, we look for any links or similarities between the properties. Layouts, families, the whole works."

Chang groaned but said nothing.

"What else?" Jackson asked.

A moment of silence settled over the group.

"Forde?" Jackson spoke her name as a question. "I know that look. You're thinking something."

She looked down at the photos again. "It probably doesn't mean anything."

"Spill it, Forde."

Callie hesitated. A bunch of holes was most likely a random act of vandalism, but what if it wasn't? She pointed to a single photo, the one in the dining room. The largest of the holes had defined edges. "It's different. See what I mean?"

"Because it's bigger?" Hendo asked.

"Yes, there is that."

"Could be the drywall broke away."

"Maybe," she said. "But the shape of the hole isn't jagged. It looks different, more uniform, and look at the edges. Does it look like two of these sides were cut to you?"

Each detective took the photo in turn. While Chang allowed she could be right, he had a quick explanation. "Yeah, it's smoother here and here, like a cut, but not sure that tells us anything. Maybe one kid likes to swing a hammer, and another kid used a pocketknife or something. It's not like there was anything missing from these walls."

Zel spoke up next, his words slow. "I see what you mean, Cal, but I think you're reading too much into it. My guess is someone kept banging on this one. Maybe the wall crumbled more easily. Maybe they thought it would be fun to cut open the wall. Who knows how the minds of teens work anyway?"

"Tell you what," Chang said. "We'll ask the kid after we catch him." He addressed Jackson then. "I don't think whoever it was spent much time in the last house. Seemed in a hurry based on what was taken. Probably because the neighborhood watch has been stepped up. A kid in the neighborhood might know that."

Callie looked over at Chang. "You think it's someone who lives in the neighborhood?"

"Makes sense, don't you think? Or maybe it's a friend of a kid who thinks these families have enough to spare, a kid who wants to score a little cash by pawning laptops and necklaces."

"And the holes?" Callie felt Jackson's gaze on her as she refused to give up about the holes.

"A cheap thrill, the equivalent of joyriding. Or just destructive. Whichever."

Again, no one spoke until Hendo cleared his throat. "We're not locked in on anyone yet, still looking at a few possibilities. We just thought you two might have a little insight."

"If it's teens," Callie said finally, "it's probably no more than three." She wasn't convinced, but the break-ins were simple enough for a child. No alarm. An open window. In and out.

"That's what I keep saying." Chang swept up the photos and deposited them back in the folder. "Shouldn't be too hard to get a list of kids in the neighborhood and go from there." He stood. "Barring that, I think we focus on tracking down whatever had enough value to be fenced. It wouldn't hurt to expand our radius of pawn shops, either."

"And background on the houses and families," Jackson said. Straightening, he nodded at Callie and Zel. "Thank you for your input. Hendo and Chang will take it from here."

Callie followed Zel out the door, her head down. Teens up to no good made sense. She reminded herself that this wasn't her case anymore. Probably just as well. She had a case of her own. And all she had were questions and no answers.

Chapter Seventeen

Now

Gordon put on his best smile, the one his former girlfriend used to love before she didn't, before she decided that nice smile or no, she could do better. Maybe she was right, but it stung, nonetheless. "Do you know when Mr. Cox will be available?"

The man's secretary cocked her head to one shoulder. "He's pretty busy right now." She looked past him to Jeremy. "Would you like to make an appointment? He might have some time next week."

"Nothing earlier?"

"I'm afraid not."

Since the smile wasn't working, he tried another tack. "Maybe you're available? We're looking for locals to be on our podcast."

"Me?" Her fingers fluttered to her neck. "Oh, no. I couldn't do that."

"Why not?"

"I wouldn't want to overstep. Mr. Cox has already been through so much, you know, what with that video coming out. He's a good man."

"Then who better to tell the public all about him, let them get to know him through your eyes."

She looked from Gordon to Jeremy back to Gordon. "You're serious?"

"Serious about what?"

Gordon whipped around. A man with graying temples, black-framed glasses, and the beginnings of a Pillsbury paunch stood in the doorway.

"Mr. Cox," the podcaster said, springing forward and sticking out his hand. "Exactly the man I'm here to see."

Barton looked from Gordon's outstretched hand to Jeremy. "No comment," he said and kept walking, stopping at his secretary's desk. "Linney, let me know when my two o'clock arrives, will you?"

"Of course, Mr. Cox."

Gordon hurried after Barton. "I'm not a reporter, Mr. Cox. I have a podcast, the *Catch a Criminal* podcast. Maybe you've heard of it?" He waved at Jeremy to follow him. "I'd really like to have you on. You can set the agenda, talk about anything you want."

Cox slowed before spinning back to face him. "Oh? How about if I want to talk about the bill Congress is voting on right this minute, the one that, if it passes, will create weeks of extra work for my staff?"

Heat rushed to Gordon's face. "Oh, uh, I didn't mean *anything* anything. The case anything."

"I see." He shoved his hands in his pockets. "What did you say your name was?"

"Gordon. Gordon Little."

"I'm sure you're a very nice young man, Mr. Little, but I don't give interviews." With that, he once again looked at his secretary. "I'll be in my office."

Fingers itching, Gordon refused to give up. "Look, I understand why you don't give interviews. I do. But my focus is on Tina and Lisa. About who these women were."

The man eyed him from under arched brows. "Didn't you just say your podcast was called *Catch a Criminal*? Wouldn't that be your focus?"

"Well, y-yes," he stammered, trying to think fast. "I mean, I'm going to try and find who really killed them, but I think it's important for the audience to know who Tina and Lisa were as people, to empathize with their families and friends about their loss, to—in a sense—bring them back to life for the listeners." He paused. Had he sounded cheesy? He shrugged inwardly, deciding he might as well go big or go home. "I want the audience to know you, too, and what you've gone through."

"Why?"

"Because it's been fifteen years and they deserve it. You deserve it. And Harry Lawson deserves it."

Had Barton's skin paled? Gordon couldn't be sure, but he thought the man seemed to be wavering.

"What about Lynnleigh?"

Gordon drew in a breath.

"She agrees."

The man looked away, his shoulders sagging. When he met Gordon's gaze again, his eyes glistened. "I never thought Harry killed my wife."

It took Gordon a moment to react. "We can talk about that, about Harry, and what happened."

"I'm scheduled to meet with the police."

Cox's secretary gasped behind them. "When?"

Cox gave the woman a sad look. "Tomorrow. They want to go over everything again. See if I remember anything new."

Gordon tutted. "I'm sure it'll be hard having to relive the investigation a second time."

Cox smiled, but there was no joy in it. "Isn't that what you're asking me to do, young man?"

Damn, Gordon thought. He circled back. "Yes and no. I do want to find who killed your wife and Lisa Lawson. The police and I have that in common. But I want to do more than that. I have a wide audience. It's bigger than this town. That means more ears to listen, to care about your wife, to be angry on her behalf, and to want to solve this case. Let them know you as a couple, see your life. It's been fifteen years. Both your wife and Lisa Lawson deserve to be more than victims. They deserve the public to know them as people, not only as a sad tragedy."

Cox rubbed his chin with a slow motion and Gordon dared to hope, adrenaline surging through his veins. He had more to say, but in that moment, he was reminded of a piece of advice he'd received the previous year after his last story pitch had been shot down. *You talk too much, Gordon. Learn to speak your case and shut up. That's when the magic happens.* Even so, it took all his willpower not to beg. By the time Cox finally answered, Gordon's lungs were close to bursting.

"If I talk to you, and I mean if, I don't want my wife's memory exploited in any way."

"I would never do that," Gordon said in a rush. "Never."

Another few seconds passed before Cox gave a slow nod. "I'll think about it. If we go ahead, it'll be a few days at least. I'll get back to you."

* * *

"I think you got him," Jeremy said without looking up from his phone.

"I hope so, but I'd be happier if he'd said when we'll know. The more we can promo, the better." Gordon turned the car west, putting Hampstead behind them. "Next stop, the elusive Brock Avery." The former prosecutor and his wife lived on a mountain not too far outside of town, the kind of spot with sparkling trout streams, uninterrupted hiking paths, and endless sunset views. He knew all about it because Mrs. Avery liked to post on social media and seemed to have a limited repertoire of captions. *Another perfect sunset. Hiking for days.* Her husband, however, was conspicuously absent online.

Jeremy looked up. "I thought you said he was out of town."

"He is, but his wife isn't."

"His wife? I don't know, Gord."

"What? She might know something."

"And he might be pissed we're harassing his wife and not talk to us at all."

Keeping his head pointed toward the curving road ahead, Gordon frowned. Jeremy had a point. Still, on the Hamilton Hayes case, he'd gotten as far as he had because he'd stuck his nose in again and again, buzzing around like a pesky mosquito on a hot summer's day. So far, that had been working here, too.

"I'm just saying, he's key. Going at his wife might not be the best way to get to him," Jeremy said.

Gordon said nothing. Avery was conveniently out of the country and

89

hadn't spoken since issuing a formal statement through his lawyer.

The statement had been short, limited to two sentences only. "I am deeply sorry that the evidence the prosecutor's office received fifteen years ago did not include the video that would have cleared Mr. Lawson. My apologies to his family and the good people of this county we worked day and night to protect."

He'd left on an extended European golf trip within days, avoiding the press at every opportunity. It was the smart move, and Brock Avery had proven more than once that he was a very smart man.

Gordon slowed the car at a rounded bend in the road, sped up, and slowed again at the next curve. "His lawyer was vague about when he was getting back, but it's not only us that wants to talk to him," he said now.

"What do you mean?" Jeremy asked. "Most of the media is gone."

"I mean the police."

"Oh. Right."

The sun beat down on the windshield, and Gordon reached over and turned up the AC. He didn't mind the heat so much, but the humidity in Virginia was relentless. Eyeing another blind curve ahead, he wrapped his fingers around the wheel again. The car climbed up the mountain, and his ears popped at the increased elevation.

Next to him, Jeremy rolled down his window, sticking his head out and sucking in the hot air.

"You okay?" Gordon asked.

"Fine. Just this road isn't doing my stomach any favors." After a minute, he rolled the window up again. "Better. But I mean it about Avery. I think the only chance we have with this guy is if we play the long game. Let him hear how we aren't pointing fingers…we're not, are we?" he asked suddenly, looking over at Gordon. "I mean, it's okay if we are. The sponsors will be happy with anything that brings in listeners, but if—"

"That's not what we're doing. Everybody already knows the cops fucked it up. No reason to beat a dead horse unless it helps us find who killed Lisa and Tina."

"That's what I thought," his friend said. "Just checking. I just don't think this is a good idea."

Gordon knew Jeremy well enough to respect his instincts. He waited.

"If he believes we're really serious about solving this case and make him feel more like—I don't know—part of getting it right, he's more likely to talk to us. I mean, we know he already basically pointed the finger at the cops with that evidence we received stuff, so there's no chance he's going to walk into a situation that might make him look like the bad guy. He was just doing his job, blah, blah, blah," Jeremy said.

"I don't care whether he looks like the bad guy or not."

"I know that and you know that, but he won't talk to us if *he* knows that. You showing up at his house, ambushing his wife, is going to look like an attack."

"He's not going to talk to us anyway," Gordon countered, slowing the car again.

"Probably not," Jeremy said with a shrug. "But you're making sure of it if we do this. It's up to you, though."

They rode another mile in silence, Gordon mulling over Jeremy's words. He had a line on one of the deputy district attorneys and someone from the public defender's office, but getting Avery to give them five minutes would be a real coup. He'd thought a sound bite from the wife might motivate Avery to respond, but what would she really know, if anything? Most likely, she'd slam the door in their faces and call the cops for trespassing. Jeremy was right. This was a bad idea.

"You're right. I'm going to turn around." Checking the rearview mirror, he shifted in his seat. A dark sedan rounded the curve behind him. Scanning the road ahead, he told himself there would be a turnout somewhere ahead. Slowing for yet another curve, his eyes went back to the mirror. The dark sedan took the curve at a faster speed than he did, closing the gap between them. "What's the hurry?" he muttered.

"What?" Jeremy asked, looking over his shoulder, and laughing. "You drive like you're eighty, bro."

"Yeah, yeah, yeah." Gordon's hands tightened over the wheel. The sedan inched closer. "If we get to a straightaway, I'm going to slow down and let them pass, then try to find a place to turn around."

"Yeah, okay." Jeremy looked down at his phone again. "I'll see if I can find a place to stop for lunch."

Gordon took the next curve faster than he wanted and the next, but the car behind them never slowed. Finally, he came to a section of the road that led straight up the mountain. A quick look behind him showed the sedan only one car length behind him now. Confirming there were no oncoming cars, he flipped on his right blinker, rolled down the window, and stuck out his hand to wave them on. He reached up and adjusted the mirror, watching the sedan as it drifted left to pass. He let out a breath, holding the wheel with both hands again.

"There's a barbecue place about five miles away," Jeremy said.

"Wings?"

"Yep."

The sedan pulled parallel. Gordon lifted his hand in a wave and turned to offer a small smile that faded quickly. Darkened windows made it impossible to see the driver.

"Fifteen different flavors," Jeremy was saying. "And there's brisket. You know I love brisket."

Gordon pressed his lips together, feeling squeezed by the sedan now. He didn't like the way the rocks hung over the narrow shoulder, but he moved over another inch anyway.

"Go already," he said under his breath.

Jeremy squirmed in his seat, phone and barbecue suddenly forgotten. "What the hell?"

"Yeah, I know." Gordon heard the shaking in his own voice. "This guy's an ass," he added and dropped a hand to the horn, blasting once, before gripping the wheel again. He pressed the brake then, and the sedan shot ahead, but his relief was short-lived. The sedan slowed, too, coming even with Gordon again. His mouth went dry. Next to him, Jeremy gripped the armrests, his body stiff.

Five hundred yards ahead, both cars would reach the next curve. He slowed again. The sedan slowed with him. Gordon's heart thundered in his chest. How had he gotten himself trapped between deadly rocks and some maniac?

Three hundred yards. They hadn't passed many cars since they'd started up the mountain, but that didn't mean there wasn't one coming just around the curve. He shot another look at the sedan, but the other car showed no signs of moving. Gordon slowed again. This time, when the sedan slowed, it crowded the rest of the space separating the cars, forcing Gordon to move even nearer the rocks.

"Gordon," Jeremy warned.

One hundred yards. A scraping sound jolted them both and he jerked the wheel left, slamming into the sedan. For one brief second, the other car seemed about to spin sideways, but just before the driver lost control, the car swerved back into the lane, righting itself and zooming ahead, disappearing around the curve.

Gordon hit the brakes, bringing his own car to a stop. Leaning over the wheel, he struggled to catch his breath. He didn't know how long they sat there—maybe minutes, maybe only seconds before he realized they couldn't stay there in the middle of the road.

With trembling hands, Gordon restarted the car and drove another mile until he came to a turnout. Neither spoke until the car faced downhill again.

"Do you think…" Jeremy started, letting the question hang there.

Gordon didn't answer right away. A sedan with dark windows. It wasn't that unusual a car, was it? And what had the car really done to them? Most likely, his car had a large scrape on the side, but that was the worst of it. It could be someone trying to scare them, or it could have been someone who thought it would be fun to mess with a guy with Indiana plates. Maybe.

"I don't know," he said finally. "But if Avery does ever agree to talk to us, there's no way I'm driving up this mountain."

Chapter Eighteen

Fifteen Years Earlier

"Were you in the courtroom today?" John asked Maura.

"For a bit." She rinsed her plate under the faucet before loading it in the dishwasher. "I couldn't stay." There was a brief pause. "To tell you the truth, being there makes me feel kind of sick. It's like watching a train wreck. You know it's happening, but there's nothing you can do about it."

Callie's gaze shot to her dad. He nodded once, face grim.

"Avery had the Wilkins kid at the table today."

"Ben? He's barely out of high school."

"Just finished his senior year. Pre-law, I heard."

Callie knew Ben Wilkins. He was in her older brother's class, although he hadn't been around since long before her brother left for the Army. Why would he? Still, she wondered why it mattered that Ben was at Brock Avery's table. Hadn't her father just said he was pre-law? She didn't have to wait long for him to explain.

"Putting the kid at the table sends a message. One that everyone seems to get but Harry."

"What do you mean?" Maura asked, wiping her hands on a towel.

"Every day up to now, he's had Bobby Blankenship with him as second chair. That makes sense. Blankenship has been with the office for more than five years. His record is respectable, although he's never handled a case like this before." His shoulders drooped as he spoke. "Not that there've been a lot of cases like this, but there's a whole lot of difference between prosecuting fender-benders and knocked-over mailboxes 'cause some guy spent his whole paycheck on pitchers at the Grill and prosecuting a double homicide."

Maura watched her husband, frown lines fanning out from her soft brown eyes.

"Up to now, Avery's done most of the heavy lifting. He let Blankenship question a few neighbors or customers of Harry's store a couple of times. What's he like? Are his moods erratic? Stuff to lead the jury to believe Harry's been one bad customer away from losing it. Amateur enough, even a public defender as green as Thompkins got in a few sustained objections. Knowing Avery, that was by design."

Her mother's hand went to her waist. "What are you getting at, John?"

"Today, Blankenship wasn't there. Ben Wilkins was." He looked at her. "He's just a kid," he added.

Maura's face softened, her expression wistful now. "I remember when Ben and Charlie met in Kindergarten. Stayed friends even when they were in different classes, had different interests. Remember how he'd show up sometimes in the summer and stay for what seemed like days?" She reached out and pushed a lock of hair behind her ear, her smile lopsided. "Charlie and Ben were thick as thieves."

"That was a long time ago, Mo. I don't remember seeing him around when they were in high school." The flat tone of John's voice made Callie's mother blink, as though being woken from a trance.

"Ben's dad needed him at the farm," she said.

"Sure, that was it."

When her mother didn't respond, Callie bit her lip. Charlie had run with a different crowd than Ben in high school, broke every rule and then some. That hadn't sat well with their father. John felt he had a position in town. Maura had done her best to play peacemaker, but most times, the nights ended in harsh words and slammed doors. It was an old fight between her parents. Callie had thought her brother leaving for the Army would bring a sense of relief, a calm to the household, and while it had, the hole he'd left was bigger. Although she'd never miss the friction between father and son, she did miss the boy who made her laugh, who teased her, who protected her.

"No one will ever mess with you as long as I'm around," he'd said once. There'd been nothing menacing in the way he said it or the way he gestured toward the party full of half-drunk teenagers, but she believed it just the same. If her brother and her father didn't see eye to eye, maybe it was because they were too much alike. Both smart. Both strong. Both stubborn.

As for Ben, she remembered him as quiet and tall in that gangly way that boys are before they fill out, with skin that was often speckled with clusters of pink bumps. She couldn't remember the last time she'd seen him—four years ago? Five?

"Avery's telling the judge, the jury, and everyone in that courtroom that it doesn't matter who sits at the table with him, he's got a slam dunk of a case," her father said now. "The kid is an intern at best. He should be answering phones or looking up crap for Avery to spit out for no good reason. Instead, Avery's got him in the courtroom as decoration, a prop. The kid probably doesn't even know it."

Maura frowned. "There's no reason for you to be nasty, John. And maybe Brock wants to teach Ben something. Isn't that what interning in the prosecutor's office is supposed to be? Learning?"

"Maura, it's a double homicide—the worst case we've had in as long as I can remember. Throwing a twenty-one-year-old into this circus could only be for one of two reasons, the most obvious being you want to lose and we both know Brock Avery has never wanted to lose a thing in his life."

A sigh escaped her mother's lips. "And the other?"

"You're not worried about losing, because you already think you've won."

"Even if that's true, John, Avery isn't on the jury. He can't know how this is going to go."

"Can't he?" Callie had never heard her father speak of Brock Avery like this before. After all, they were on the same side of the law, albeit with different perspectives and methods. "Harry doesn't stand a chance."

Her mother's hands floated up to her heart. "You say that like you don't believe Harry should be convicted."

Callie's body went still, her heart thudding in her chest. Would her father say Harry didn't do what everyone said he did? She knew it wasn't his case, that his involvement was minimal, but it was the first time it occurred to her that he might not agree with the charges. Maura had pushed him to have it stopped, telling him to think of Lynnleigh, but he'd clammed up. She'd answered with her own silence. When they did talk, it sometimes felt more like the dropping of small bombs than a conversation. There were no major blowups. Her parents were careful not to cross that line, but with each passing day, they came closer, and she worried more.

John grunted at last. "The evidence is solid."

"That's not an answer, John," Maura said, her tone part disappointment, part something cold that Callie didn't understand.

Callie tensed, frozen in her chair.

"Maybe not, Maura," he said, getting up and throwing his napkin on the table. "But it's the only one I have."

Chapter Nineteen

Now

"You're not coming for dinner?" John Forde's voice crackled over the line.

Callie tore her eyes from the whiteboard and fell into the closest chair. "I can't, Dad. I've got a case."

"The break-in? Hardly urgent, Cal. You have to eat."

"Not that one. Hendo and Chang are on that now."

"Huh."

A silence fell between them. She sighed, knowing he'd wait her out, badger her until she told him what he'd guess on his own, given enough time. "Zel and I picked up the Lawson and Cox case."

"Huh," he said again. "Not Jackson?"

"Chief Waters didn't like the optics."

"Waters," John said with a humph. "A blowhard if ever there was one."

Callie smiled. "Well, you'll be glad to know he hasn't changed." Holding the phone to her ear, Callie returned to the whiteboard. She lifted a hand, her finger tracing the line drawn between the two women who'd been murdered. She'd added so many lines and spokes, the board looked like a map with pictures. She stepped back, her gaze lingering briefly on the photo of Anthony Battle before moving on to the two pictures at the bottom of the board, the traveling salesman and the drifter. So far, they'd found no connection between either of those men and the two murdered women, but she hadn't given up.

"Tell me, Cal."

"Nothing to tell, Dad. Technically, it's been reopened but it might as well be a cold case. We're starting over." She looked up to the ceiling and swallowed a sigh. A part of her wanted to voice her frustrations, but it had taken so much work to get her dad willing to be a part of the world again that she didn't want to burden him. And with the Chief breathing down her neck every few hours and that podcaster promoting his next episode, it was too much. Patty Handler would be featured along with a few others. Callie just hoped she wouldn't live to regret her own role in their agreeing to be interviewed.

"Have you spoken to Barton?" her father asked.

"Tomorrow."

"And Avery?"

"Still in Europe. He's supposed to be back in a few days."

"And Ben?"

She drew in a breath. The press had sought out Ben Wilkins for many reasons, not the least of which was his standing in the community as a defense attorney. The fact that he'd briefly interned for the prosecution wasn't a secret, but after so many years, had been largely forgotten until the video. To his credit, he'd stuck to no comment so far. But they both knew talking to Ben wasn't as easy as it sounded, not when everyone in town knew about their past relationship.

"Not yet."

"What about Lynnleigh?"

She let her eyes close for just a moment. She'd worked hard these last few months to put distance between her job and her father. She'd kept their conversations at a high level or focused on cases like the break-ins. Callie didn't mention the domestic assault that landed Hillary Tildon in the ER or the fire the drug-addled mom started at her apartment on Somerset while her three kids slept in a single bed in the cramped bedroom. Like her, John Forde had been a detective who cared about the victims. If he allowed emotion to enter into his investigations, it was only as fuel to keep him going.

But now, confined to a wheelchair, his emotions could be unpredictable. For years, there had been only withdrawal. Although he'd come back to them, there were still mood swings. The therapist helped. He kept a journal now. Callie had expected him to laugh at that idea, but he'd surprised them all. Her mother confirmed he wrote every day. And last week, he made noises about taking online classes at the college. It was progress. And while Callie didn't think John Forde could ever not be a detective, they'd all followed the therapist's advice to help him seek out a purpose, whatever that turned out to be.

"I've gotta go, Dad."

"You know," John said, talking over her, "I was never convinced Harry was guilty."

The phone nearly slipped from Callie's hand. "What?"

"It was a good case. I'm not saying it wasn't. Jackson and Weston did their job. Avery thought there was enough to indict, and he got a conviction. It made sense at the time. Where there's smoke, there's fire. But…"

"But what, Dad?"

He took his time answering, and when he did, she got the feeling he was the one measuring his words this time. "I didn't know Harry as well as your mother. Well, she knew Lisa fairly well, so… He was a difficult man, had seen difficult times. But he was a soldier at heart. And I know he loved Lisa. I believe he would have done anything to protect her and their daughter." He paused again before continuing. "Like I said, they had a solid case. A witness."

"Anthony Battle." She told him about Battle's most recent claim that he'd mixed up the day, that he'd made an honest mistake.

"You don't believe him."

"No, I don't, and…." She stopped herself before she said too much.

"And you wonder why no one questioned using him as a witness a little more. I'd probably feel the same if I was you, but we can't always choose our witnesses. And in this case, Harry's alibi was already shaky for a bunch of reasons, not the least of which is that even the idea of Harry Lawson going to a grocery conference sounded absurd. He wasn't a friendly guy. Why would he put himself at an event with hundreds of people? It didn't make sense."

She started to say something, but her father wasn't finished.

"You know, I spoke to him once before they zeroed in on him. It was after the service, and I managed to get a minute alone with him."

Callie's mouth went dry. She hadn't seen anything about a conversation between her father and Harry in the files.

"He told me if he ever found out who killed his wife, he'd make them pay in ways they could only imagine. Obviously, I'd heard that kind of thing before. It's a good line. Any man who wants to direct guilt away from himself might say the same. But the way he said it, the fury he could barely control, I believed him. Harry Lawson just wasn't that good an actor. So, I reminded him that if he did that, his daughter would be alone. He'd be in jail. I remember the way he looked at me then, the way his voice sounded. 'It was my job to protect Lisa, and I didn't. I failed my mission. Don't you understand, Forde? I failed. He's still out there. He could hurt Lynnleigh.' He had his hands on my shoulders by then. I couldn't have moved from that spot if I'd tried. I remember the way his eyes burned behind the tears, and his voice dropped to a whisper. 'I can't fail again,' he said. 'Not again.'"

"Not again," she whispered, then louder. "What do you think that means?"

"I don't know, Callie." She heard the sorrow in his words. "I wish I did."

* * *

"Captain, can I have a word?" Jackson waved her in. "I need to ask you about Anthony Battle's alibi."

He settled back in his chair. "I figured you'd get to that."

"Amber Wall, Anthony's girlfriend. She was his alibi."

"Yep. Worked at the Home Depot in Charlottesville and swore Anthony went to the Stop n'Gas to get beer a little before two and came right back. Never left her apartment until the next day. That jived with the time he claimed to have seen Harry. Course, I didn't take her word for it. I checked at the Tavern, too, but Buck said he didn't come in that day or night. No one saw him that Saturday outside of the beer run."

Callie's gut told her Anthony Battle had been less than honest, but she didn't doubt Buck's word. If he said Battle wasn't in the Tavern that night, then he wasn't.

"Did you run his prints?"

"Nothing to indicate he'd been in the Lawson home. No hairs. No fingerprints."

"He could have worn gloves."

"If we were talking about someone other than Anthony Battle, you'd be right, but he isn't that smart. Never was."

"Smart enough to lie on the stand and then deny he lied fifteen years later."

Jackson scratched his chin. "The cashier thought Harry had been there, too. By the time we asked, he couldn't be one hundred percent it wasn't the Saturday before, so he couldn't be called to testify, but it was enough to corroborate Battle's story."

Thinking about Anthony's alibi again, she asked, "Could Amber have been lying?"

"She wouldn't be the first girlfriend to cover for a boyfriend, but I wouldn't have thought it at the time. She seemed like a nice girl, and we were already looking at Harry by then." There was sorrow in his eyes. "But yes, it's possible."

Callie's heart ached for the captain. He wasn't the first detective forced to look at evidence through a different lens, one that illuminated his mistakes.

He let out a breath. "Amber Wall didn't stay with Anthony. Maybe a few more months, less than a year. I was a bit relieved when it ended."

Callie lifted her brows. "You kept an eye on her?"

The captain nodded. "Like I said, she seemed like a nice girl, and Anthony Battle was the kind of man no family wants to see their daughter bring home. Her parents weren't happy about her involvement in the case, but they were even less happy about her involvement with Anthony. I believe Amber's mother called him a monster. I don't know if that was true or not, but I've been around long enough not to question a mother's instincts. Anyway, knowing young people, the parents' dislike was probably part of the attraction, but no matter how I looked at it, she was mixed up with trouble. I checked in every now and then to keep her mother happy. At first, Amber didn't like it, but over time, she didn't seem to mind, and eventually, she kicked him to the curb. The whole family moved away a long time ago. Pennsylvania or New Jersey, maybe? I might have heard Amber got married but couldn't say for sure about that."

She'd heard the same. The Wall family hadn't lived in Hampstead long. Amber's father followed construction jobs, but there didn't seem to be any pattern to it. She'd tracked them to New Jersey and then Illinois, but the trail had gone cold after that. Maybe her father had retired, or the jobs dried up. And Amber was older now. Callie didn't even know if Amber was still living with her family, had married, or what. "Do you think she'll talk to me if I can find her?"

"I don't know why she wouldn't."

She stood. "Thanks, Captain."

"Nothing to thank me for." He looked down at his hands a moment before rising with her. Guilt and regret rolled off him in waves. She'd seen less of him these last days. Part of that was due to his being outside the investigation, but it was more than that. His role in the original investigation isolated him now, made him a target in the press, a pariah in town.

"Waters brought up early retirement," he said now.

"No," she breathed. "He can't. You can't."

Sad-eyed, he lifted one hand. "He might be right. Maybe I've been at it too long. Might be time for a change."

Callie didn't know what to say. Jackson wasn't perfect, but no one in the Hampstead Police Department was or ever had been. Not even her father. And Jackson's steady presence kept them in line, kept them moving forward. He closed his door before she could get out another word.

"You're wrong, Captain," she said to the empty hall. "We need you." Her voice softened. "I need you."

Chapter Twenty

"I'm an old man now," Dean Marks said, a wry smile splitting the caverns of his sunken cheeks. He patted his hand on his chest. "Ticker's old, too. Got a pacemaker and a cabinet full of pills to prove it. That's not even the worst of it. My wife has me on a gluten-free, fat-free diet. Now she feeds me tree leaves, and if I'm lucky, chicken or salmon." His stooped frame gave an involuntary shudder. "I hate salmon."

Gordon laughed. "So do I."

"Good man," Marks said. "There's hope for your generation yet."

"Right," the younger man said with a smile. He slid forward on the slick leather chair facing the former dean and glanced briefly at the mic he'd set up between them. Reaching out, he adjusted the boom arm, bringing the mic closer to Marks. After shifting the pop filter again, he tapped a few buttons on his laptop. The dean touched a hand to the headphones Gordon had given him. "Are you comfortable?" he asked the elderly man.

"I'm afraid that's an impossibility at my age," Marks said with a chuckle, "but I'm fine. Just not used to these, is all."

Gordon laughed a little with him. Although sometimes it felt like he spent half his life in headphones, he knew that wasn't entirely normal—especially not for a man like Dean Marks. "Should we get started?" he asked.

"I'm ready. But I must remind you, I'm not as young as I used to be. My memory..." He lifted his palms. "I get things mixed up sometimes—at least that's what they tell me."

Gordon did his best to reassure the man. "Don't worry about it. If you don't remember something, we'll move on. Fifteen years is a long time for anyone. Lots of people have forgotten the details." This wasn't exactly true, but Tina Cox's former boss was an important addition to the podcast. He saw her five days a week for years. What was that phrase? Work husband? Dean Marks was Tina Cox's work husband. "We'll start with you telling me about how long you were at the college."

"More than fifty years," the man said before launching into a long-winded summary of his rise from new professor to Dean.

After nearly ten minutes, Gordon was finally able to steer the conversation back to Tina. "So, those last ten years, Tina was your assistant?"

"She was a godsend for sure. Mary, my previous assistant, didn't come back after maternity leave, and there was no time to find anyone else. As it turned out, Tina was the one who was hard to replace. Such a shame." His voice and head both dropped in remembrance.

Giving the man a minute, Gordon waited before asking, "Those last several weeks, did you notice anything different about Tina? Did she seem upset about anything? Or especially happy? Or possibly distracted?"

"Not upset. Distracted maybe. She misfiled a document. And forgot to reschedule an appointment. Very unlike her, but we were all busy. The end of every semester is a bit of a madhouse on a college campus. And that year, we'd increased enrollment for the first time, and we were working on the class schedules for summer and fall. There was a new building, new professors. Old ones leaving. My son was one of those. He left that summer for a new position. Came back as the Dean of the hospital last year. We're lucky to have him."

Gordon looked down at his notes. Byron Marks. He was the Dean's youngest child, his only child with his third wife, Diedre. His other children were older by at least a decade and, unlike Byron, lived far away from their father. There could be any number of reasons for that, of course, but if the stories Gordon had heard were to be believed, it might have had something to do with the fact that while the former dean continued to age, his wives didn't. By the time he'd married for the third time, his wife and his oldest daughter could have been sisters. Still, unlike the other wives, Diedre had lasted, and from what he'd witnessed that morning, doted on her older husband.

The elderly man picked up a picture from a nearby table. "A handsome man, my son. Even married, the women were always buzzing around. Unfortunately, he's followed in his father's footsteps a bit, but hopefully, like me, his third wife's the charm." His smile grew rueful as he replaced the photo.

"The thing is, Byron's quite brilliant. He's been published in most of the science journals. When he's not teaching or researching, he's speaking at conferences, other hospitals, and…" his words faded and he offered a grin. "Sorry, young man. You didn't come here to listen to the ruminations of a proud father."

Proud father. The words hit him in the gut, but he shoved the unwelcome thought aside. "It's okay. You have four children, right?"

"I do, although you wouldn't know it by them. The others tolerate me. Cling to their mothers. Though to be fair, I wasn't the best father in my younger days. I'm better now." He clasped his gnarled hands together and inclined his head toward the laptop. "Might be best to cut all that. Ramblings of an old man. Especially all that about Byron. Diedre warned me not to talk about him. Or her, for that matter. Sorry."

Gordon did his best to steer the conversation back to the murders.

"Tina thought of you like a father, didn't she?"

His lips turned up then. "I do believe she did. Her own father died when she was young. And she craved approval. Any dime store psychiatrist could have figured that out."

Gordon suspected it might have been a little more complicated than the former dean made it sound, but he probably wasn't wrong. "Did she ever come to you—as a father figure—with any problems or anything of a personal nature?"

Snow white brows drew together. "I'm not sure what you mean."

"Neither am I," Gordon admitted. The old Gordon would have asked

Jeremy to edit out any comments like that, but he knew better now. Showing his own humanity enhanced his credibility rather than hurt it. He wasn't a journalist after all. Those standards didn't apply. "I suppose I'm thinking of something like a fight with her husband or a friend. Had she had any trouble with anyone? She admired you. Trusted you. So, I was wondering if she ever needed advice when things in her life weren't going the way she'd hoped."

"Ah. I see what you mean now. I'm afraid I'm going to have to disappoint you, young man. While I was very fond of Tina, I didn't know much about her life outside the office. Even when she worked late, most of our discussions were centered around work. Occasionally, a new restaurant—Lord knows there are precious few of those—or a book or something like that."

Although the man's answer didn't surprise Gordon, he was, in fact, disappointed. Still, he had another angle he wanted to pursue. The hairdresser's inference that some of the wives were not fond of the staff—or at least not Tina. "What about your wife, Diedre? Would Tina have confided in her if she had a problem? Or if something or someone was bothering her?"

Again, the man's brows knitted. "I'm not sure what you're getting at. Was someone bothering Tina? I don't mean to be rude, but it was my understanding that the other woman was the one mutilated, the reason they were both killed. Tina was a victim of…" he paused as though searching for the right word. "Of circumstance shall we say."

Gordon didn't know what he was getting at either. He decided to be honest. "Most likely, that's true, but Tina had been upset about something." He decided to draw on his interview with Patty Handler and another of their friends. "She and Lisa Lawson's friendship had become strained in the weeks before they died. I was hoping maybe somebody close to Tina might be able to shed some light on what was going on. Maybe it has something to do with what happened to Lisa and Tina."

"I see." He pressed his fingertips together on the desk. "I don't think Diedre will be able to help you with that. She wasn't very involved in my work. Or with the staff. She was friends with a few of the other wives, but they kept to themselves. I doubt she was even aware of Tina's last name until she was murdered."

Something told Gordon that the Dean didn't know his wife as well as he thought. As the third wife, Diedre Marks would absolutely know the name of the attractive young woman who worked in his office each day. And if the hairdresser was to be believed, Byron's wife, along with Diedre and the other wives, made sure that Tina Cox knew her place. Even so, he let it go.

"Had Tina taken any sick leave or personal days in the weeks before she died?" He didn't expect to learn anything, and when the old man didn't answer right away, Gordon considered reminding him of the question or letting it go altogether. Before he could, Dean Marks sighed and lifted a hand.

"That was a long time ago. I can't be sure."

"I understand. Anything you can remember?"

"She did come in late a few mornings, but it might have been weeks earlier or even months. I wouldn't remember at all, but she used to joke that working in my office was the only thing she was on time for. And she worked late, too, whenever I asked." Gordon watched the old man's face soften at the memory. "She knew just how I liked my coffee. Organized all my papers. Proofread every letter." He gave a slow shake of his head. His hands shook as he sat back, holding onto his chair. "Still hard to believe she's gone."

Gordon nodded, silent. There was nothing more to learn. They'd already been at it for more than an hour, and it was clear the old man was tiring. After thanking Dean Marks and adding closing remarks, he switched off the microphone and shut down the laptop. Looking up, he spied a frowning Diedre in the doorway, arms crossed.

"Gerald," she said. "You should rest now."

He waved his hand. "Five more minutes."

She stood a second more before spinning away.

Gordon knew he'd stayed longer than he should have, but he'd wanted to let the man talk, enjoyed it even. It didn't matter that once or twice, he got lost in his memories or failed to remember at all. They'd edit out those parts. "I really appreciate you seeing me today. I hope I haven't made things difficult for you with your wife."

"Young man, at my age, everything is difficult."

"Right. Well, thanks anyway." He packed up the boom arm and the rest of the equipment and placed the strap of his bag over his shoulder. "I can show myself out."

"Good day."

Gordon was leaving the room when he heard Marks calling him back.

"Young man. Young man." The podcaster stepped back inside. "I just remembered something. Tina did come to me once. I'd forgotten all about it until now because, as far as I know, it never went anywhere."

Shifting his weight, Gordon considered taking out the laptop or, at the very least, his phone, but changed his mind. Even the old man was already discounting what he had to say. "What was that, Dean Marks?" he asked.

"She asked me if I knew of any fertility specialists."

Gordon said nothing. He already knew that Tina and Barton had struggled to conceive, that this was one of Tina's greatest sorrows. It made sense she would have sought out a fertility specialist, although he couldn't understand how this would line up with the pregnancy rumors.

"And what did you say?"

"I told her I didn't know much about fertility specialists. For better or for worse, the ability to father children has never been one of my problems."

Something about the way the dean answered made Gordon wonder about Barton. "Did she say she thought her husband was the problem?"

"Oh no. Tina would never have suggested that, but I got the feeling Barton didn't know she was asking."

"When was this?"

"Oh, I don't know." He rubbed a hand across his beard. "A couple years before, maybe?"

Interesting timing, Gordon thought. Could be a new avenue to explore. His stomach rumbled then, and he thought it might be a good time to visit Buck again. He shifted his weight, adjusting the heavy bag. Still, another couple of minutes wouldn't hurt. "Did she ever say if she met with one? A specialist?"

"No. She never mentioned it again."

And there it was. He'd wasted his time again. "Okay. Thanks anyway, Dean Marks."

"You could ask my son."

Gordon blinked. "What?"

"He was affiliated with the hospital, you know, had connections that were different than mine. I told her to talk to him. I believe Tina and Byron became friends after that. He was quite broken up about her death, of course, as we all were. Perhaps he can help you."

Chapter Twenty-One

Now

Callie couldn't stop thinking about Lisa Lawson. Opinionated. Protective. Loyal. Private. These were all words she'd heard to describe Lisa. Was that enough to incite the kind of violence that had taken her life? She looked down at her list of names, the same that sat in the Venn diagram on the whiteboard. She and Zel had checked off two dozen already, but other than Patty Handler, none had anything new to add. There was still one left to talk to, one she'd saved for last, but before she pursued that interview, she opened the box of original transcripts. With trembling fingers, she flipped through the report until she found it. Just under two pages.

Jackson: "How long had you known Lisa and Tina?"

Maura: "We went to school together, all the way up. They were always best friends, as far back as I can remember."

Jackson: "And you were also a friend to both women?"

Maura: "I was. We saw each other a lot when we were younger, and then we got busy. We started having movie night. Sometimes someone couldn't make it—a sick child, or other engagement, or something. But most months, we got together."

Callie read her mother's brief description of the movie club Patty Handler had told her about.

Jackson: "And you know Harry?"

Maura: "Yes."

Jackson: "Have you ever known Harry to want to hurt Lisa?"

Maura: "No. Never."

Callie thought this matched her memories of the conversations she'd overheard between her parents. She wondered if Jackson had been surprised by this answer and if it had deterred his investigation of Harry in any way.

Jackson: "Have you ever known Harry to be violent?"

Maura: "I've heard stories, but no, not personally."

It was an evasive answer, and Callie had to admire her mother for it. She already knew that not everyone was so discreet.

Jackson: "Did you see Harry on the day that Lisa was killed?"

Maura: "No."

Jackson: "Did Lisa or Harry ever tell you that he would be attending a grocery convention in D.C.?"

Maura: "No."

Jackson: "Did Lisa have any enemies that you know of?"

Maura: "Enemies? That's a strong word, so no."

Jackson: "Okay. Do you know of anyone who didn't really like Lisa?"

Maura: "Not specifically, but I'm sure there were some people who didn't love her. Lisa wasn't a gossip and kept to herself when it came to stuff like that, but she didn't have a filter either."

Jackson: "What do you mean by that?"

Maura: "I don't know. If you asked her if the schools should keep the new math program they started last year, she'd give you an earful. She'd been on the school council for a while and knew all about it."

Jackson: "So, not everyone liked her?"

Maura: "Does everyone like you, Detective?"

Jackson: "I don't know. Probably not."

Maura: "Does that mean they want to kill you?"

Jackson: "We're getting off topic here, Mrs. Forde. I'm trying to establish who might have wanted to hurt Lisa Lawson."

Maura: "I can't tell you the answer to that other than whoever it was is a bad person. A very bad person."

Jackson: "Thank you for your time, Mrs. Forde."

Maura: "Is that all? Aren't you going to ask me anything about Tina or Barton?"

Jackson: "Do you want me to ask you about them?"

Maura: "I want you to treat them the same. Lisa and Tina were both murdered. They both had husbands who aren't perfect. Why are you only asking me about Harry and Lisa? Is it because he was in the Army? Is it because of that idiot Jerry Morgan?"

Jackson: "You know I can't talk to you about our investigation, Mrs. Forde."

Maura: "Two women were murdered, Detective. Two."

Jackson: "I'm well aware."

Maura: "It doesn't seem like it."

Callie looked up from the page. She could imagine her mother sitting primly on her chair, hands folded on the table in front of her, the very picture of decorum. But the set of her mouth and the darkness in her eyes would have told a different story. Had Jackson seen it? Had he understood how deeply Maura believed pursuing Harry was a miscarriage of justice? Had Callie's father warned him? The next words told her Jackson had taken the path of least resistance.

Jackson: "Fine. Did Tina have any enemies?"

Maura: "No."

Jackson: "Did you ever know Barton to be violent?"

Maura: "No."

Jackson: "I think that does it then. Thank you for your time."

Maura: "Harry didn't do this, Detective. I know it."

Jackson: "I appreciate your opinion, Mrs. Forde. Thank you again for coming in."

Callie put the pages aside. Captain Jackson didn't get much from her mother other than a lot of sarcasm, as far as Callie could tell. She bounced her leg up and down, her gaze returning to the whiteboard.

"Jesus, Callie. Do you live here?" Zel stood in the doorway with a large cup of coffee. "It's not even seven."

"I couldn't sleep." For the first time, she told him about the conversations—and fights—she'd overheard between her parents after the murders. "I wanted to read Jackson's interview with my mom. Thought I might learn something new."

"And did you?"

She picked up the pages, holding them a moment before sliding them back into the file. "Not really.

"Well, I don't think I'm going to make your day then."

"No?"

"I just found out the podcaster and Lynnleigh Lawson are friends. Apparently, they went to college together."

"Well," she said, "that explains what he's doing here."

"Yep."

"I guess we're going to have to move up our timeline, try to talk to Lynnleigh before she goes on the podcast."

"Agreed, but that's not all. Rumor has it the podcaster went to see Barton Cox. He's never spoken to the press before, but that could change and..."

She sat back. Barton was due to be interviewed at the station later that day. "And," Callie finished for him, "we need to know what he's going to say before the rest of the world."

Chapter Twenty-Two

Now

Gordon walked through the park, his bag slung over one arm and balancing a cardboard tray with the other. He passed the swings and children's play area, both empty at this early hour. He settled on a bench near what looked like a small cave and tilted his head to the rising sun. The air was already thick with humidity, promising another sweltering day. Taking one of the coffees, he lifted the lid and took a large swallow, burning his tongue. Gordon had been in Hampstead only a few weeks but already, he felt the exhaustion that came with deadlines creeping over him. He saw it in the mirror, felt it in his bones, and yet, he was also exhilarated. And hungover. A scorched tongue was worth the caffeine.

The night before, Buck had poured Gordon one more beer than necessary, but he hadn't really minded so long as the barkeep kept talking.

"Yeah, I know who Marks is. Not that he hangs out around here. If he's friendly with the ladies, he doesn't do it in my bar." Buck had propped his elbows on the wooden counter and leaned closer. "I hear you've been making waves, my friend."

"Have I?"

"No skin off my back, but I'd be careful if I were you. It's one thing to come to me. I'll tell you what I know, and I won't tell you what I don't. In a town like this, you got your honest folks, your old-timers, and your self-centered assholes—just like everywhere. And you got those who don't like strangers.

The first kind, they'll be okay, but others won't be so understanding."

"The self-centered assholes."

"You learn quick. Watch out so you don't get burned."

"And how will I know when I'm gonna get burned?"

"When it starts getting hot," Buck had said. The laugh that followed a few seconds later made his long beard rise up and down over his belly. He'd still been chuckling when he moved down the bar.

Gordon shook his head and drank his beer.

Now, nursing a headache and a coffee, his gaze fell on the rock that rose from the ground and the fence around it. Thick branches laden with bright green leaves hung over the entrance. In spite of himself, he found himself curious about it. He'd check out the historical marker he'd spotted later. As parks went, he figured it wasn't bad, nicer than the one in his hometown anyway. It was cleaner for one thing, and its location in the center of town meant everyone could enjoy it.

From the corner of his eye, he saw her, and he felt the same rush of anticipation that came every time he thought of her. He watched her walk toward him with that purposeful stride of hers, arms swinging at her side, head held high. He'd always loved that about her, that show of confidence, no matter what. She stood over him now.

"Is one of those for me?" Lynnleigh asked, eyeing the coffee cups on the tray.

"One sugar, no cream, and a blueberry muffin."

She smiled and sat down. "You remembered."

"How could I forget? You practically bit my head off that time I brought you a stale banana nut muffin? Remember?"

She laughed, the skin around her eyes crinkling. "You could have gone to the bakery. It wasn't that far."

"There was a line. The convenience store was faster."

"What would it have been? An extra ten minutes?"

I wanted to get back to you. The words were on the tip of his tongue, but he bit them back. What good would it do now? "You're right," he said instead. "Forgive me?"

"Water under the bridge."

He raised his cup to hers. "To old friends."

Her smile widened. "To old friends."

A pair of bluebirds flew near, twittering and pecking at the grassy mound near the cave before flapping their wings and disappearing among the leaves again. Gordon swiveled toward Lynnleigh. "Thanks for coming this morning."

She shrugged. "It was time."

He knew he shouldn't ask, but he couldn't help himself. "Why me, Lynnleigh? There are bigger podcasts, those news magazines, all kinds of ways to get press for this story. And we didn't end the best..." His words trailed off.

Her shoulders rose and fell again. "I know you, Gordon. I don't know those people. They don't care about me, and even though we broke up, I know you care. We were in college. Stuff happens." She waved a hand in the air as though brushing aside the events from that semester. "You understand loss. We share that. It had to be you."

These things were true, and he'd suspected as much. Still, she hadn't mentioned Hamilton Hayes or his success. He didn't know why, but he was disappointed, as though his success—limited though it was—had played no part in her decision. It hurt more than he realized.

"I'm glad," he said, deciding to swallow his pride. "I do care, and I always will."

"I know." She didn't look at him, but he thought he heard a catch in her voice, a hesitation, and his heart skipped.

Although they'd spoken on the phone a couple of times and exchanged multiple emails after she'd reached out, he hadn't seen Lynnleigh since that semester years earlier. She'd cut her hair. It was shoulder-length now, falling in waves across her cheeks. Gone was the dark eyeliner she'd worn in college, along with the nose ring, although she could have lost all of that by senior year, and he wouldn't know. He'd dropped out by then, his grades an embarrassment. Turned out, going to class actually mattered. His parents had put their foot down, and he couldn't stomach the thought of loans when he'd already changed majors four times. Not like Lynnleigh. She'd graduated, gone to work in Chicago at a big company before coming back to Virginia to be closer to her dad. But Harry Lawson had died in his cell a few months after her return. Then came the grocery store conference video. The news articles were the first he'd heard of it. He'd wanted to reach out then, but he didn't know how.

"How's it been going?" she asked. "Have people been nice?"

"Fine. Good."

"No one's tried to kill you yet?"

He gave her a sharp look, but she was staring past him, a faraway look in her eyes, and he breathed a sigh of relief. He'd told no one about the car on the mountain, although Jeremy thought he should put it on the podcast.

"If listeners think you're in danger, think how many new subscribers we'll get," he'd said.

It was a fair argument, but his instincts told him to leave it alone, and he didn't want to give Lynnleigh any reason to worry.

He forced a laugh before switching subjects. "Did you hear the first episode?"

"Yeah. The hairdresser was good. People will respond to her. That thing about Tina and being late," Lynnleigh said with a shake of her head. "I remember my mom used to say she would give Tina fake times, like if movie night was at seven, she'd tell Tina six-thirty. I think Tina caught on, but my mom kept doing it." Her tremulous smile slipped.

"I went to see Randy McKay."

"The insurance guy? He's the one who did the policy on my mom, right?"

"One and the same."

Her face darkened. "He didn't help my dad at trial at all."

Gordon couldn't disagree, but his interview with McKay was not what he'd expected. It threw everything in the transcript into a new light, and he'd decided to hold it a little longer before airing. He remembered how eager the man had been to talk.

Randy had run a hand through his sparse hair, his gaze darting to the shiny mic. "Is that on?"

"As soon as you tell me you're ready."

The small man had drawn in a breath and straightened his shoulders. "I'm ready."

Gordon had given him a small smile and hit the buttons. He'd gone through a brief introduction and thank you before getting down to business.

"Randy, most of the people in this town know that Harry Lawson took out a life insurance policy on his wife only six months before she was murdered. You testified about it at his trial, didn't you?"

"I did, but there was a lot I didn't get to say about it. And everyone took what was said at trial as the whole story. Some people even avoided me for a while, like I'd done something to Lisa and Tina." Deep lines had appeared between his brows. "I wish I'd spoken up more then, but no one seemed interested. Not the police. Not the prosecutor. Not even Harry's attorney."

Gordon had sat forward, his pulse quickening. He hadn't expected much from this interview. In truth, he'd wondered if it would even be included in the final cut, but now he was all ears. "If you had spoken up, Mr. McKay, what would you have said?"

"Well, for one thing, I would have said that Harry Lawson didn't give a rat's ass about money. That whole suggestion that he'd set Lisa up for money couldn't be further from the truth. Harry could live in a hole in the ground and be fine if his wife and daughter were okay. He took out that policy because he suffered from nightmares. And in some of those, Lisa died. Not murdered but died. Car wreck in one. She got sick in another. I remember him crying when he told me about them."

"You're saying he took out a policy on his wife because he had nightmares that she was going to die?"

"Yes, and I know what you're going to say next, that I just said Harry didn't care about money, so what was with the policy?"

That is what Gordon was going to ask, and he told the man so. "Not to mention that it's a fairly sizable policy. You can see how that might seem suspicious."

"Sure, but the money wasn't for him. It was for Lynnleigh. Lisa dying was one part of the nightmares he was having, but not the only part. More than once, he dreamed that Lynnleigh was taken from him."

"Taken from him?"

"Like he was an unsuitable parent. He knew what people said about him. That he was paranoid. And he'd gotten in that barfight. He tried to control his temper, but he worried there'd be another fight, and he couldn't escape without an arrest the next time. If something happened to Lisa and he couldn't take care of Lynnleigh, where would she be? He wanted that money for her, so she'd be taken care of."

The earnest way the man spoke told Gordon everything he'd shared was true. "Okay," he said, "I get that he was having nightmares and he was afraid for his daughter. But his brother is nearby, right? Lynnleigh would have been taken care of. Did that not occur to him?"

"I said the same thing, but Ned had kids of his own. Harry wanted to make it easier for Ned if she had to go there. She'd have college money." He waved a hand in the air. "The thing is, it doesn't have to make perfect sense to you or me. It only had to make sense to Harry. And Lisa understood that. She didn't like the idea of spending money on a policy, but she agreed if it gave him peace of mind."

"And did it?"

"I think it did."

There was a moment where neither said anything. Gordon knew Jeremy didn't like dead air, but he suspected the audience would be with him, thinking about a man seeking assurances his family was taken care of.

"Why didn't you say any of this at trial?"

"I tried, but Brock Avery kept cutting me off. He kept all his questions to the facts 'cause he knew the facts didn't look too good. But people do things for all kinds of reasons—some good and some bad—and while Harry's reasons for taking out that policy might have been a bit strange, the intentions were good." He paused. "I didn't know Harry that well before he came to me, and he could be an intimidating guy. The first time he came in here, I wasn't sure what to think." He lifted his hand toward Gordon. "He was sitting right where you are, explained what he wanted and why. He was a no bullshit kind of guy."

"You said he was crying."

"Yeah. About the dreams. I think he was pretty haunted by what he'd seen in the Army. My uncle was in Afghanistan, so I have some experience with how it can affect a guy. My uncle's okay now, but it was tough at first. In Harry's mind, he couldn't be okay until he took care of the people who were important to him. Kept saying protecting them was the only thing that mattered, that he wouldn't make that mistake again."

"What mistake was that?"

"I don't know. He never said."

Gordon knew it would be next to impossible to dig up whatever haunted Harry Lawson, but he'd try. Somebody had to know.

"Okay, but I still don't understand why he wouldn't also want a policy on himself. Wouldn't they need that if something happened to him?"

"That was my argument, and a good one. Many couples have life insurance policies on both parties, with the larger policy on the breadwinner. But Harry wasn't a regular guy. And Lisa wasn't a regular woman either. I'm only guessing here, but I got the impression he viewed himself as the weak link in the family. He figured his wife would be fine if something happened to him, maybe even better off. Not to mention, he wasn't sure he could pass a mental evaluation." His sigh was deep. "I know how it looked at trial. I know how it looks if you didn't hear Harry talk about his wife and daughter. But that's not the man I met or worked with." He held up his hand. "I'm aware there was another side to the man, but the man I knew couldn't have done what they said he did. Never."

After the interview, Gordon had gone back to the transcript. Twice, Avery had stopped McKay before he could expand on his answers. Did he know that McKay might offer another interpretation of the policy, or was it simply instinctual? The podcaster couldn't be sure, but it added weight to McKay's interview. He told Lynnleigh about it now. When he was finished, she wiped away her tears.

"Thank you for telling me, Gordon," she said with a sniffle. "I never doubted whether or not my dad loved us, you know. I always believed in him, no matter what anyone said, but other than my Uncle Ned, Aunt

Maggie, and Barton, I always had the feeling the rest of the town thought he belonged behind bars. I wish I'd known."

"Well, for better or worse, McKay suffered accusations of his own. He told me about a letter to the editor saying that selling a policy to Harry Lawson was nothing short of irresponsible. I think business was tough for a while."

Lynnleigh's gaze slid away, and she sat back against the bench. "When will the episode air?"

"Tomorrow. Jeremy is adding the music today, and we'll do a final edit tonight."

"Good," she said, slinging her purse over her shoulder.

No matter how one looked at it, the size and timing of the policy was strange, but McKay had humanized Harry. He reminded himself it wasn't his job to clear Harry Lawson. The video did that. But he could do this for Lynnleigh. He rose with her, considering whether or not to tell her Barton had agreed to consider an interview. And he had three more of Lisa's friends lined up after that. But the sponsors wanted her, the daughter.

"Lynnleigh, you need to be on soon." He waited. His request wasn't a surprise, but he knew it wasn't welcomed, either.

"Give me another day or two, okay?"

"Are you still getting those texts?"

She'd had a handful of threatening messages, all from untraceable numbers. None were specific. None were crass, but all were clear enough. Leave the past in the past.

"Not in a few days. That's not it. I just want to do this right. For both my parents."

Her answer wasn't unexpected. The girl he'd known in college shied away from personal attention even back then, but she'd stand on a soapbox for the ones she loved. He wondered if she'd been that way before the murders, before her father was found guilty. Not for the first time, he considered the domino effect an event, traumatic and otherwise, could have on the lives that felt its impact. Even a gesture or a word could make ripples. He'd seen that firsthand.

"Gordon, stop biting your fingernails," his father had said once. "You're not a toddler anymore. Young men don't sit around gnawing on their fingers, for Chrissake."

"I'm not trying to, Dad. I don't even know I'm doing it sometimes."

His father had snorted. "Well, your brother doesn't bite his nails, now does he?"

Gordon had cringed. Another comparison to Max. He loved his older brother. He did. But he didn't know why his dad had to keep reminding him how he didn't measure up. Coach didn't do that. At least he gave Gordon a pat on the back for trying and told him to keep at it.

He'd stolen a glance at his mother, but her head had been bowed, her eyes glued to the remains of her dinner. "No, Sir," he'd said at last, swallowing a sigh.

"Exactly right." He'd thrown his napkin on the table and pushed away from the table. "Well, about time to get to your brother's game. And don't be lollygagging around. We're not waiting for you again."

Gordon's brother had been the star child before his death, and after, he'd graduated to near saint status while Gordon's already negligible status had tumbled to less than nothing. He'd tried to be better, to fill in the chasm that had opened up in their lives, but if he hadn't measured up before, he failed miserably after. He couldn't be sure when he began to embody the things his dad said about him. Was it before Max's death or after? For a long time, he wanted his parents to notice him, to be proud of him. He still did if he were honest, but not the way he used to. The truth was, he didn't always know what he wanted.

He nodded at Lynnleigh now. "It's okay. I've got a couple of other interviews I can do before you, but people know I'm here and you're here. They're expecting it." He paused. He needed to give her something. "I talked to Barton Cox."

Her head snapped up, her eyes wide. "Barton? Did he agree to be on the podcast?"

"He didn't say yes yet, but he said he'd think about it," he admitted.

"Oh. Okay. That's something, I guess." She rocked back and forth on her heels. He recognized the motion.

"What is it?" Gordon asked.

Her narrow shoulders rose and fell. "I don't like dredging up old memories for Barton, making him relive all this, too, but…" Gordon said nothing, waiting. "But I always wondered how he had the strength to stay silent. He stuck by my dad—maybe not so much after he was charged, but he never joined in on talking crap about him. He could have. He'd lost his wife, too, but he still stayed out of the spotlight."

Gordon found himself nodding along with her words. "From what I saw in the transcript, he was only called to the stand once."

"Yeah, I don't know if it's true, but I heard he told Avery he wanted no part of prosecuting his friend, that he didn't think he'd done it, and none of it would bring his wife back anyway."

Shaking his head, Gordon said, "More generous than I would be. If it was my wife, I'd want justice."

"Well, Barton is, well, Barton." Her hand tightened over the strap of her bag, and she half-turned. "I'll check in tomorrow."

"Sure. Tomorrow." Feet rooted to the ground, Gordon watched her walk away, feet bouncing and hair swinging. Tomorrow seemed like a long time away.

After leaving the park, Gordon drove out to the house that once belonged to Harry and Lisa Lawson. It was empty now, abandoned among tall weeds and fallen trees. The Lawsons hadn't lived in town but just outside, far enough to have few neighbors but close enough to still be part of the community, for Lisa and Lynnleigh anyway. A development company had snapped up the property, filing paperwork for multi-use zoning not long after the trial, but when the paperwork stalled, the investors dropped out, and the land went neglected.

Taking out his phone, Gordon hit record, describing what he saw as he walked.

"There's an old shed in the back, if you could call it that. It's mostly rotted now. There's what looks like a fire pit." In the quiet, he heard trickling water and walked past the shed. At the edge of the lot, he came to a stream bubbling over rocks and a stone bench.

"I'm sitting on a bench near a stream." Heavy branches hung over his head, filtering the battering sun. "It's peaceful, calm." Gordon didn't need Lynnleigh to tell him that this was her father's place, where he came to seek calm and perspective. The stream glittered in the mid-morning light like jewels, dazzling the eye. It was cooler here, too, like an oasis, and he was glad no builder had yet bulldozed the property. He looked around for some sign of Harry or Lisa, a mark on a tree or a carving, but other than the bench, there was nothing. It was simple and plain, the way he imagined Harry and Lisa were.

Gordon didn't move for a long time, drinking in the natural beauty. He breathed in the scents of moss and warm dirt and listened to the birds flapping in the trees. An hour slipped by, and still, he stayed. Lynnleigh had grown up on this land, had no doubt spent countless hours down at the water's edge, holding her father's hand, skipping barefoot over the stones. And one day, it had all ended.

Brushing his hands across his thighs, he forced his thoughts from Lynnleigh to Barton. His life had changed, too. He had a new wife now and a new family. Gordon didn't know much about Cindy Cox, other than she was a few years behind Barton in school and had grown up only a few blocks from him, albeit in a smaller and shabbier house. Presumably, they'd known each other their whole lives. Like Barton, Cindy married young, settling down with a boy who'd gone to Hampstead College. The marriage had lasted less than five years, though, and the college boy had moved on to a bigger job in a bigger city. As far as Gordon could tell, most of the locals didn't even remember him, but none of them could ever forget Cindy.

"Cindy Cox acts like she's the First Lady of this town, if you know what I mean. Got a chin that points straight up at the sky when you see her walking." The hairdresser had snorted and leaned in close, although there was no one else in the woman's kitchen. "Lurla, who does her hair, says Cindy throws a hissy if her extensions aren't just the right shade of blond. You know what I call that shade? Bimbo," she said with a cackle. "I swear, Tina would die all over again if she saw who Barton ended up with. He's a beaten man if you ask me. Beaten."

Gordon had heard a few other similar comments, but all had come from women who loved Tina. One even hinted the timing of Cindy's first marriage seemed suspiciously close to the birth of her first child, but Gordon didn't bother to find out either way. It wasn't the type of information he found interesting or, in this case, relevant. What mattered is that Barton Cox married Cindy almost one year to the day after Tina was murdered. He knew there were a hundred different explanations for why he might have married again so soon, but Gordon wouldn't make assumptions. Not that he hadn't heard them.

"Men are just lonelier than women, aren't they?"

"As long as Tina and Barton had been together, it's no wonder the man couldn't be alone."

"Rebound."

But the comment he'd found most interesting came from a mother at the children's school.

"I've known Cindy my whole life, and that girl's sole ambition in life has been to be the biggest fish in a small pond. Back in high school, she somehow made captain of cheer even though she wasn't even close to the best. Would only try out for the lead role in any school play. Now it's being PTA president or chair of the park committee. She wants the biggest and the best—goes up to DC to buy all her clothes." The woman had paused. "I'm not blaming her for any of that. She didn't grow up with much, so it's natural she'd want to have a better life. It's just that for Cindy, better isn't enough."

He'd thought about that a minute before asking, "And marrying Barton satisfied that need?"

"To be the best? Yeah. I mean, after he married Tina and grew his business, he turned into the kind of catch a girl like Cindy would drool over. My mama always talked about how he was a rich guy who did good, and there weren't many of those around."

"Did good in what way?" he'd asked, although he was already familiar with some of Barton's financials.

"Well, he supported the renovation of the Hampstead Hotel. You should have seen it before they redid the lobby and put in a cocktail bar. Kind of a dump, but it's nice now. And there's the park. He was part of the team that raised money to clean that up, pledging his own money, too." She'd snapped her fingers. "And he's in real estate, like building better houses. I think he was part of that development out near College Drive. You get the idea. Barton Cox put his money back into this town, which people love."

"Let me guess, Cindy loved it, too."

"Ha! She was probably first on his doorstep with a casserole after Tina died. Not that she was alone, mind you." The woman had blanched then, her hand rising to her throat. "You're not recording this, are you? This is just between us, right?"

Chapter Twenty-Three

Now

Ben Wilkins set his cup down on the table. "I was wondering when you'd get around to me."

Callie swallowed the hard lump in her throat. "Is now a good time?"

He waved a hand at the seat across from him. "Sure. I don't have to be in court today."

She gave a short nod and slid into the booth. She'd known he'd be there, same as he was every morning. She used to meet him here, back when they spent more time together than apart, but that was a long time ago. Her brother had never seen his sister with his old friend, but somehow, she always thought he would have approved. But then her father was shot, and the world shifted. She didn't meet Ben here or anywhere. It still hurt more than she'd like.

Zel had offered to do the interview, but Callie couldn't let him. It wasn't like she didn't run into Ben in the station or at the courthouse from time to time. He was a defense lawyer, and she was a cop. But rarely did she see him one-on-one anymore. The drumbeat of her heart echoed in her ears now, and she willed it to slow, turning her focus to flipping open the notebook she'd placed between them. "I only have a few questions."

"Fire away. I'll answer what I can."

Taking a deep breath, she looked into the lightness of his eyes. There were more wrinkles now, tiny starbursts above his cheekbones, but those only accentuated the smooth skin of his brow and the strength of his chin. She gripped the pen tighter, and thankfully, before she could get lost in her thoughts, Shelley appeared with a clean cup and steaming pot of coffee. "Want some, Callie?"

"Yes, thanks."

"That podcaster was in the other day." Callie shifted toward Shelley. "I might have given him a piece of my mind."

The detective smiled. Shelley had never been short on opinion. That made her like most folks in town. The difference was that Shelley paid attention better than most. "How'd he take it?"

"Like any five-year-old getting a slap on the hand," she said with a grin. "But he listened. I heard the first episode. I don't think he's half bad."

"We'll see," was all Callie said, and Shelley backed away with a nod. After she'd left, Callie got down to business, facing Ben again. "You worked for Brock Avery during the Lawson case, right?"

"Yep. My dad knew Avery and thought it would be a good way for me to figure out if law school was for me."

"Were you privy to interviews with witnesses?"

"I sat in on a few."

"With who?"

"Wow, Callie, you're not holding back, are you?" he said with a shake of his head. She waited. "Okay, well, Harry's brother. That was a tough one. Dean Marks. I wasn't there for his son's interview, though. Avery handled that one himself."

"Did he do that with a lot of witnesses?"

"Some."

Callie sat back. Why would Byron Marks warrant special treatment? She'd have to take another look at his connection to both women.

"What about Anthony Battle?"

"Once," he admitted. "Surprisingly, that was my one and only legal run-in with the man."

"Oh? Never came to you to defend him?" Battle's arrest list wasn't long by some standards, but long enough that he'd been in court enough times to need a lawyer. Outside of one sexual assault charge that was reduced to sexual battery, most of the charges were petty, and his sentences had been limited to stiff fines and short sentences. Crowded jails meant he'd been out more than he'd been in. He'd stayed out of trouble for the last couple of years—either because he'd cleaned up his act or because he'd gotten better at not getting caught. Callie's money was on the latter.

"I'd be surprised if he did. He may have been pivotal in the case against Harry Lawson, but there was no love lost between him and Avery. 'He's like gum on the bottom of your shoe,' I remember him saying once."

"Didn't stop him from making a deal."

"No, it didn't. That's how the system works." He shifted forward, leaning across the table. "Have you been to see him?"

"I have." Even at ten in the morning, Battle had smelled of whiskey and sour sweat. His living room smelled worse, if that was possible. She told him about the brief interview and Battle's claim to have been confused. "We're trying to find Amber, his ex-girlfriend, see if she can tell us anything more."

"Good luck with that, I guess."

Callie wasn't ready to let go of Battle yet. "Anything else you remember about him?"

"Not him exactly, but something else Avery said about him. He said, 'Normally, the kid's about as worthless as a paper bag in a rainstorm, but maybe this will change things.' I think he hoped Battle would understand he was being given a second chance and make good on it. His mother had even promised to keep an eye on him."

So much for second chances, she thought. Fifteen years earlier, a drunk and disorderly charge hung over the man's head. That, combined with a pair of previous arrests, would have landed him in jail. It went away with his testimony, of course, and the rest wasn't enough to hurt his credibility in court. As the sole witness who could swear Harry was not in DC as he claimed, the prosecution treated him with kid gloves.

"Did Avery really believe it? That Anthony Battle might walk the straight and narrow after the trial?"

"Who knows? The Brock Avery I knew wasn't a cynic. He was more of an optimist, in spite of his job."

"That doesn't make sense."

"It didn't to me either, which might be why I leaned toward defense, but I think he believed that carrying out justice was a form of making the world around him right. Only problem was, he sometimes had blinders on about who was guilty."

She couldn't help herself. "And defense attorneys don't?"

If she thought he might take offense, she was surprised a second time that morning. A smile spread slowly across his face, bringing back those crinkles she'd already grown to love. "Same old Callie, I see."

She returned his smile. "Why mess with a good thing?"

His throaty laugh rang out over the din of chatter around them. "I've missed this," he said after he caught his breath.

A warmth rose from her belly to her cheeks. He missed their banter, or he missed her? Flustered, she picked up her coffee, lowering her lashes.

"Well," he said, "that went over like a lead balloon."

It was her turn to laugh. "Now, who's blunt?"

"Touche." He shook his head. "I only meant we always were a pair, right?"

The smile on her face slipped. *Were a pair.* Another reminder their relationship was in the past. She flushed again, immediately embarrassed that she'd thought—even for a minute—that it might be something more.

"I've got to get back," she said. "Is there anything else you can tell me about working the Lawson case?"

He sat back and sighed. "Right," he said, drawing out the word. "The case." He drummed his thumb against the table before speaking again. "Here's what I can tell you. My access to the evidence was piecemeal. Avery divided the responsibilities in a way that meant none of us had total access to the complete file. In my case, I was assigned to Tina's friends, who in most cases were also Lisa's friends. That list was long, so it was split, too. My job was to write up the reports with recommendations on whether or not they would make good witnesses. Most of them were never called to the stand."

"Why not?"

He shrugged. "Circumstantial or not, Avery already had a strong case. His most damning evidence was Harry Lawson himself. He didn't do himself any favors getting up on the stand, and everyone knew it."

"So why did his lawyer let him?"

Again, Ben lifted his shoulder. "You could say she didn't know who she was up against, that she was green, too young—any of the above. She could have had fifty years in court, and it might not have made any difference. According to what I heard, Harry Lawson insisted. Innocent people tend to do that."

Callie gave a short nod and reached for her wallet.

He waved her away. "I've got it."

"Thanks." She slid from the booth. "Can I ask you something?" He nodded once, and Callie's eyes moved to the large window overlooking Main Street. Like most days, it was neither empty nor crowded, which pretty much described Hampstead in general. Predictable. Average. Quiet. But this case was none of those things. She looked down at Ben again.

"Did you think he was guilty? Back then? Did you ever question why everyone was so sure Harry Lawson butchered his wife and her friend?"

His thumb stilled along with the rest of him. "Ah, that question." He swallowed the rest of his coffee and wiped his mouth with his napkin. When he did finally answer, she heard honesty and raw emotion in the quiet way he spoke. "I was young, Cal. I was an intern. Today, with my experience, I'd have spotted the holes. I'd have had questions. But not then." He paused. "I didn't want to believe it. Somehow, it was easier to believe a stranger had come to town and chosen that house at random. But the evidence said otherwise. It was the knife, the manner of the injuries." His voice dropped lower. "Even now, knowing Harry was innocent, I don't know how to explain either of those facts. But did I ever question what everyone said was true?" His shoulders sank lower. "I guess the answer is, not enough. Not enough."

Chapter Twenty-Four

Now

"Mr. Blankenship, you worked in the prosecutor's office when the Lawson case came to trial, didn't you?" Gordon asked.

The man nodded, his gaze never wavering from the oversized TV mounted on the wall. On the screen, cars plastered with logos raced around a rainy track. The camera lens, speckled with water, moved from a wide angle to follow the leader, making Gordon dizzy. "Yeah," the former lawyer said. "Assistant District Attorney. Made it up to Deputy before I retired."

Gordon shifted on the folding chair the man had dragged into the tiny room. They sat in Mr. Blankenship's man cave—a converted shed with low ceilings and little air flow—although it did have lights and power. Facing the muted TV was an equally massive chair with deep cushions, a side table on one side, and a minifridge on the other. From the fridge, Blankenship had produced two cold beers. Gordon's sat on the floor next to his computer. He held his recording equipment in his lap.

"Brock Avery was the District Attorney then?"

"Yep. I left the same time he did. Hard to find a man better at what he did than him."

Gordon stopped short of reminding Blankenship that Avery had prosecuted an innocent man. How good did that make him? Instead, he steered Blankenship away from Avery and back to the trial. "So, as I understand it, you helped out on the Harry Lawson case?"

"All hands on deck for that one. Even the interns and secretaries worked overtime. One of the biggest trials this county had ever seen. Still is as far as I know."

"Is there anything you can tell me about the case or the evidence that led you to believe Mr. Lawson was guilty?"

The man's head rotated toward him. With his body still facing forward, he reminded Gordon of a large owl, his eyes glowing in the glare from the TV. "What kind of question is that? The police believed he was guilty. The District Attorney thought he was guilty. Hell, the whole town thought he was guilty. He'd been a loose cannon for years."

"Yes, that was the consensus, but I was wondering if there was anything specific, one piece of evidence that made the district attorney's office choose to indict?"

Blankenship stared at him, unblinking, and Gordon wanted nothing more than to get out of that shed, away from the dank light and too-close walls, but he wouldn't. Jeremy couldn't edit recordings that didn't exist. Besides, Lynnleigh needed him, was counting on him.

Gordon licked his lips. "What I mean is, surely there have been times the police have thought they had whoever did whatever crime it was, but your office couldn't go forward with what they had. That didn't happen here, so I'm wondering if there was one thing that convinced the district attorney that this case had enough to go to trial."

"It had Avery. That was enough."

The younger man fought the urge to roll his eyes. He still had yet to meet the famous Brock Avery, but he was already growing weary of his reputation. "I understand, but Mr. Avery is still out of the country, so I'm asking you." He paused. "As someone who played a key role in the case and who worked closely with Mr. Avery."

For the first time, the whole man shifted toward him, his body following along with his gaze. For a split second, Gordon worried he'd laid it on too thick, but the man nodded again. "Yeah, we worked together a lot. I was second chair for him plenty of times."

"So, you know the reason the case went forward…"

"The knife for one thing, and the insurance, but mostly because it wasn't hard to picture Harry Lawson losing his shit." His light eyes darkened. "If you'd seen those pictures of Lisa Lawson, you'd think it was him, too. He was the kind of guy who obsessed about things. I don't think he was always that way, or maybe he was, and he just got worse, but take that insurance policy. Pretty funny business there. That's a man who's obsessed with his wife and not in a good way." He paused to take a swig from his beer. "I'm not a psychologist or anything, but the opposite of love is hate. It's not that big a stretch. He'd already lost most of his old friends, and you've seen his record." His shoulders rolled forward as he set his bottle back on the TV tray. "I'm not saying anyone wanted to believe they knew someone who could do something like that, but…" his words fell away, and he shrugged.

"But you did?"

"Yeah. We all did. And if the murder weapon had been anything other than the exact knife that Harry admitted he owned, the only one like it in the county, maybe Avery would have thought twice. But it wasn't."

Gordon found himself nodding now. In spite of Harry being cleared by the video, the murder weapon remained a problem. That particular brand and style of knife had unique markings, and it didn't help that it was still missing. "I can see the logic. Can I ask, though, if there was ever a moment when the police or your office considered that someone other than Harry Lawson might have committed those murders?"

"Nope. Not based on the evidence we had, and as you know, that evidence did not include one bit of proof that Harry Lawson was in DC other than his word. The only thing we had was a registration badge that was never picked up. And we had a witness placing him here in Hampstead."

"That witness lied."

"I don't know anything about that."

Gordon guessed the man didn't want to know. "Can you think of anything else?"

"No. Only this. If the same case came before our office a second time with the same evidence, we'd have done the same thing."

"Okay," Gordon said, swallowing his sigh. It wasn't like he expected anyone from the prosecutor's office—even someone who'd retired—to cast blame on Avery or anyone else, but he couldn't help feeling a bit let down. He'd come to try and understand the thinking behind the original indictment, but he hadn't learned anything new, which meant his listeners wouldn't learn anything new either—at least not until Jeremy worked his magic. Already, he knew he'd cut the majority of this interview. There wasn't enough meat to make it more than a snippet. As it was, they'd been forced to heavily edit the hairdresser and the Dean. It was either that or have longer episodes or two-parters. Neither was ideal for the format he'd been pushing with the sponsor. He got to his feet. "Thanks for speaking with me."

"Sure," Blankenship said, his head swiveling back toward the screen in that strange way he had. "Good luck."

Gordon stood awkwardly a few seconds longer, but the man had already lost interest in him, the sound of the race at full volume now. Gathering his equipment, he let himself out. In spite of learning nothing new, there was something that nagged at him about the interview. Was it the way Blankenship had shrugged off Anthony Battle's lie? Or the insistence that the office had done everything by the book? Shaking his head, he steered the car in the direction of the motel.

Driving past the college with its historic red brick buildings and tree-lined paths, he thought about his own brief time in school and meeting Lynnleigh. He remembered the way his stomach had flipped over the first time he'd seen her. Sweat had glistened on her forehead as she'd run past him, ponytail swinging. After that, he'd seen her everywhere. The college deli, tailgates, even outside a local shopping mall. It had taken him weeks to build up the courage to introduce himself. He'd been instantly smitten, of course, but it had turned into something else for him. Something deeper. He couldn't eat. He couldn't sleep. When she'd broken it off, he'd gone to class even less, drank even more. But that's where it ended because he'd left school not long after that. Yet, he'd never forgotten that feeling, that driving need to be near her, to touch her, be as close to her as he could be.

He recognized now that his obsession with Lynnleigh wasn't wholly about her but was partially a manifestation of issues he'd been avoiding. His sister had helped with some of that and Jeremy, too, but he had yet to fully untangle the unhealthy grip his father had on him, the way the man could reduce him to nothing with only a few words. That kind of desperation for approval wasn't healthy. Maybe he and Lynnleigh's father had more in common than he'd realized. Harry had issues, too. Big ones. An obsession to protect his wife, for one. But he didn't kill Lisa or Tina. Someone else had committed that crime. Someone who used Harry's knife.

* * *

Gordon rocked backward on the chair. "What we still can't explain is the murder weapon."

Jeremy frowned. "What do you mean?"

"It was never found, right?"

"Man, we've been over this already. That thing is gone."

"I'm not talking about where it is now. I'm talking about when it was stolen." He tapped on the notepad in front of him. "Harry Lawson testified that the knife was stolen two weeks prior to the murders."

"But never reported."

It wasn't lost on Gordon that this had been a layup for Avery at trial, but the video cast a different light on Harry's testimony. If one accepted the argument that Harry's knife was the murder weapon and Harry didn't kill the women, then the only logical conclusion was that Harry had told the truth about the theft, too. Gordon picked up his copy of the trial transcript and read aloud now.

Avery: "This is a picture of the knife you owned."

Lawson: "Well, that's what it looks like, yeah, but that's not my knife."

Avery: "We know that, Mr. Lawson. This is an image from a website, but it's the same type of knife. Is that correct?"

Lawson: "Yeah, looks the same."

Gordon summarized the next section. Avery walked over to the large screen that had been brought into the courtroom and displayed the same image. He showed it from different angles, described its unique features, and resumed reading.

Avery: "Now, Mr. Lawson, are you a hunter?"

Lawson: "I don't like hunting."

Avery: "Fishing?"

Lawson: "I've done my share."

Avery: "Of course, you have. We are blessed in this county to have bountiful streams and nearby lakes. Why, most folks in this room today probably picked up their first fishing pole before they set foot in a classroom."

Gordon imagined there might have been a titter in the audience and a few nodding heads.

Avery: "How old were you when you learned to fish?"

Lawson: "My father took me on my third birthday."

Avery: "Just as I thought. Grew up fishing. And how old were you when your father taught you how to clean a fish?"

Lawson: "I don't know. Nine or ten, maybe."

Avery: "And you use a knife to do that, don't you?"

Lawson: "There isn't any other way."

Avery: "Did you ever take your Gerber knife with you when you went fishing?"

Lawson: "Sometimes."

Avery: "Would you consider yourself good at cleaning a fish?"

Lawson: "I'm not bad."

Avery: "Is it possible you're being modest about your ability to carve open a rockfish?"

Lawson: "I know what you're doing. But lots of people in this town—hell, this whole damn state—know how to clean a fish."

Avery: "That may be, but not all of their wives have been brutally murdered with a Gerber LHR knife. In fact, I'd venture to say you're the first."

The record showed Lawson had broken down then.

Jeremy whistled. "Went for the jugular with that."

Gordon agreed, thinking about how he could bring this testimony onto the podcast. He wanted the people who'd been sitting in that courtroom to remember the way the man had cried, his wide shoulders shaking. Most of them probably thought his tears were either an act or more the result of guilt about what he'd done. But now they could look at all of his testimony in a new light. His inability to rein in his emotions had been real, not the result of guilt, but grief.

The young man knew better than anyone what it felt like to have your actions judged, misunderstood. After Max's death, he'd walked around on eggshells, afraid to see the hollowed-out face of his father, the red-ringed eyes of his mother. For a time, their suffering meant they left him alone until a call from his coach and the school counselor. They were worried. He'd missed school. He'd missed practice. No one inside the house considered Gordon's grief. Gordon was lazy. Gordon didn't want to work hard. Gordon let them all down. He heard it so many times, it became a self-fulfilling prophecy.

"When are you going to get a real job?" his father had asked after the first season of the podcast dropped. He'd tried to explain, even asked his dad if he'd listened. "Why do I want to hear about corrupt politicians? And I sure don't want to hear about the man's crimes. Don't I get enough of that on the news every night?"

"Honey, Gordon is doing his best," his mother had said. If he'd thought she was sticking up for him, she disavowed him of that. "He'll try harder, won't you, dear?"

Judgment was a funny thing. Would the men and women who sat on that jury think something different now? Would they feel bad about their judgment? He didn't know, but he hoped so. He picked up the transcript again.

"Listen to this part."

Avery: "Isn't it true that you received comments on your service report that you were quite adept with a knife, that you were, in fact, categorized as an expert with a knife, particularly in combat situations."

Lawson: "I was well trained. But that doesn't mean I used a knife on my wife."

Avery: "I didn't ask you that question, Mr. Lawson, but since you brought it up. How many men and women have you killed with that knife?"

Lawson: "Do I have to answer that?"

Judge: "I'm afraid you do."

Lawson: "Four."

Avery: "Is that including your wife and Tina Cox?"

Gordon described the next section. "Thompkins, the public defender, finally did something, and the judge must have been feeling sorry for Harry by then, because he sustained her objection. He returned to reading.

Avery: "So, it's your testimony that while you were in the service, you recorded four separate kills, all with a knife?"

Lawson: "Yes."

Avery: "Why not a gun?"

Lawson: "I don't really like guns."

Avery: "But you own a rifle."

Lawson: "It belonged to my dad."

Avery: "So, you don't like guns when you kill, but you do like knives?"

To the public defender's credit, she stood up again.

Thompkins: "Your Honor, where is this going? We're willing to concede that the defendant was good at using a knife. In fact, I'd be willing to bet that many in this very room know how to use a knife. But that isn't a crime and never will be."

Again, the judge cooperated with the defense.

Judge: "I happen to agree. Sustained. Please move on, Mr. Avery."

Avery: "No more questions at this time, Your Honor, but we reserve the right to recall the defendant."

Gordon's voice trailed off, and he shook his head before looking up at Jeremy again. "Without the knife, the whole thing is innuendo. Bringing in his service record, talking about fishing, all of that. None of those things is motive or opportunity."

"Yeah, well, you have to give the prosecutor credit. He reminded the jury that Lawson had killed four other times, and every time was with a knife. He didn't need the knife in evidence to do that."

Gordon said nothing. Harry didn't kill his wife, but his knife was used. Either he gave it to someone and was lying about it being stolen, which seemed unlikely, or he told the truth. If only Gordon could figure out who might have taken it. He flipped through the transcript, reading aloud again.

Avery: "Was anything other than the knife taken?"

Lawson: "The case it was in."

Avery: "Nothing else? Not cash? Not food? Not a keyring or a coaster?"

Lawson: "No. Nothing."

Avery: "I see. Do you lock your store at night, Mr. Lawson?"

Lawson: "Sure."

Avery: "So, how do you suppose the alleged knife thief got in? Was there a broken window? A door that had been jimmied?"

Lawson: "I already told you there wasn't."

Avery: "I see."

Gordon paused. Without having been in the courtroom, he had to picture the prosecutor stepping back from the witness box and shooting a meaningful look at the jurors before continuing. The moment would have been charged, each of the twelve men and women leaning forward in their seats. He let out a breath now and continued.

Avery: "Your knife was stolen, which you kept locked up in your store, which showed no sign of a break-in. Is that about right?"

Lawson: "You're making it sound wrong. You're—"

Judge: "Mr. Lawson, you need to sit down."

Lawson: "But he's—"

Judge: "Sit down, Mr. Lawson."

The trial record showed that the witness did sit down.

Judge: "Clerk, could you read back the last question, please?"

Clerk: "Your knife was stolen, which you kept locked up in your store, which showed no signs of a break-in. Is that about right?"

Judge: "Mr. Lawson, please limit your response to answering the question at hand."

Lawson: "Yeah, that's right."

Judge: "Thank you, Mr. Lawson. Mr. Avery, do you have any other questions?"

Avery: "Only one, Your Honor. As far as I can tell, after this knife was allegedly stolen, you did not go to the police, you did not find evidence of a break-in, and you told no one at all that it was missing. Isn't it true that your knife was never stolen at all? That you used it to murder your wife and her best friend?"

Lawson: "I would never have hurt Lisa. Never. And I—"

Judge: "Mr. Lawson, I warned you to keep your seat."

Lawson: "Sorry."

Judge: "Thank you, Mr. Lawson. Do you need the question read back to you?"

Lawson: "No, Sir. I did not kill my wife or Tina Cox. That knife was taken. You're right, I didn't call the police, and that's 'cause they wouldn't have found anything. Like you said, no one broke the window like the other time, and nothing else was taken. But just 'cause I didn't tell the cops doesn't mean I didn't tell someone."

Gordon imagined Avery whipping around to face Lawson in that moment.

Avery: "Oh? And who would that have been, Mr. Lawson?"

Lawson: "My wife. I told Lisa."

Avery: "Well, we only have your word for that, don't we? Seems like that's about all we have for anything, isn't it? Your word. Such as it is."

Thompkins: "Objection."

Judge: "Sustained. Mr. Avery, please keep your personal opinions to yourself."

Avery: "I apologize, Your Honor. No further questions."

Gordon laid the pages down and licked his dry lips. He had to admire Brock Avery. In spite of not having a murder weapon, he'd played it to the hilt, implicating Harry, putting the image of him with that knife in his hand front and center in the jurors' minds. And even Lawson's claims that he told his wife about the missing knife would have been like a drip versus a waterfall. It was masterful, really, and should have been useless to him for the podcast, and yet, he kept coming back to it. Somebody stole that knife. There was nothing random about that act or the murders. There was something there. If only he could figure out what it was.

Chapter Twenty-Five

Now

The man followed Gordon back to his motel, slowing outside the lot before driving on. Gordon Little had been a busy boy. Lynnleigh, the Lawson property, Blankenship—not to mention the director of the preschool and that old Dean the day before. In spite of himself, he was curious about the podcast, curious about what people had to say. But he was most curious about what Lynnleigh would say. She was the key. Without her, the story would die a natural death. He was sure of that.

He swung his car onto the main road until he neared the girl's neighborhood. She'd grown into a strong woman, like her mother, and had a way of looking at you as though she could see inside. He'd only seen it a couple of times, but it had taken all he had not to squirm under that gaze. Maybe if she'd had a normal childhood, she might have been different. Less intense. He'd seen her laugh once, seen the way she dragged her fingers through her hair when she was amused—so like her mother. He wondered if anyone else had ever noticed that? Her mother? Her father? Unlikely. Everyone knew the man hadn't been right in his head for a long time. It was a wonder anyone wanted to spend any time with Harry Lawson. The older he got, the worse he got. And now he was dead. No real loss in the man's mind. Lawson would have ended up in prison one way or the other, his death no real surprise. He'd always seemed fated for tragedy, if you asked him.

The man wasn't entirely heartless. He hadn't wanted to do what he did.

Even now, he believed that in his gut. If there'd been another way, things might have been different. People's perceptions mattered. He wished that wasn't true, but he knew from experience it was. A leader is respected. A criminal isn't. He wished it could be different, that he could go back and change it all, but he couldn't. It was her fault. She'd made him do it. And now the girl was causing problems. He couldn't let that happen.

He took the turn into her neighborhood. It wasn't wise—he knew that—and he considered his timing. Was he too early? Too late? Slowing at the yield sign, he pulled forward slowly. Lynnleigh's house, three houses down on the right. There was a car parked out front, a standard-issue four-door sedan. Hampstead Police. Heart thudding in his chest, he pulled forward into the cross street, eyes scanning the road for her mailbox, but his view was blocked by the car. Damn.

Inside the sedan, a head moved, then another. His breath came faster. The detectives got out of the car and walked up the driveway to the front door. Their pace appeared purposeful but unhurried. What did that mean? Had they even looked in the direction of the mailbox? He didn't think so, but he couldn't be sure. A moment later, they disappeared inside. He checked the time on his phone, his stomach roiling. Had he made a mistake? Done something wrong? Deciding he couldn't be anywhere near when things went down, he drove away from Lynnleigh's house and the small cluster of homes, putting Hampstead in his rearview mirror. With shaky fingers, he flipped on the radio, rotating the dial until he found the local news. Mile after mile, he listened to weather reports and traffic reports, a sick disappointment in his belly. The breaking news report, when it came, made him sit up taller. Details were sparse, and the police had issued a "no comment," but it was enough. Only after it was over did his pulse slow and his grip on the wheel relax. She would understand now. They all would.

Chapter Twenty-Six

Now

Callie pulled up outside Lynnleigh's small house, a hard knot forming in the pit of her stomach. Lynnleigh Lawson hadn't been friendly on the phone, but then again, why would she be? Her mother was gone; her murderer still at large. And now her father was gone, too. None of it was Callie's fault, but she was a Hampstead detective, and today, she would be the face of Lynnleigh's pain. Some might say that wasn't fair, but Callie knew better. That's how it worked. The police had failed the Lawsons. While she may not have been part of the squad then, it was her job now.

Zel reached out and touched her arm. "Cal, hold on a minute." Her head came around, her eyebrows arched. "I've been thinking about something."

"Okay. What about?"

"I hope you don't think this is crazy."

She settled lower in her seat to give him her full attention. Zel's sunny personality brought a balance to their partnership. It also meant he was happy to let her take the lead most of the time. Yet anyone who doubted his detection skills would be making a mistake. She knew better than anyone how intuitive her partner was. And when he did question a decision or had "been thinking," she knew it was a mistake not to listen.

"Let's hear it."

"Well, the thing is, through all of this, the first investigation and now, we've been assuming that the killer had something against Lisa. Maybe someone local, or maybe someone passing through who had a run-in with her. Could have been someone random out of their minds on something, but if that were the case, there should have been other signs and evidence. My point is that other than the circumstantial stuff pointing to Harry, we haven't found a single reason someone in this town would want to murder Lisa Lawson, much less stab her dozens of times."

Everything he said was true. Still, she said nothing, waiting.

"So, I'm wondering if we need to look in another direction. Maybe the person the killer wanted to hurt most wasn't Lisa but Harry. He beat a man to protect his wife's honor. He did everything for Lisa and Lynnleigh. We know he didn't have many friends, but he had plenty of enemies. Maybe they thought Harry would be home, and Lisa and Tina paid the price. Or maybe Lisa was the target. What better way to get to Harry? To break him?" He paused, his previous words having poured out in a rush. "It would explain why Tina wasn't killed in as violent a way, too." He followed with an apology. "It's just a theory. No worries."

Callie stared at her partner, her lips parted. She turned the idea over in her mind: Harry's volatile personality, Harry's irrational behavior, Harry's dwindling group of friends, and she wanted to slap herself in the forehead. Harry wasn't the killer, but maybe he was the intended victim. Why hadn't she thought of that? Jackson and Avery had been single-minded in their pursuit of Harry, and in a way, she'd been doing the same thing. She remembered her mother's insistence with Jackson fifteen years earlier that he ask her about Tina and Barton. Maura had been making a point, but she'd been right. There were four victims that day—five if you counted Lynnleigh—Lisa, Tina, Harry, and Barton. It was time she started considering whether any of them could have been the target.

"You're one hundred percent right. We need to consider all possibilities. Be open to more than one idea of how this happened. Keep reminding me, okay?"

"You got it," he said and glanced up at the house. "Now, let's do this.

Lynnleigh made them wait, and when she did finally open the door, she jerked it back in one angry motion as though they'd woken her at three in the morning.

"Detective Forde," Callie said. "And this is my partner, Detective Zeleniak."

"I know who you are, Callie, I mean Detective Forde." The words were delivered without malice, but there was no warmth either. "Unless you have something new, Chief Waters already gave me an update. Do you?" One hand held the door. The other landed on her hip. "Have something new?"

"We have a few questions. If you wouldn't mind."

The girl's face remained closed, but after a few seconds, she waved a hand toward the hallway. "Come on then. Might as well get this over with."

The pair followed her into a small den outfitted with a couch, two chairs, and a desk. The young woman took the smallest chair and waited for them to sit. Settling back onto the sofa, Zel pulled out his notebook and pen.

"We're sorry for your loss, Ms. Lawson," Callie said and added, cringing, "your losses, I mean."

"Call me Lynnleigh. You knew me in high school. You were my tutor that summer before my freshman year, weren't you?"

"I don't think I helped much."

"Pretty sure I didn't make it easy. Things were…" Her words faded, and she twisted her hands in her lap.

Callie waited a beat before saying, "So, Lynnleigh, there's no point in beating around the bush. The case of your mother's murder has been reclassified as unsolved. Detective Zeleniak and I are leading the investigation and have been going over the case files."

Lynnleigh frowned. "Then you know they targeted my father right from the beginning. His being charged was no accident."

"I wouldn't put it quite that way," Callie said.

"How would you put it then? Your office ate up the evidence spoon-fed to them."

Zel sat forward. "You're suggesting your father was framed."

"You bet I am. My father's knife going missing. The ID at the gas station store. Pretty convenient. Somebody set him up."

Neither detective spoke for a moment. Callie had her own questions about why Anthony Battle had lied about the ID, but until she knew more, she wasn't ready to share. "I understand why you might think that, and we'll investigate that possibility," she said.

Lynnleigh folded her arms across her chest, expression stony. "There were others no one ever investigated."

Callie's mind flashed back to her whiteboard and the web of names. The drifter, the salesman, Jerry Morgan, and Battle. Then there were the Marks, father and son. One had been Tina's boss. The other, an apparent friend. How good a friend was still unknown. Buried in the discovery files, she'd discovered that Tina had made an appointment with Byron a year and a half before her death. There were no follow-up appointments and nothing to indicate why she'd been to see him, but a note in the margin indicated they'd known each other outside of that one appointment. By itself, it meant nothing. Still, she kept his name on the board. There were others, too. Still, she wasn't there to discuss suspects.

"There's something else I wanted to ask you about, Lynnleigh, something about your mother and Tina. They'd known each other since they could walk and were best friends."

"This isn't new territory, Detective."

"We've heard from several sources that they hadn't been getting along for a few weeks, had been fighting."

Lynnleigh uncrossed her arms. "I don't remember that."

Callie shared the little she'd heard. "You didn't hear anything or see any tension?"

"No, but I was in middle school. I was more interested in going to the mall than paying attention to my mother and her friends."

Callie allowed a small nod. "Sounds a lot like my teenage years."

"Yeah, well..." She clasped her hands together. "I wish I could go back. I wish I had paid better attention, seen something, anything, but I can't."

"Maybe not," Callie said, "but you might know something you don't even realize."

"You don't think I've thought of that?" Her voice, so sure earlier, wobbled now. "Even if it wasn't fifteen years ago, I didn't know that much about what my mom did every day. I mean, I knew she taught preschool and tutored sometimes. I could tell you who most of her friends were, that her favorite color was blue, that she liked to watch cooking shows, that she checked out books she thought I would like, that she still brushed my hair sometimes, that she—" the words faltered and thick tears flowed. Her head dropped. "She told me the only thing she ever wanted in life was my dad and me, that she couldn't be any luckier." Her head swung from side to side above her shaking shoulders. "We were the lucky ones. She was the best mom, the best wife." She lifted her eyes to them. "And someone took that away. They killed her—someone evil—killed her. And you let them get away."

There hadn't been much to say after that.

"Well, that went about as well as could be expected," Zel said. "Something tells me Lynnleigh Lawson is not a big fan of the Hampstead Police—not that I blame her. She didn't need to lose her father. She's had it tough."

"Yeah, she wasn't happy to see us." Callie tossed Zel a sad smile. It was just like her partner to recognize Lynnleigh's pain. He didn't like pouring salt in a wound or twisting the knife. He saw the good in people always. She wasn't sure how he managed that, considering the work they did, but that's who he was. His wife once said that she couldn't decide if he was woefully unsuited for life as a detective or entirely what the job called for. Callie only knew that he was a bright spot in her life, exactly the attitude that kept her going even when she wasn't sure she had it in her. She circled the car, slapping her hand on the hood. "Making friends wherever we go," she said, using one of his favorite expressions.

He laughed and wagged his finger at her. A small plane roared overhead, and Zel paused to look up, raising a hand to shield his eyes from the sun. He watched it a moment and glanced over at her, mouth open, but whatever words he planned to say were lost, drowned in an ear-shattering explosion that threw Callie backward. Before her eyes, Zel flew straight up into the air like a rag doll, legs splayed wide. He dropped down again with a thud, landing some twenty feet further from where he started. Shards of metal and bits of paper floated around him like confetti. There were shouts and calls and eventually a siren, but Callie saw only her partner, lying still on the pavement, his body bent in two, silent and still.

Chapter Twenty-Seven

Now

The door to the motel room banged open, and Gordon looked up to see Jeremy panting, hair askew, and skin ashen. He threw a look over his shoulder before slamming and locking the door in a single motion. Gordon watched his friend draw the curtains closed, throwing the room into darkness.

Gordon got to his feet, switching on the lamp. "I was working here, you know."

Jeremy waved his hand and stayed near the window, peering out at the parking lot from behind the heavy drapes.

He studied his friend. "What's going on, Jer?"

"You didn't hear?" Jeremy looked over his shoulder.

A tickle of worry stirred in Gordon's brain. "Hear what?"

Jeremy's eyes closed briefly as though he needed strength, and Gordon tensed. Jeremy let the curtain drop and pulled over a chair. Slowly, Gordon sat across from him, his heart beating faster now.

Jeremy clasped his hands together in his lap. "I need you to stay calm, but somebody set off a bomb at Lynnleigh's house."

Gordon sprang to his feet but once up, didn't know what to do. "What? No. That can't be right. I just saw her this morning."

"She's okay," Jeremy said at the same time Gordon found his phone. "At least that's what I heard. She was in the house, and the bomb was in her mailbox. There's a cop who got hurt."

Gordon's hand shook as the phone came to life. Seven unseen messages, the last from Lynnleigh.

Someone decided to carry out their threat, but I'm fine. The police are putting me somewhere temporarily—I don't know what good that'll do. Be in touch as soon as I can. You've got to find out who did this, Gordon. Fast. Before someone else gets hurt.

He sank down onto the bed, every ounce of energy draining from his body. She was alive. With trembling fingers, he tapped his phone, searching through the local news stories. All were brief, mostly limited to time and location. The sole person injured, a Hampstead detective, remained unnamed. Gordon considered scrolling through social media, but realized he didn't need to. This was a small town, and news would have travelled fast. He looked over at his producer and friend. "What did you hear?"

Jeremy didn't need much prompting, telling Gordon how he'd stopped at the store to get sandwiches, chips, and beer, and came away instead with snatches of overheard conversation and innuendo.

"It's horrible," a woman in the wine and beer aisle had said, leaning toward a tall, heavyset man. "That poor girl. Hasn't she lost enough already?"

The man had answered with a scowl, and where her voice had been tremulous with sympathy, his had been flat, emotionless. "You can't walk into a hornet's nest without expecting to get stung, Beth. Isn't that how this whole thing started?"

The woman had visibly recoiled. "What are you saying? That she deserved to have a bomb planted at her house?"

"Now, c'mon, I didn't say that. You know I'm not a violent man. But there's been a lot of finger-pointing since she brought that podcast fellow to town. He's got people's gums flapping, and that's not how we do things around here. Maybe someone thought it was time to send a message."

The woman had gasped. "She just wants to know who killed her mother, Billy. Besides, it's not her fault someone blew up her mailbox and injured Todd Zeleniak. Marcie must be worried sick."

"Yeah, well, Lynnleigh Lawson is lucky she's not the one who got hurt.

She'd be wise to watch her back in the future."

"For Chrissake, Billy. You sound like you're the one threatening the girl."

"Me? No way. I'm just saying you can't go around accusing people of things and not expect any blowback. It isn't right."

"None of this is right." The woman had straightened her shoulders. "In the future, I'll be careful not to express an opinion around you," she'd huffed and stomped down the aisle, her cart's wheels clicking along the slick floor.

"Well, shit," the man had muttered before reaching into the case for a twelve-pack of Miller. That's when he'd spotted Jeremy. "What the hell are you looking at?"

Jeremy shrugged now. "And that's it. I got outta there as fast as I could." He shook his head. "But Jesus, Gord, should we be worried? That car the other day on the mountain? That was some serious shit—and now this."

Gordon didn't need reminding about the sedan, but he didn't have a good answer either. He'd received threats when he'd investigated the Hamilton Hayes case, too, but the publicity that surrounded that case protected him. Lisa Lawson and Tina Cox didn't warrant that kind of attention, and Hampstead didn't come with a large police presence.

"Threats are part of it. You know that, Jeremy," he said, hoping he sounded braver than he felt. "And we haven't gotten any credible ones lately, have we?"

"Nothing serious, but..." his friend trailed off, jumping up to take another peek outside.

Lynnleigh was okay. He told himself that over and over until he felt calmer, better able to analyze the situation. The bomb was bad, but it told him something. Whoever killed Lisa and Tina didn't like the attention the case was getting. Was it because of the podcast? Was this his fault? He couldn't be sure. Should he have taken that sedan more seriously? Had he put Lynnleigh in danger? He felt bad about the cop, but what could he have done?

He texted Lynnleigh, waiting for the dots to indicate she was typing, but none came.

"What should we do?" Jeremy asked. "Do we call the sponsor?"

"Yes." Gordon lifted his head, glad to finally have an answer, to take action. "Yes, I'll do that now." Fifteen minutes later, Gordon reported back to his friend. "They want us to get some soundbites from locals on what they think this means for the case and post them on the website and social media. Build momentum leading up to the next episode."

Jeremy nodded. "That makes sense."

"Yeah. To be honest, they seemed less interested in the fact that someone got hurt than they did in the increased subscriptions it'll bring in. They're writing a press release about our next episode and making sure the AP is tipped off about the bomb."

"Meaning more reporters."

"I guess." The sponsors were right. Additional coverage would bring additional listeners—in theory, anyway. They'd even promised to provide his contact info to the major papers in case they wanted to interview him. The tragedy of the bomb could bring more interest in the case, not less. He wasn't sure how he felt about that. Someone had been hurt and could have been killed. Things had just gotten real.

Chapter Twenty-Eight

Now

Callie escorted the girl into the safe house, an empty two-bedroom bungalow on the opposite side of town. Hidden from the prying eyes of neighbors, it was the best she could come up with on short notice. Lynnleigh took one look at the dusty tabletops and worn rug and rolled her eyes.

"How long do I have to be here?"

"Just until we clear your house. One night, most likely."

The girl stood in the middle of the room, one bag in each hand. "I'd rather just stay home."

"Forensics needs to finish going over every inch of your house, and we need to be sure it's clear of any other threats."

"So, after that?"

Callie wanted to shake the girl. What part of keeping her safe didn't she understand? "You can go home when I say you can." She stopped short of telling her that she'd have an officer assigned to keep watch. Something told her the girl wasn't going to like it.

Sighing, Lynnleigh's gaze travelled the room. "Fine," she said, dropping her bags. "You can go now."

Callie gritted her teeth. She'd expected the girl to be worried, maybe even grateful. At the very least, to show a little more concern. Sure, Zel would be fine. A broken wrist was the worst of it, along with a concussion serious enough to keep him overnight, but he'd be back at work in a few days. Yet Lynnleigh had barely asked about Callie's partner, satisfied he wasn't dead. If the bomb had been studded as some were, his injuries might have been worse. Much worse.

"I'm not your maid," the detective said now.

"Just my babysitter."

The two women stared at each other. This wasn't the timid girl she remembered, the one who'd shunned the spotlight, who'd kept her emotions hidden from the world. This one lifted her chin, her mouth set in a hard line. She didn't mind making waves or hurling accusations. It wasn't the kind of behavior that garnered sympathy. It was the kind that attracted enemies—dangerous ones.

"You're not helping yourself," Callie said now.

"Maybe not, but I didn't ask for your help. You're supposed to be investigating the murder of my mother, aren't you? But instead, you're here." Her hands flew to her hips. "Doing nothing."

Callie blinked, heat rising from her belly to her chest to her cheeks. She didn't have to put up with this, did she? What the girl had been through was terrible, but that didn't give her the right to behave this way, did it? Callie's hands curled into fists. On the verge of giving the girl an earful, she clamped her mouth shut. That wasn't why she was here or why she'd volunteered to get the girl settled. She had a job to do. Her father's face rose up in her mind, his words ringing in her ears.

"A good detective plays many roles, Callie. Good cop. Bad cop. Angry. Compassionate. Everything in between. All are part of the job, if and only if they serve a purpose." A new detective back then, she'd squirmed in her chair, not particularly interested in yet another mini lecture on what kind of detective she should be. She'd been in her new job less than three months and had sat through nearly a dozen of these "talks" already. She'd stifled a yawn.

"Am I boring you?"

"No, just tired is all."

He'd frowned. "Are you having trouble sleeping?"

"God, no, Dad. Just normal tired." She'd gotten to her feet. "Look, I should get back."

"Sit down, Callie. I'm not done."

She'd groaned. She knew that tone, the one that said anything other than sitting would be taken as a sign of disrespect. She sat.

"As I was saying, emotion is only good so long as it serves a purpose. If it drives you to keep digging, for example. As an interrogator, emotion is useless for anything other than playing a role. Behind every bad cop or good cop scenario should be a plan. If anger makes you play the scene better, fine, but it should never be allowed to take over. Do you understand?"

"Sure."

"Never forget the reason you are conducting an interrogation, Callie."

"To catch the perp."

"No, that will happen. There is only one goal in every interview and interrogation—whether it's a witness or a suspect. Find the truth."

She repeated it silently in her head now. *Find the truth.* Flexing her fingers, she let her anger go—or mostly.

"I won't be staying long," she said, calmer. A standoff with Lynnleigh wouldn't help her reach her goal. What she needed to know wasn't just who might have threatened Lynnleigh, but why now? What she needed was the truth. "I have a few questions first."

Lynnleigh flopped down in the closest chair. "Fine."

Finding a spot on the old couch, Callie tapped her pen against her notebook. "I'm assuming you know that bomb was intended for you." The girl said nothing. "As a device, it wasn't designed to inflict a fatal injury, which leads me to believe that whoever planted the bomb had another motive."

Lynnleigh's left brow rose, and her lips parted. "Which is?"

"Well, one answer is simply that it's a hate crime. That the person who put the bomb associates you with your father. In spite of the new evidence, we both know there are still some people who refuse to believe your father wasn't guilty."

"Which makes me the murderer's girl, his evil spawn, right?"

"That's one theory."

"That's really creepy."

Callie couldn't disagree, but she moved on. "The second, and more likely theory, is that whoever did this is sending a message, one to back off."

Lynnleigh's body came forward in the chair. "Back off what? I'm not doing anything." Gesturing toward Callie, she said, "You're investigating the murders. Gordon's doing the podcast. I'm literally sitting in my house doing nothing. I have a job in marketing. There's nothing threatening about that. I don't really date. I don't have many friends, not here at least. Why do I matter at all?"

Everything the girl said was true. "That's what we need to find out."

"How?"

"By retracing your steps of the past couple of weeks, looking at what you're planning going forward."

Lines appeared across the girl's forehead. "I haven't done anything unusual."

"Have you talked to any reporters about the case?"

"Not recently. I did a few when the news first broke."

"Have you talked to anyone at work about the case?"

"Not really. I work remotely."

Few friends in town. Working remotely. The anger and defensiveness made more sense. Not insensitivity, but a wall. The only person she seemed to be talking to was the podcaster. Then it hit her. *Gordon's doing the podcast.* Hadn't Zel said they knew each other in college?

"How well do you know Gordon?"

Lynnleigh's gaze dropped to her hands. "Okay, I guess. We went to school together before he dropped out."

"But you stayed friends."

"Not really. Well, sort of."

"Is that how he came to be doing this podcast? Because he heard about your father's case and put two and two together?"

Lynnleigh pulled one leg up onto the chair and licked her lips. "Not exactly."

It clicked then. "You asked him here, didn't you? You're the reason for the podcast."

"I had to," she said, chin thrust forward. "No one was trying to find out who really killed my mother and Aunt Tina. I lost both my parents." Callie bristled but resisted the urge to point out that the police would have reopened the case with or without the podcast. "And my dad. It wasn't fair what they did to him." Her voice faded away to a whisper, a single tear slipping down one cheek.

In spite of the girl's outwardly prickly personality, Callie's heart broke for her. Lynnleigh had lost both her parents and her "aunt." She thought about the terror of learning her own father had been shot, unsure if he would live or die, the fear that had consumed her. Yes, she knew all about heartache, but at least she still had her father—even if the shooting had changed them all.

Lynnleigh wiped the tear away with an angry swipe. She was tougher than most, Callie realized, and the tiniest bit of admiration for her grew.

"Okay. I understand."

The girl's chin quivered. "You do?"

"I do." She allowed a small smile. "I mean, it's not true that no one's investigating. It kind of happens to be my job right now, but I think I understand." The girl cocked her head. "You lack faith in the Hampstead police. Is that it?"

Her shoulders sagged with the truth. "Why shouldn't I? I mean, I know you didn't personally work the case or put my father in jail, but your department did, your boss. Why should I believe you have any interest in admitting your mistake and doing anything other than going through the motions?" She was on a roll now, and Callie let her talk. "I mean, if you investigate and find nothing, then people start to believe the new evidence is bullshit, and my dad was guilty after all, right? Isn't that how it works?"

"That's a bit cynical, isn't it?"

"Not from where I'm sitting. It's realistic."

Callie tried to put herself in the girl's shoes. Would she feel the same if the situation were reversed? It was hard to say. Either way, she needed to get back on track. *To find the truth.*

"All right. So, you called your friend Gordon to look into it with his podcast."

"He'd done that Hamilton Hayes case. And he cares about me. So, yeah, I emailed him."

"That makes sense." She tapped her pen faster, thinking. "How many people know that the podcast was your idea?"

"No one. I made sure Gordon didn't tell anyone. I don't even want to be a part of it, but he said he couldn't do that."

"People will have put it together. It's not that much of a stretch. Could be the reason for the bomb." Lynnleigh didn't comment, and Callie pressed on. "When are you supposed to be interviewed?"

Lynnleigh's shoulders rose and fell in a shrug. "I think he teased it at the end of the last episode, the one where he had that bed and breakfast lady on."

A tingle crawled up Callie's spine. "Before that episode aired, had you had any threats of any kind?"

"Some random text messages from numbers that went nowhere. Once I had a note under my windshield wiper, but that was pretty soon after I moved back to town."

"What kind of note?"

"Hold on." She got up from the chair and went to her purse. "Here," she said, holding it up for Callie to see. "I don't know why I didn't throw it away, but..."

The detective leaned in. The paper looked to be torn from a lined spiral notebook, the kind you might find in any school-aged child's backpack. The note, written in black marker, consisted of one word in block letters. LEAVE.

"Did you report this to the police?"

"What for?" Before Callie could answer, she pulled it back. "What could they do? I had gone into town to run a few errands and left my car parked over on Fulton. It ended up taking longer than I thought, and I was gone for like three hours. Anyone could have put it there, and it's not exactly a busy street. I had eggs thrown at my house once, too, but that's the world we live in, right?"

Callie said nothing for a moment. The idea that they lived in a world where people could be harassed just because someone didn't like them was not a world she understood, but a note left on a car months ago and a couple of broken eggs was a long way from a pipe bomb in a mailbox. "Does your friend Gordon know about the note and the messages?"

"He was a little worried at first until I told him nothing had happened."

"Okay, tell me about the teaser." Callie would go back and listen for herself, but she wanted to hear Lynnleigh's take on it now.

"Not much to tell. I think he said something like 'be sure not to miss the next episode when Lynnleigh Lawson—me—drops a bombshell on the investigation into the murders.' Blah, blah, blah."

Callie winced at the bomb reference but tried instead to focus on the teaser itself. "And what is this supposed bombshell?"

She shrugged again. "It doesn't really have much to do with the case. It's kind of personal, actually, but Gordon thought it would bring more listeners. And he said he might start working it into his theory."

Gordon had a theory? A visit to the podcaster was definitely next on her schedule.

"Can you tell me what the bombshell is?"

The girl's face flushed pink. "Like I said, it doesn't really have anything to do with the murders, but it's important to me."

Callie said nothing, waiting.

"Alright, if you really want to know. When my father was in prison, he had some health problems. Maybe you heard about that?" Callie gave a brief nod. "It was only six months ago, right before he died, you know. I met with the doctors, and they told me there was a chance he could get better if they could do a bone marrow transplant. He said no. He forbade it, actually. He had a life sentence and he said he'd already accepted his fate. All he wanted was for me to have a happy life and not to worry about him. But he was all I had left, you know. I mean, I have my aunt and uncle, and they've done what they can for me, but...it's not the same."

Again, Callie nodded. "So, what did you do?"

"I got tested anyway, to see if I would be a good match. And the thing is…" Her voice fell away, and she stared down at her hands again. Goosebumps rose on Callie's arms. Lynnleigh's head shook from side to side. "The thing is, I wasn't. Turns out my dad wasn't my dad at all." Raising her eyes to meet Callie's, she laughed bitterly. "That's the big bombshell. All those people who hate me because they think I'm the daughter of a killer are wrong. He wasn't even my dad."

Chapter Twenty-Nine

Now

Callie opened the file in front of her and looked across the table at Barton Cox. "Thanks for coming in today, Mr. Cox. I know none of this has been easy for you."

"It's not easy for anyone, is it? How's your partner, Detective?"

"He'll be fine."

"And Lynnleigh? I tried to check on her, but she wasn't home."

"She's fine."

He blinked at her a second. "Oh. That's good then. She's a sweet girl, doesn't deserve any of this. She and Tina were very close, you know."

"That's what she said." Callie shifted, cleared her throat, and pressed record on the phone between them. "Okay?"

"I am."

"Good." She stated the date and time. "Now, Mr. Cox, fifteen years ago, when the police arrested Harry Lawson, you refused to testify against him. Can you tell me why?"

"He didn't do it. I told the detective that."

Jackson's notes backed up the man's claim. "How could you be so sure?"

"Harry Lawson was absolutely incapable of lying. If he said he didn't do it, he didn't. They all thought I was in denial, and maybe I was, but not about that."

"Did you offer to testify for the defense?'

"I didn't. I'll never forgive myself for that. I don't think anyone was all that interested in putting me on the stand anyway. You need to remember, I was grieving. It took everything I had to get up in the morning and keep my business going. They saw a broken man. Why would they listen to me?" He spread his palms wide. "I know that's a poor excuse. I did support Harry in every way I could. I'm sorry I didn't do more now. When I finally came out of my fog, I wrote letters on his behalf, but he didn't have enough grounds for appeal. I went to visit him once, but he wouldn't see me. I think I would have been too much of a reminder for him."

Callie had heard that Barton never wavered in his support of Harry, and that appeared to be true. "Did you spend a lot of time together before the murders?"

"I'd say so. Our wives were inseparable, so I'm not sure we had much choice."

"Did you ever do things together, just the two of you?"

His brows drew together. "Without Tina and Lisa?"

"Say meet for a beer or go to a game or something."

"No. Harry didn't like being around crowds."

She rolled a pencil between her fingers. "Did Harry have any enemies that you know of?"

"Harry? Probably more than a few, but I wouldn't know their names. He ran a grocery store, and I'm an accountant."

"Did you know anyone he spent time with outside of you and your wife and his family?"

"I don't know that he did." His half-smile turned apologetic. "Harry was a complicated guy."

"I've heard that before."

"We did have one thing in common. Our love for our families." Gesturing toward the files, he said, "Detective, I assume you have whatever files or evidence there is from the original investigation. There's nothing I'd like more than for you to find out who did this to my wife and to Lisa, and I'm more than willing to help in any way I can, but I've done my best to avoid the spotlight. The truth is, I'd like to keep it that way."

"What about the podcast?"

For the first time since they'd sat down, she saw him rattled. Pink-faced, he said. "Well, word travels fast, I guess. I haven't committed to anything."

"But you're thinking about it?"

"I am." He ran a hand over his face and let out a long sigh. "I don't have to explain myself to you, Detective. We both know that, but I want to. The reason I'm considering going on the podcast is so Tina won't ever be forgotten. On the news, they plaster her picture on the screen, but that's it. Did you hear the episode with her hairdresser and the one with Dean Marks?" She told him she did. "Then you know what I mean. The stories about her keep her alive, so yes, I'm considering it. But that's all."

"You're right," Callie said, her voice soft. "You didn't owe me an explanation."

He cleared his throat. "Well, thank you for that," he said.

"I'm wondering, though, how your current wife feels about all this."

Again, he seemed to falter, searching for his words. "Cindy is a good woman. I love her. I do. Tina's ghost will never go away for her. I think that's why she tries so hard to be seen, to be known. She works so hard trying to live up to Tina's memory. Running this fundraiser and that one. It took me a long time to understand, but I do now. And she's been there for me. Really been there." His eyes misted behind his glasses, and he averted his gaze. "But Tina deserves to be seen right now. It's the only way to help find her killer and get closure, real closure for all of us—including Cindy." At that, he stood. "I'm sorry, Detective. I have another appointment."

"Right, but if you don't mind, I have just a few more questions." He hesitated, his hand resting on the back of the chair. "It won't take long," she said.

"I guess I have a couple more minutes."

Callie opened the folder to the autopsy report. She didn't want to do this. Asking a man about his dead unborn baby was not high on her bucket list of work goals, but in the hopes that she wouldn't have to bother this man again, she had no choice. "There is something else I need to ask you about. It's a difficult thing."

CHAPTER TWENTY-NINE

For a moment, he didn't understand.

"It's about Tina's condition at the time of the murder."

The blood drained from his face. "Oh, I see. You want to ask me about," he paused as though considering the right word, "the fetus?" He caught the look on her face, cheeks pink again. "It's easier for me if I think of it that way. Makes it seem less real somehow. I'm not sure if you're aware that we'd been trying for a very long time."

For a second, she didn't speak. "At the time of the murder, Tina was nine weeks pregnant."

"Yes. Is there a question about it?"

"I wondered why you didn't want that brought out at trial."

"Why? It wouldn't have changed anything. Whoever was convicted—whether that was Harry or someone else—they were already getting life. I didn't want to be the face of an added tragedy." He fell back against the chair. "And I'd just recently learned Tina was expecting. We hadn't told our families, our friends. It was between us. Our last thing between us. It wasn't for the public. In a way, I still prefer it that way. It's a grief that's mine alone, not shared, if you know what I mean."

It made some sense. "I think I understand." She slid the report back in the file. "Mr. Cox, can you think of any reason why anyone would want to harm your wife?"

He frowned. "Don't you mean harm Lisa?"

She understood his assumption. It was the one shared by the police fifteen years earlier, and while it still made some sense, Zel had reminded her they didn't know that the killer was targeting Lisa. "No, I mean Tina."

"Why would you ask that?" His skin, pale moments earlier, flushed red.

"We need to consider every possibility, Mr. Cox. It's possible the perpetrator was angry with both women. Maybe some of that anger had worn off before the killer attacked your wife, or they heard someone coming." The man continued to stare at her. "I'm sorry. I don't mean to upset you, but as I said, we need to take another look at everything."

"Everything," he repeated dully.

"So, can you think of anyone who might have been angry with Tina? Did she have any enemies?"

"No. Absolutely not. Everyone loved Tina."

"Had she had any run-ins with anyone around town or up at the college?"

"She didn't say anything if she did."

Callie hated to give credence to gossip, but since Barton had admitted listening to the podcast, she decided it was fair game. "What about with the Dean's wife or daughter-in-law or any of the other wives or husbands?"

"You mean the stiffies?" he asked, sitting back. "I didn't even know what that was until I heard the hairdresser on that podcast, so no."

"Did you know Dean Marks and his family?"

"I'd met them. Dean Marks seemed like a good man. His wife didn't say much."

"And Byron and his wife, uh," Callie paused to check her notes, "Amanda. Did you ever meet either of them?"

"Former wife, if I'm correct. The man…" Barton checked his watch and frowned. "Never mind. What does any of this have to do with my wife's murder, Detective?"

"Maybe nothing," she said with a shrug, "but according to Dean Marks, he'd suggested your wife talk to his son about fertility issues. Did you ever meet Byron or Amanda?"

His jaw tightened. "No, Detective, I did not." The man pointed at the report she'd recently closed. "And in case you forgot, my wife was pregnant, so…"

"Yes, so," she repeated.

He placed his hands on the table, poised to push himself up. "Is that all, Detective? I'm very late."

"One last question." Ignoring his audible sigh, she said, "Your wife and Lisa had been best friends their entire lives, but I've heard from multiple sources that they'd been fighting and hadn't been getting along. Is it possible that they'd had a disagreement, something that might have led to their murders?"

Rising from the chair, his eyes burned with frustration. "You've got to be kidding. Is this about that Handler woman on that podcast? None of this has anything to do with what happened to my wife, Detective. First,

Dean Marks and those wives, and now this." He paused, seeming to gather himself. "Let's say it was true they were fighting—which it's not—are you actually implying they brought this on themselves somehow, or wait, no," he stopped again, his eyes bugging behind his glasses now. "Are you suggesting they hurt each other? This is insane." He took a step toward the door and halted, looking back over his shoulder. "I thought with Harry gone, you all could see the forest for the trees and maybe actually find who did this, but now... I don't know what to think."

After he was gone, she stayed in her seat, replaying the interview over and over in her head. Maybe Barton was right and any bickering between the longtime friends had nothing to do with the murders, but he was wrong about there not being any friction between the women. Patty Handler hadn't imagined the two women arguing in the hall at that fundraiser or Tina's tears. Nor had the hairdresser imagined Tina's reluctance to get to her friend's house. But husbands were not known for their observation skills. There were plenty of jokes about missed anniversaries and birthdays, and any other number of meaningful dates to prove it. And Barton's job came with long hours and a large list of clients. Any problems between Lisa and Tina would most likely have gone unnoticed by both Harry and Barton.

Still, whether Barton realized it or not, something had been bothering Tina. Callie was sure of that, and she had to ask herself: in light of the pregnancy—one that Tina had been dreaming of for years—why did she seem so unhappy?

* * *

Still smarting after the interview, Callie looked up to find Hendo and Chang standing over her desk.

She felt something close to relief. "Another break-in?" she asked.

"No. A call from one of the homeowners."

"Which one?"

"Dan Braun."

Her brow creased. Dan Braun owned the first house hit, the one that had been vandalized in addition to being robbed.

"You know that dining room wall, the one with the big hole you said looked like it was cut?" Hendo asked.

"Sure."

"They figured they'd take the whole thing down instead of getting it patched, open up to the den or something. When they started the demo, they found a box inside the wall."

"A box?"

"Yeah, about the size of a shoebox. Looked like it had been opened recently. Owner swears he's never seen it before."

Callie uncrossed her legs and sat forward, her mind ping-ponging with possibilities. "Are you thinking your thieves came across this box? Or that's what they were after all along?"

Chang had said nothing up to that point but chimed in now. "Why would a bunch of teenagers want an empty shoe box? And how would they know about it?"

"You know what," Hendo said, tapping his partner on the arm and dragging him toward the door. "How about this? We'll call Mr. Braun and see when we can check out this box for ourselves, and in the meantime, we can swing by the diner for some club sandwiches. I could use some real food for a change. Lauren's been sick all week, and I don't know if I can eat cereal for dinner one more night."

Watching them head out, Callie slipped on her own jacket, but before she could get off the floor, Jackson found her.

"Good. You're still here."

The look on his face told her she wasn't going to like what he had to say.

"The Chief called a press conference in fifteen minutes. He wants you there."

Chapter Thirty

Now

The man stood across the street from the makeshift podium, his hands shoved in his pockets. All around him, townsfolk gathered in clumps, low murmurs rising and falling as they waited for the chief to appear. Local and regional media had staked out a spot near the front. Scanning the heads, he searched for the podcaster. There, just outside the circle of traditional media. Next to him stood his friend, holding up a microphone. A stirring made him look up at the front doors.

The Chief, two uniforms, a man in a suit, and Detective Forde joined the two uniforms already stationed on the steps. Chief Waters took his place in front of the podium, clearing his throat.

"As many of you have already heard, a pipe bomb exploded late yesterday afternoon in the mailbox of Lynnleigh Lawson." He went on to describe the incident briefly before turning it over to questions. It was clear to the man—even from his distance—that the Chief rather enjoyed the role. He preened and puffed his chest, imbuing even the words "No comment" with great import. When he got to the podcaster, the man sensed a shift in the crowd.

"Chief Waters, do you think the person who planted the pipe bomb is the same person who murdered Lisa Lawson and Tina Cox?"

The crowd around the man went quiet.

"Well, Mr. Little, that's a good question. Of course, we'll consider the possibility, but more likely, it's someone who doesn't like the attention this case has brought to Hampstead." He swung back toward a young woman in the front row, raising his finger in her direction.

The podcaster was not to be deterred. "Chief Waters," he said, his voice louder than before, "What do you say to the rumors that this investigation has stalled?"

The chief pressed his lips together. "The rumors are false."

"What can you tell us about the progress you've made?" He waved an arm around at the crowd. "I'm sure all of these people would feel safer knowing that you're close to making an arrest."

Hearing the comment, the man almost laughed out loud. The idea was outrageous. These people were not in any danger, whether the police knew what they were doing or not.

Blinking into the cameras, Chief Waters looked over his shoulder. "I'm going to let Detective Forde take your question, but I do want to assure all the good people of Hampstead that this department is working double time to ensure the safety of each and every one of its citizens. Rest assured, we are out there."

The man heard grumbling to his right, but he kept his focus on the podium. Unlike the chief, Detective Forde did not appear pleased to be at the microphone.

"Thank you," she said, her gaze wandering over the crowd. Instinctively, the man shrank back behind a large man sporting cargo shorts and an oversized backpack. "I'm not at liberty to give details on the progress, but in light of the video, we are taking another look at each piece of evidence and—"

"What about the witness who said Lawson was in town?"

The man's head tried to follow the sound of the voice, but he couldn't pick out the speaker.

"That witness has allowed that they may have been mistaken."

"You say mistaken, I say lied," came another voice.

A few titters rose up around the man, and nearby, two women leaned in conspiratorially.

"It was Anthony Battle who said that."

The man pulled his hood farther forward, hiding his face.

"The drunk?"

"One and the same."

"I always thought he had a thing for Lisa. Do you remember that?"

"How could I forget?"

The man slipped further back in the crowd, keeping his head low.

At the podium, Detective Forde spoke again. "As I said, we are taking another look at all the evidence that's already been collected as well as expanding our search and interview pool."

A reporter in a pink jacket raised her hand and shouted, "How is that different than the first investigation?"

The Detective gave a short nod. "Good question. In some ways, it's not. The evidence in our possession is solid, but where some of that appeared to point to Harry Lawson, we can now look at things in a new light, consider the murders from a variety of angles and perspectives, flip things on their head. That includes motive and opportunity."

The woman in pink seemed skeptical. "Look at and consider. That doesn't sound like you've gotten very far, Detective."

"From where you are, maybe not, but from where I sit, we're seeing things more clearly and asking the right questions. At this point, it would do more harm to the investigation than good to share more."

Next to him, a tall man rolled his eyes. "Cop speak for we have nothing."

The man wasn't sure he agreed, but there would be no shortage of opinions and talk—he knew that—although what other people thought about the investigation mattered little to him.

On the stage, the detective backed away, allowing the chief to wrap things up. A couple more reporters got the chance to ask their questions, but the man had heard enough. As he made his way down the sidewalk, it was the detective's earlier words that rang in his head. *Flip things on their head. That includes motive and opportunity.* He lowered his chin to his chest and began to walk faster. He may not have learned anything new about the investigation, but he did know one thing. He couldn't allow that detective to get any closer to the truth. He was going to have to end this charade sooner rather than later.

Chapter Thirty-One

Now

The chief droned on, spouting crime statistics and other data that had nothing to do with the investigation. Callie stood behind him, her hands clasped behind her back, fingers twisting and twisting. Why couldn't he wrap it up? Even the crowd was growing restless.

Her mind drifted to the podcaster. His questions were better than most, not as good as some. Had it been a mistake to allow Patty to talk to him?

"How are we supposed to feel safe?" a woman in a headband was shouting. On her hip, she balanced a small child.

"Yeah," another resident yelled. "A house got robbed in my neighborhood. What are you doing about that?"

To his credit, the police chief knew how to talk. Giving an actual answer was another thing. A few more shouts rose up, and Callie knew he must have finally decided to throw in the towel because he passed the microphone back to the official press rep. Of course, he said even less than the chief.

A bead of sweat slipped between her breasts, and Callie danced on her toes, scanning the crowd one more time. She knew half the press, mostly regional, but there were a few new faces. There was the podcaster, of course, and his producer. A group of women stood near the back, and Callie winced. Her mother was among that group, along with Patty and the rest of the movie club ladies. She searched her mother's face for some kind of reaction, but her face was closed, her arms crossed over her chest.

Tearing her eyes away from the women, she searched the rest of the faces but didn't see the one she was looking for. Barton Cox. If he was there, she didn't see him, although she couldn't blame him. Hadn't he avoided the press in the past?

A movement at the back of the crowd drew her attention then. A ruckus of some kind. Pushing and shoving. Raised voices. Her gaze snapped to the uniformed officer on the far corner, but he didn't hear. She stood up taller, trying to make out what was going on. Another shout, this one louder. A handful of townspeople seemed to be arguing, fingers pointing. One man landed on the ground, and the woman with him screamed. More heads turned. Now the uniform on the corner paid attention. A fist caught a second man in the temple, and both collided with a third. It was then that she saw him. Slipping out from the fray was a man in a dark hoodie.

Callie didn't have to think. She ran across the stage, skipping down the steps, and plunged into the crowd. Popping up and down, she saw the dark hood weaving in and out. A moment later, the man in the hoodie spotted the approaching officer and took off in the opposite direction. She moved faster, pushing people out of the way. Her mind raced. She'd been by Anthony Battle's house that morning, but the place had been locked up tight. The neighbors hadn't seen him, or his ex-wife, and he hadn't shown up at any of his usual haunts the night before. Not that she'd been surprised. If she hadn't shown up on his doorstep days earlier, he might have already been gone.

"What do you want?" he'd said.

"To ask you a few questions."

"I'll let you know when my lawyer arrives," he'd said, closing the door, but she'd been too quick, inserting her boot first.

"You can talk to me now, or I can haul your ass downtown, let everyone see us bringing you in with your lawyer. That podcaster's been hanging around. Maybe he'll talk about it on his show. Do you want that, Anthony?"

The whites of his eyes had bulged. "I don't wanna talk to you at all."

"You don't have any choice. It's now or down at the station."

In the end, he'd let her in, swearing he'd made a mistake when he said he'd seen Harry that day.

"Perjury is a crime, Anthony," she'd said, but he refused to say any more about it.

"I answered your question. We're done."

"Fine," she'd said. "There is one other thing. I wanted to ask you about a run-in Jerry Morgan had with Harry."

His eyes had narrowed to slits. "What about it?"

"Is it true you were egging Jerry on, making jokes about Lisa in his ear?"

"I was there. That's all. I didn't do nothin'."

"So, you didn't say anything about how Lisa was always on her high horse, always looking down her nose at you, how everyone knew she couldn't stand Jerry. How she deserved to be put in her place."

"Maybe I did. Lisa Lawson was a grade A first class b—" He'd caught himself then. Wagging his finger, he said, "No, you don't, Detective. You think you're so smart." He'd pushed the door toward her, forcing her backward. "If you have anything else to ask me, you can reach out to my lawyer."

Callie had conceded, knowing she'd already gotten more out of him than she'd dared hope. "I'll do that, Anthony. Don't leave town."

"Oh, yeah? Is that a warning?"

"As a matter of fact, it is."

But he had disappeared, going underground. His lawyer claimed he couldn't be reached and wanted to know if Anthony was under arrest.

Breaking free from the crowd, she searched the street in front of her. A flash of black. Arms pumping, she raced down the street to the corner, looking right and left and back again. Pockets of men, women, children flooded the street, all leaving the press conference. She jumped up and down on her feet, chest heaving, but the man in the black hoodie was gone.

Chapter Thirty-Two

Now

Gordon looked through the peephole of the motel room door and groaned. Detective Callie Forde. He'd known she was coming. Lynnleigh had warned him. Ordinarily, he would have jumped at the opportunity to come face to face with the lead detective on the case, but nothing about this day was ordinary. He hadn't finished prepping his intro, and the sponsors wanted him to tape the "bombshell" episode and get it to air. Their questions about his ratings ate at him even now.

"Will we see an increase in your download and streaming numbers?" one had asked that morning. The worst thing about the question was that it wasn't sarcastic. Every year—no, every month—there were an increasing number of true crime podcasts. Listeners could afford to be discriminating. His first podcast had made headlines with the name Hamilton Hayes. Nothing screams scandalous like politics and murder. That the ones holding the money wanted him to deliver something equally compelling was worrying, and the kind of thing he would have run from in the past. Living up to expectations had never been his specialty. His dad told him that often enough. But this time was different. It wasn't only about him. It was about Lynnleigh, and he didn't know if he could bear to disappoint her a second time.

Taking a deep breath, he opened the door.

"Detective Forde," the woman said, sticking out her hand.

She was taller than he'd realized, almost his height, with sharp cheekbones and a jutting chin. Her hair, not quite blond but not quite red, was pulled back into a tight ponytail. He'd looked her up, of course, but the department photo didn't do her justice. Lightly freckled, she had intelligent eyes, a slightly turned-up nose, and the creamy, unadorned skin of a soap model.

He reached out to shake her hand, noticing the wide-brimmed hat she carried in the other. "Gordon Little."

She cocked her head to one side. "I've been wanting to meet you." He waited, not sure what to say. "My partner wasn't a big fan of the idea, but I thought it was about time, don't you?"

"Absolutely," he said. "I was hoping to have you on the podcast at some point, but I'll take now if you're up for it."

She smiled. "Good one."

"I'm not kidding."

Her smile faded. "I don't think so." She looked past him to the room. "May I come in?"

He stepped back and pointed toward the only two chairs in the room. "Why not?"

He didn't miss the way she took in the makeshift desk, the recording equipment, or the piles of notes and pictures haphazardly stacked on the desk's surface.

She settled into a chair, and her jacket fell open, exposing her badge and gun. Again, he felt the muscles in his back tighten. It didn't matter that she looked more like a young mom than a detective. His experience with cops told him she wasn't there to play nice so much as to find out what he knew. That little exercise would probably be followed up by telling him what she thought of him and his podcast. He'd been down this road before, and he didn't like it.

"I've heard your podcast, Gordon. May I call you Gordon?" He shrugged. "Great. It's not bad. I mean, I'm not going to pretend I'm a fan of amateurs inserting themselves into police investigations, but there's a whole true crime industry out there making it a fact of life. That being said, yours is not the worst I've heard."

"Is that supposed to be a compliment?"

It was her turn to shrug.

"What do you want?" he asked.

"Let's start with Lynnleigh," she said. This took him by surprise. Was she going to lecture him about her? "You've known her a long time. Presumably, you care about her."

Gordon said nothing.

"I've known Lynnleigh since before she started high school. Not very well, but right after her mother was murdered. I was supposed to be her tutor, although I don't think I helped much." She paused, seemingly unfazed by his silence. "It isn't a stretch to say she's gone through hell. All the accusations. Her father's conviction. Dying before he could be cleared. I can't imagine." She spoke softly, leaning forward, her elbows on her knees.

Everything she'd said was true, but he kept his lips pressed together.

Sitting back again, she switched gears. "I think it's fair to say we both want to solve this case. I'm not giving you too much credit, am I?" He gave a short nod. "Right. Besides, for Lynnleigh, I don't want to guess about your other reasons. To be honest, they don't matter to me. It's enough that we have the same goal."

"It wasn't enough before today." The words came out before he could stop them. The police had done nothing but block him for days and weeks. It was almost worse than the Hayes case. In a city the size of Chicago, it wasn't hard to find where the wheels could be greased. Even cops liked going viral. But the tiny Hampstead Police Department had closed up tight, like revolutionary soldiers erecting a blockade. Yet, here was Detective Callie Forde pitching him on what? Working together? Was this some kind of trick?

"What's changed that the police want to talk to me? Why now?" He didn't mean to get worked up, but he couldn't help himself now. "I know it's not the bullshit that we have the same goal. I've had the same goal since I got here. It's your office that can't say the same. My guess is you're here because people are talking to me and not you, right? That's it, isn't it? You want to partner up because you need my help."

She'd listened without interrupting, assessing him with those sharp eyes. When she spoke, he heard no anger, only calm. "I didn't say I needed your help, Mr. Little. I merely said we have a common goal."

Gordon's eyes narrowed. He had sponsors reminding him every minute this podcast could be his last. He didn't need this detective distracting him with mind games. He got up.

"Great. We've got a common goal. Maybe remember that the next time your department treats me like the enemy."

Callie Forde looked up at him, expression unreadable. Her calm was really starting to annoy him.

He folded his arms across his chest. "I've got work to do."

"Like what?"

"That's none of your business." Her eyebrow arched, and his face flamed. He'd sounded like a petty child. Worse, he'd sounded amateur. Isn't that what his father had called him the last time he was home? An overgrown child?

"When are you going to grow up, Gordon? You can't live your life eating cereal and flitting from job to job and crashing on our sofa when you have nowhere else to go. You need health insurance. You need to get a real job. Make your mother proud for a change instead of breaking her heart."

He looked away, releasing a breath. "Look, I really do have a lot of work to do."

"I really am curious," the detective said, her voice even. "About what work you're doing."

He lifted one shoulder. It didn't matter if she was curious; he wasn't talking to her about Lynnleigh.

She stood up then, drawing herself up to her full height. "How about this?" she asked. "I have a few questions. You can answer. Or not. Then if you want to ask a few, I'll answer."

"Or not."

"You catch on quick."

"I'm guessing this would be off the record." He shifted his weight from side to side.

"You guessed right."

He glanced at the shades drawn against the outside world. Jeremy wouldn't be back for at least a half hour, and while he did have work to do, he was curious now, too. The chance to ask questions of the police might have been the Detective's hook, but it wasn't the bait that interested him. No. What she asked him would be more telling, would show him the holes in her investigation, might even shine a light on any theories she had. He had his own, of course, but he would save those for ratings. Making up his mind then, he flipped his chair around and sat, folding his arms over the back.

"I'll give you fifteen minutes."

Chapter Thirty-Three

Callie studied the podcaster facing her. He didn't like her, although she suspected his antagonism had more to do with the badge she wore than her personality. His job would never endear him to the police, so she didn't blame him. In truth, she didn't really care whether this man liked her or not. She cared about finding out who murdered Lisa and Tina. She cared about Lynnleigh.

"The pipe bomb in the mailbox. You know about that, right?" She didn't wait for him to respond. "Forensics has a preliminary report that tells us it was meant to maim, not kill. Most likely, whoever planted the bomb in Lynnleigh's mailbox wanted to scare her, maybe hurt her a little, but that's all."

There was no mistaking the relief in the flicker of his eyelids and the subtle loosening of his arms. She continued.

"This hasn't been an easy case. You're right about that, and your podcast is making it more difficult." Before he could protest, she explained. "I believe it's possible the pipe bomb is because of you and your podcast. Well, and Lynnleigh."

"What?"

"Hear me out. The bombshell that she's going to drop. Someone doesn't want that to happen."

He disagreed. "What she has to say doesn't have anything to do with the case."

"I know that, but the listeners don't—specifically one listener."

"Oh." His face clouded. "Does that mean Lynnleigh's still in danger? Is Jeremy?"

"Lynnleigh's safe. And we've got an officer assigned to watch your room until after the episode drops."

"Wh—" he started, getting up from his chair and going to the window. After a minute, he spun back around. "The guy in the grey Ford?"

"Yep."

"Not exactly subtle."

"Not meant to be."

He dropped the curtain. "What are your questions?"

"First, can you think of anything that's come up in any of your interviews that you didn't put on the air, anything that might mean something?"

Gordon paced the floor in front of the window. "Not really." He told her he'd heard from others about Tina and Lisa's strained relationship. He said he'd heard rumors of a pregnancy. He'd heard Harry had a run-in with Anthony Battle at the very same Stop 'n Gas he'd claimed to have seen Harry in on the day of the murders.

"What kind of run-in?"

"It was a couple weeks before. The guy I heard it from is ancient, though. I mean, he was probably ancient back then, too, but he said Anthony Battle started in on Harry about Lisa, how she needed a real man. Crap like that."

"And then?"

"Harry shoved him to the ground and started to walk away. Battle got up and jumped on his back, screaming something about how he wasn't so tough without his knife."

He cut his eyes to her, gauging her reaction, but she gave him nothing.

"Anyway, apparently, Harry didn't need his knife. He threw Battle off him and punched him in the gut. The guy folded like a deck of cards. End of story."

She absorbed what he'd told her. "Were there other witnesses?" He told her there weren't, that he'd done his best to get someone to corroborate the old man's story, but no one could—or would.

"But you believed him?"

"Sure, but he's barely alive, and his daughter wouldn't let me put him on the podcast. She says behavior like that shows Harry was guilty."

"Yeah, well," the detective said, getting to her feet. "That's really helpful, Gordon. Is there anything else?"

"That's all…no, wait. There is one other thing, but not sure this is as important."

She sat down again. "Go on."

"When I met with Dean Marks, he said Tina asked about a fertility specialist," Callie remembered. "So, he didn't know any but referred Tina to his son. Said he might know someone. I looked him up. Byron Marks. He's the new dean now. Anyway, his wife was the one that the hairdresser was talking about being stuck up. He's divorced from her now, so I figured he might have something colorful to say, give me a good sound bite at least."

"And did he?"

The podcaster rolled a shoulder. "He won't return any of my calls. I'm wondering why he won't talk to me. At first, I thought he was just putting me off because he was busy, but I'm wondering if maybe he and Tina weren't closer than friends."

"Huh," she said.

"Is that all? Huh?"

"Do you have any proof they were more than friends?"

"Not yet." The skin around his mouth tightened. "I think women liked him, and he liked them back if that means anything. That might have had something to do with his leaving Hampstead for a new position. And there were those rumors that Tina was pregnant."

She'd heard the same rumors, of course, but said nothing.

"Fine," he said, throwing up his hands. "My turn."

Instead of answering, she said, "I'd appreciate it if you would keep me filled in on anything else that comes up about Anthony Battle.

"What?"

"Or Byron Marks," she added.

"Why should I?"

"Because, besides sharing a common goal to solve this case, we both want to protect Lynnleigh. The only way I can do that is if I know who and what I'm protecting her from."

He opened his mouth and closed it again, his guard from earlier sliding back into place. "You want to use me. And my podcast." Gordon shook his head, disbelieving. "This was never about a quid pro quo."

Callie pulled a piece of paper from her jacket pocket. "Here's a list of names for interviews and a few questions you might want to ask."

He took one look and threw it back at her. "This is bullshit," he said, pointing his finger at her. "Look, I'm not trying to be an asshole, but we're done. I don't need a bunch of names you've already crossed off your list or bogus questions any monkey could ask."

She studied the boy-man in front of her. He had a strong nose and chin, deep-set eyes, and a handsome if serious face. She didn't blame him for being angry, but she had her reasons.

"I don't know if I can trust you."

"Trust me?" He threw up his hands. "Whatever."

It was her turn to get annoyed. "It's not whatever. It's Lynnleigh's life. I'm guessing if you'd known all this would put her in danger, you wouldn't have done this podcast. Now, she's coming on with her bombshell, making her even more of a target. The only way to protect her is to flush out whoever doesn't want us to find out whatever they think she knows or you do."

Callie's phone buzzed, and she pulled it out. Hendo.

Sending you a picture of the box.

A second later, the image came through. Dirty and crushed on one side, it was difficult to say what color the box was. Dark blue? Gray? The size struck her as unusual, too—smaller than a shoe box but bigger than a cigar box. A gift box, maybe? With her fingers, she zoomed in. There was something familiar about the box. A local store? Somewhere, but she couldn't be sure.

She stood up. "I've gotta go."

"Wait," Gordon said, his arm reaching out to her. "You really think she's in danger?"

"I do."

He raked his hand through his hair until it was standing on end, making him look even younger. "What do you want from me?"

It was the question she'd been waiting for since she'd walked through the door. "Fifteen years ago, the police interviewed a woman named Amber Wall."

Chapter Thirty-Four

Fifteen Years Earlier

Callie followed her mother across the walkway onto the freshly-mowed grass. She kept walking, breathing in the scents, until they reached her grandmother's gravestone. Maura placed a fresh bouquet of flowers at the base, crouched down, closed her eyes, and began to recite a prayer. Callie stood back, used to her mother's ritual. Same time every week. Same prayer. She hadn't wanted to come the first time or the time after, but older now, she didn't mind. In the oddest way, she found it comforting. There was a quietness, a stillness in the cemetery that made her want to be still, too.

When her mother was finished, she rocked back on her heels and looked up at her daughter, clear-eyed and calm. The tears that had fallen in the first few months after Callie's grandmother's funeral had given way to resignation and finally, to peace. Her grandmother's suffering had ended, and for that, they were all grateful. Getting to her feet, Maura rubbed the grass from her hands. They never stayed long, speaking little, but the length of time didn't matter. It was their time. Callie's father had asked to come once, and both women had looked at him with horror. He didn't ask again.

Callie was about to suggest coffee at the diner, but Maura spoke first.

"I need to do something." Her gaze traveled over the headstones dotting the park. "You don't have to come if you don't want to."

Something in the way her mother spoke made Callie ask, "Do you want me to?"

Maura hesitated. "I don't know. Maybe."

"Okay. Coffee after?"

"Definitely." With a wan smile, her mother began picking her way through the cemetery until she reached the far edge bordered by a thicket of trees. Here, the land was mostly undisturbed, the grass lush and thick underfoot. Only two graves had taken up residence in this part of the cemetery. Callie might have thought no one was buried there if it weren't for the two new headstones and a circle of grass that had the trampled look of the park after a Fourth of July picnic. Callie drew in a breath. She knew without looking who was buried here. Lisa Lawson and Tina Cox.

Her mother moved close, but Callie lagged behind. These were her mother's friends. Callie didn't know them, not really. Maura didn't kneel or fall to the ground. She stood between the two graves, her head bowed. From her vantage point, Callie couldn't see her mother's face, but she could read the epitaphs. Lisa Lawson. "Beloved daughter, wife, and mother." *Mother*.

Callie swallowed the lump in her throat, vowing to try harder with Lynnleigh—if the girl even showed up for the next tutoring session. Her gaze shifted to the other grave. Tina Cox. "Loved by everyone who knew her." Was that kind of corny? Callie thought maybe it was and yet, she guessed most people wouldn't complain about those being the final words to describe their lives. Even her father, admired by so many, was definitely not loved by everyone. Of course, just because the lady's family put that didn't make it true. Callie considered asking her mother but wondered if that would be insensitive. The last thing she wanted to do was add to whatever pain and anxiety her mother harbored around the deaths of her friends.

The sun cut through the trees, rising higher in the sky, and she wiped a bead of sweat from her forehead. Maura's head swung between the two gravestones, the low sound of her voice rising and falling with the motion. Callie took a step forward and another until the words were clearer.

"I'm worried, and I don't know what you want me to do. I went to see Harry the other day. Don't worry..." The words faded, and Callie strained to hear. "Harry made me promise." Again, the words grew muffled, and a small sob escaped, sounding loud in the quiet. After a moment, Maura's head swung toward Tina's grave. "I've heard Barton won't see anyone, that he's too distraught, but…" There was a brief moment of silence. "It's not my place. Grief is different for everyone, isn't it? Still…" Her mother shook her head slowly. "I wish, well, it doesn't matter what I wish. I love you and miss you both. The world just doesn't seem as bright somehow." An audible sigh followed, and Maura lifted her head up toward the cloudless sky. After a moment, she looked over her shoulder with a smile.

"How about that coffee?"

Chapter Thirty-Five

Now

Callie sat up in bed, the memory as close as though it were yesterday, lingering in the present. After leaving the cemetery, she and Maura had gone for coffee, neither speaking as they walked the blocks to the downtown diner. Sipping from a steaming mug, her mother had seemed distracted, staring out the window. Callie hadn't known why, but she'd reached out that morning and touched her mother's hand, covering it with her own. It wasn't like Callie. Outside of their visits to the cemetery, mother and daughter spent little time together. Instead, Callie had spent her childhood trailing after her father. She'd always loved her mother, of course, but they didn't do girl things together. When she wasn't at the hospital, Maura was too busy tending to their needs. Her father was the one who took Callie and her brother camping and fishing, letting them roam until dark. Somewhere along the line, she'd stopped hugging her mother, stopped thinking about her outside of her role as part of the parental unit. And even then, barely out of her teens, Callie regarded her mother as only that, her mother. She'd rarely thought of her as a person, someone with feelings that didn't revolve around making dinner or doing laundry.

At Callie's touch, Maura's eyes had shimmered. Her smile, sad and grateful, had sparked something in Callie that day.

"Thank you, Mom."

Genuine surprise had wiped away the tears. "For what?"

"I don't know. Everything, maybe." She'd taken a breath. "I'm sorry about your friends."

The tears were back. "Me, too." She'd wiped her eyes with her napkin. "Losing people you love is always hard. It takes months, sometimes years, to understand they aren't really gone, that they're always with you if you look hard enough. Do you remember after Nana died?" Callie nodded. "I couldn't believe I was alone, that I didn't have a mother. Ridiculous really. I wasn't a child, and the MS had taken such a toll. I knew all that. But the fact that I couldn't go to her when I needed her felt like I'd lost an arm or a leg, and in a way, for a while I had." She paused, blinking hard. "Anyway, it was your father who noticed the owl nest in the corner of our yard. Nana loved owls. She had that statue of one on her porch, and those weird little figurines in the library."

Callie remembered playing with the tiny owls for hours, Nana laughing and hooting in the background.

"I've never loved owls, to be honest. I used to think there was something creepy about the way they turned their heads and the eyes followed you." She took a sip of coffee then and wrinkled her nose. Both their cups had long grown cold. "Your dad saw the nest and made a comment about Nana, something like 'Nana would be sending pictures all day long if she could.' I knew he was right, but I dreaded it getting dark. I'd been having a lot of trouble sleeping, and I was so sure I'd be up all night if that darned owl started hooting. The funny thing is, the opposite happened."

Callie's hands had tightened around her cup. She'd never heard this story before.

"Sure enough, the owl started in, hooting and hooting. But it wasn't loud the way I thought it would be. It was soft and almost musical, so soothing that I fell asleep almost immediately. The same thing happened the next night and the next. That week, your father sent me flowers for our anniversary, which was very nice, but what I remember most is that the delivery man was wearing a t-shirt with an owl on it. Next thing I know, I started seeing owls everywhere, and I knew. Nana was everywhere I was." She'd smiled shakily and ducked her head. "This probably sounds silly to you, but I believe it with all my heart. Whether the owls were actually sent by Nana or not isn't the point, though. I felt her with me, her spirit, and that was enough." She'd looked at her daughter with soft eyes. "I think she's with you, too."

Callie had squeezed her mother's hand, her own eyes wet by then. "Thank you, Mom," she'd said again. "For everything."

As Callie turned on the shower now, the memory tapping at her brain, she wondered if Lynnleigh or Barton ever saw signs of Lisa or Tina. Or Harry. It wasn't the kind of question a detective would ask, but she hoped it was true—for both of them.

Chapter Thirty-Six

Now

"Are you comfortable?" Gordon asked Lynnleigh.

"I guess." She didn't look at Gordon so much as look through him. She raised her hand to her mouth, biting at a fingernail. "At least I'm back in my own house."

He leaned in. "We don't have to do this."

Her eyes widened. "Won't that get you in trouble?"

She knew enough about sponsors and podcasts to understand that he would, in fact, be in trouble if he teased a bombshell and failed to deliver. His stomach twisted at the thought. "I'll come up with something," he said with more confidence than he felt.

"No," she said, and he hated himself for the relief that flooded through him. "I have to do this." She bit her fingernail again. "But I'm not going to lie. I'm more nervous than I thought I'd be."

"Five minutes," Jeremy said.

The three of them sat in the den, a small, cozy room with decent acoustics, according to Gordon's producer. The uniformed police officer assigned to watch Lynnleigh sipped coffee in the kitchen, a first for Gordon and the show.

Gordon gave Jeremy a thumbs-up. Lynnleigh wasn't the only one fighting nerves. This episode was live, his first in this format. This wasn't completely unheard of in the world of true crime podcasting, but it was rare enough.

There'd be no sound mixing other than the intro and closing minutes, which they'd prerecorded. It was risky, but the sponsors loved it. He did, too, if he were being honest. Already, there'd been more chatter online about the case than in previous days and weeks. Still, he had his reservations about whether he could pull it off, worried about staying on track, missing a key question. Of course, the goal was to have Lynnleigh do most of the talking, but he'd have to draw her out. Experience told him that might not be as easy as it sounded.

"Lynnleigh," he said, "I want you to think about this like it's just you and me talking, like old times. Forget about the microphone and all that business."

She pointed at the oversized mike set up in front of her. "How am I supposed to forget about that? It looks like something out of a porn magazine."

Jeremy's guffaws brought a smile to her face, and Gordon relaxed along with her. "One minute," the producer said, his laughter fading. "Get ready."

Gordon and Lynnleigh both watched Jeremy raise a hand to count down the seconds.

"Five, four, three, two, one, and we're on."

The theme music played then, and Lynnleigh jumped, the sound loud in the quiet of the tiny house. Together, they listened to the sound of Gordon's voice recap the case and earlier episodes. As it came to an end, Jeremy pointed at him to go.

"Today, folks, we're here live talking to the one person most affected by these terrible crimes, Lynnleigh Lawson." After a brief summary of her background, he said, "Now listeners, I need to be up front with you. Lynnleigh and I are not meeting for the first time. We knew each other in college, before I left school, but haven't seen each other again until this case." He and Jeremy had worked hard on the wording. It was important to reveal their previous connection, but the last line put distance between them. It was good enough. If anyone wanted to dig further, let them, he thought.

"Welcome, Lynnleigh."

"Thank you, Gordon."

"I imagine it's hard for you to do this, to talk about losing your mother and then what was done to your father."

"Actually, it's not. I don't want to forget my mother. Not ever. And talking about her helps me to keep her alive in my memory. As for my father, it's not so much that I like talking about the injustice that killed him as that I have to. This town labelled him a murderer, charged him, and convicted him. Those people may not have taken out a gun and shot him, but they killed him just the same. They—" She stopped at the sight of Gordon's hand gesture to slow down. Taking a deep breath, she nodded and started again. "They stole him from me. So, while talking about all this is hard, it's not as hard as doing nothing. He deserves better than that. They all do."

"Tell me about your parents and Tina."

This was the easy part for them both. They'd gone over what she would say, the memories she would share. There weren't any earth-shaking revelations, but anyone with a beating heart would surely understand the suffering this young woman had endured. Lynnleigh had snorted when he'd explained the rough script for the episode.

"Manipulating the audience? That's your plan?"

"You say manipulation. I say getting them on your side."

"Before I drop the bombshell, you mean."

"Exactly."

Up to now, she'd played along, but Gordon knew Lynnleigh better than to expect there wouldn't be any surprises. She'd been told to sit down too many times in her life not to say and do what she wanted now. Even nervous, she could prove unpredictable. His script, loose as it was, could go up in smoke before he could pull the plug.

"Thank you, Lynnleigh. I want to ask you something that might be hard." He allowed a pause, imagining the harried mom in the carpool line shushing the children and leaning closer to the dash. This was the part he loved. "You were only a child when your mother and her best friend were murdered. When your father was arrested, did you ever doubt his innocence? Did it ever enter your mind that maybe it was possible he could have done it?"

"Never."

"And after he was convicted? Did that plant any seeds of doubt?"

"None. I always knew he was innocent even when everyone else told me he was guilty." There was no doubting the sincerity in her tone. "It wasn't just because he was my father, but no one would listen to me."

"That must have been difficult, to feel ignored."

"Sure, but the hardest part was that the police didn't look for anyone else. If they had, maybe they would have found the real killer."

She opened her mouth to say more, but he held up his hand. He couldn't afford for her to rant, no matter how much she was entitled to. Keeping the listener focused was the only thing that mattered right now.

"Let's go back to when you were a child for a minute. If you didn't believe your father murdered your mother and Tina Cox that day, did you suspect someone else? I know you were young, but maybe you witnessed someone make threats."

"No, nothing like that."

"Okay. How about the rumors that things had grown tense between your mother and Tina? Had you noticed that?"

He saw the way she struggled to keep her composure before answering. He'd known this part might be difficult for her.

"Not really, but I had just turned fourteen. Aunt Tina was over all the time, sometimes with Uncle Barton, but most times not. She liked spending time at our house, spending time with me."

"She was your godmother, wasn't she?"

"Yes. She and Barton didn't have any kids yet, so she liked being able to spoil me. She would take me on shopping trips, and once she took me up to DC to the zoo. I don't know why anyone would want to hurt her or my mother." Her voice broke, and she reached for the tissue box Gordon had placed next to her.

He allowed the sound of soft crying to fill the air for only a few seconds.

"How did Tina get along with your father?"

"Fine. My dad was pretty quiet—even with my mom—but I think he liked Tina. They did stuff together sometimes, the four of them."

"Your parents and Barton and Tina Cox?"

"Yeah. They'd all been friends since high school, or at least my mom and

Tina had. I think my dad and Barton became friends later, after they all got married."

It wasn't part of the script, but a new thought occurred to Gordon in that moment. "During the trial and even now, Barton has refused to make any statements about the case."

"That's true. He stood by my dad."

"So, I imagine you share this tragedy. Are you close?"

Lines creased her forehead. "Not really. He has a new family, so…"

"Right, but surely he was there for you when all this was going on."

If he'd thought her face would clear, he was mistaken. "I don't really remember. My aunt and uncle did as much as they could. The principal at the high school and one of my teachers. But he'd lost his wife, so I think he was having a tough time, too."

"Well, we're still hopeful he'll talk to us soon." It was a shameless plug, but that was the name of the game. He made a note on the pad in front of him and moved on. Again, keeping the listeners engaged rose to the forefront of his mind. "Let's talk about this year and the discovery of the video putting your father in Washington at the time of the murders."

"I'm very grateful for that."

"I'm sure you are, but it didn't come in time to save your father, did it?"

"No, it didn't." She briefly gave the highlights of her father's declining health in the last years he was alive. "He needed a transplant. If he'd been able to get one, he might be here today."

"Isn't it true you were tested to see if you were a match?"

"Yes. He didn't want me to. That was just like him. The surgery wasn't without risk, and he told me he couldn't allow me to do that when he wasn't ever getting out of prison anyway. Every time I saw him, I could see he was dying. It wasn't just the illness. He was dying on the inside, too. He'd given up, but I couldn't let him do that. He was all I had left."

"So, you got tested against his wishes."

"Yes, he didn't know about it."

"Well, that's pretty amazing of you, but if you could have been a donor, why didn't he get the transplant? Were you too late?"

Again, he imagined some listener raising his or her hand to their throat, pulse skipping faster, and he almost smiled before he remembered Lynnleigh in front of him. What was wrong with him?

"No, that wasn't it." The words were a whisper. She drew herself up then, as though she needed the air for strength. "The thing is," she said in a shaky voice, "I was told that family aren't always a complete match, and that's the only way to really guarantee success."

"Are you saying you weren't a match then?"

"I wasn't."

"That must have been incredibly disappointing."

"It was. It's funny, apparently, family is only a good enough match about thirty percent of the time. Siblings are usually only twenty-five percent."

"I didn't know that." He did, of course, because they'd talked about this part already. A glance at Jeremy's face told him the number of streamers was high, and he nodded in return. Some of those would be frowning, but more would be near tears, thinking of the poor girl who wanted nothing more than to save her father, only to find out she wasn't a match? "So, how much of a match were you?"

"Zero."

"Zero." Gordon said the word slowly as though hearing it for the first time. He glanced at Jeremy again, who gave him a thumbs up. Maybe his acting was improving. He didn't know if that was a good thing or a bad thing. "How is that possible?"

"That's what I wanted to know. I had them redo the whole test, sure they'd mixed something up, but no, I wasn't a match. Not at all." She took another deep breath. "The doctors gave me a possible explanation, but I couldn't believe it. Well, I didn't want to believe it, so I ignored it for a while."

"But you couldn't ignore it forever."

"No, I couldn't. I had the doctors do another test to find out if it was true."

"If what was true?"

He was about to ask the question a second time when she spoke at last, a kind of wonder and disbelief tinging the words. "That Harry Lawson wasn't my father."

Even though he was alone with Lynnleigh and Jeremy in that tiny den, he heard a collective gasp in his head. Maybe a listener had to sit down or pull their car over. It was that shocking, that unexpected. In spite of himself, he knew she'd landed the episode.

"Wait," he said now, "are you saying that Harry Lawson wasn't your father?"

"Not my biological father, no. That didn't make him any less my father—my real father. Not to me anyway."

"You loved him."

"He was a great dad. I know people talked about how he wasn't right, how he was paranoid after he came back from the Army, and maybe that was true. I don't really know. Like I said, I was fourteen, and all I saw was a dad who loved me and my mom. I had a friend who asked me once if he scared me, if I was afraid to be alone with him. He was my dad. Can you believe that?"

"That's horrible."

"Well, we weren't friends after that. I've done a lot of research on PTSD, particularly as it relates to veterans, and my dad did have some issues, but he was dealing with them. My mom was helping him, and there are some vets who have it much worse than he did. He came home to a stable life, to a business. That's not nothing."

"Okay. I'm going to ask the obvious now." Although she knew what was coming, she seemed to physically steel herself. For his part, he did his best to keep his tone impassive. "There are many who will listen to this episode and think maybe your father found out you weren't his daughter, that he was angry about it. Add in his PTSD, and they might even call it a motive."

"He wasn't here that day. The video proves it."

"Okay. What do you have to say to those who think that doesn't prove he wasn't involved or that he didn't hire someone to kill your mother? Maybe he couldn't do it himself."

"I'd say that's bullshit."

Gordon knew how much she loathed this line of questioning, but he'd warned her. "I'm not disagreeing with you, but there will be naysayers, although my sources tell me there's a person of interest in the current investigation."

"What? Who?"

He could tell he'd taken her by surprise, but it had to be this way, no matter that it might be misleading. According to the detective, indicating the police were making headway—true or not—took some of the heat off Lynnleigh. If more attention swung their way or his and away from Lynnleigh, that was fine with him.

Evading the question, he said, "Lynnleigh, I think the listeners will understand how shocking this news about your father must have been, but it does bring up another question. Do you have any idea who your biological father might be? Are you searching for him?"

"I don't. I wouldn't say I'm actively searching, but I went back through my dad's records. He would have been deployed in the month I was conceived. I never knew that before."

"And where was your mom living?"

"On the base with the other wives, although I think she spent a lot of weekends back here in Hampstead."

"So, you could have been conceived here or there."

"Yes."

"I reached out to one of her friends from the base—the one she stayed in touch with—but she didn't remember any other men around. She said the wives were always together. The only time my mom wasn't with the group was when she came home to Hampstead to visit."

"So maybe someone your mom knew from home?"

"I don't know." Twin lines appeared between her brows. "There is this one thing. My mom's friend said my mom came home one weekend like she did every month, but when she got back, she was different. Shut herself inside her house. Wouldn't see the other wives. Her friend got so worried, she eventually got a message to my dad. He was able to get a pass and came home right home. He was devoted to my mother always, and according to this woman, my mom got better, and later that year, I was born."

"Wow." He stared at his old friend. "That's a lot, but without knowing more...I don't know what to think."

"Neither do I, but I-I have an idea."

"Anything you want to share?" She bit her lip, dropping her gaze, and he decided not to pursue. "Lynnleigh, is it possible your biological father might not want that information to come out?" He was spitballing now, but it occurred to him the public might wonder the same thing. Lynnleigh's lack of surprise by the question told him she'd already considered the idea.

"Possibly. It's unlikely, though. I mean, it's already been so long, and as far as I can tell, my mother never told anyone Harry wasn't my father."

"What about Tina?"

"Oh," she said with a blink. "I didn't think of that, but if there was anyone, it would have been her."

"And Tina might have told Barton who might have told Harry, assuming he didn't already know." His voice was gentle. "Is that possible?"

"Ye-es," she said slowly, "but I think Harry already knew, had for a long time. That's why he didn't want me to do the matching test. He knew I'd be upset if I found out the truth." She paused to take a breath. "We had this bond—you know that kind where you can be with someone without saying a word, but it feels like you're having a whole conversation? It used to drive my mom crazy. The point is that I loved having him as my dad, but I got the feeling he loved having me even more. My mom and me were his world." Again, she hesitated. "One time, I might have been seven or eight, he told me that he couldn't have chosen a better daughter. I remember laughing and saying something about how that was stupid because he didn't get to choose, that he was stuck with me. And he smiled and told me again how he would choose me every time. I thought he was being sappy. He got like that sometimes, but now…" Tears shimmered in her eyes. "I think he was trying to tell me even then."

Gordon swallowed the lump in his throat. He'd never known that kind of love from a parent. Maybe Max had, but even that had been different. It had been more worship than love, hadn't it? Had that been what Max had been trying to escape? Shaking off the memories, he nodded at Lynnleigh.

"That sounds nice."

"It was."

"Lynnleigh, do you have any other ideas about why your mother and Tina were murdered?"

"Like a million," she said with a bitter laugh, "but that's only because I can't stop thinking about it. Not that I want to. Think about it, I mean. It's gruesome. I've read the police reports so many times I could probably recite them like a book report. It's not healthy. I know it's not, but I can't help myself."

"We've also read the police reports," he said then, using the change in topic to shift away from Lynnleigh's lineage and open up another line of questioning about the case. "As you know, the police are reinterviewing everyone they talked to in the first investigation. I've been looking at that list myself. As a reminder, folks, the original file is available through the public records act since the case was closed for fifteen years. Anyway, there are a few names on the list I'd like to talk to but haven't been able to locate." He listed three names: Barney Hicks, Amanda Marks, and Amber Wall. "Listeners, reach out through our website if you can help us locate any of these witnesses." Mentally, he made two check marks. He'd applied pressure with the implication of a person of interest, and he'd just asked the public to find Amber Wall—exactly as the detective requested. If he'd added a couple of extra names, that was for him.

"Lynnleigh, we can't thank you enough for being here today and—"

"Wait. I-I didn't finish."

He cocked his head to one side. "Oh? We're all ears. What didn't you finish?"

She met his gaze, lifting her chin. "Someone set a pipe bomb in my mailbox."

"Yes, that's right," Gordon said and reminded the audience of the attack that had landed a detective in the hospital.

"I'm not afraid," she said. "I just wanted to say that. You can't hurt me."

Gordon's heart skipped a beat. Had Lynnleigh just issued a challenge?

"Well, you're very brave," he said, rushing over his words. "We're about out of time and—"

"I remembered something from that week, too, something really important about my mom and Tina, so whoever did this to them and is trying to hurt me now, I'm going to find you and expose you. I will never give up. Do you hear me? Never."

Gordon's mouth hung open now. She'd blown up any idea he or the Detective had of keeping her safe. In the corner of the room, Jeremy made slashing motions at his neck and pointed to his watch. Gordon scrambled to close out the episode. "Well, Lynnleigh, it sounds like you have another bombshell to drop."

"You could call it that."

He lifted his hand in a questioning gesture even as he said smoothly, "Can't wait to hear it, but we're out of time for today, so listeners, you'll have to tune into our next episode to hear more from Lynnleigh. As always, if you like our podcast, don't forget to leave a review. If you have a comment or question, you can contact us on our website or send us an email." He rattled off the addresses, and Jeremy cued the closing music, ending the show. Gordon's focus never left Lynnleigh as he waited for Jeremy to give him the sign they were off the air.

"What the hell, Lynnleigh?"

"What do you mean?" she asked with a nervous laugh.

"Did you really remember something, or did you just promise a bombshell you can't deliver?" She looked away, and he knew. "Godammit, Lynnleigh."

"Nothing is happening, Gordon. So, what if I poked the bear? I had to."

Jeremy, packing up the equipment, stopped and stared at them both. Gordon understood his producer's concern. True crime podcasts didn't always deliver answers. That was the nature of the business, but podcasting wasn't politics either. Making the kind of promise Lynnleigh had just made— a revelation that could break open the case—with no way to deliver ate at the credibility of Gordon and everyone associated with the show. Sponsors tended to frown on that sort of thing. Shit.

"I am so fucked," he said with a groan, regretting the words as soon as they were out of his mouth.

"Don't worry," she said, eyes like marbles now. "You'll get your bombshell."

"Lynnleigh, I'm sorry. It's not that. Well, not only that." He did care about the show, more than he was willing to admit, but claiming she'd had some revelatory memory had painted a giant target on her back. That terrified him. "Lynnleigh, that pipe bomb wasn't a joke. This is serious. You can't play games here. You could get hurt."

Eyes searching his, her face softened. "I'll be fine," she said finally, reaching out and touching her fingers to his cheek. "I promise."

Chapter Thirty-Seven

Now

Callie banged on the steering wheel. "No, no, no," she said over and over again, her voice growing louder. She was going to have Gordon's head for this. The idea behind the live episode was to get the news out as a means of protecting Lynnleigh. No more bombshells. Divert attention away from her. And now the girl had gone and done the very thing that put her in the most danger. She'd made herself the focus for another few days at least. Taking a breath, she listened with relief as Gordon closed out the show. Finally.

Sitting in the parking lot outside the station, she tapped at her phone. Lynnleigh picked up on the second ring.

"Please tell me you're coming in right this minute to share the incredible memory that's just surfaced."

"Sorry to disappoint, Detective."

The girl's response wasn't a surprise, but that didn't stop Callie from groaning out loud. "Why? Why would you say that?"

"Why would you let Gordon say that bullshit about the police having a person of interest? Trying to get whoever it is to make a mistake, right? No different except you were playing softball, and I'm playing hardball."

The girl was infuriating, not the least because she wasn't wrong. "How do you know it's bullshit?"

"Isn't it?"

"You know what I want you to know, Lynnleigh, to keep you safe." Callie wasn't sorry she hadn't shared any of her leads, particularly her interest in Anthony Battle. Lynnleigh might have gotten him killed before she could find Amber Wall and the truth around his involvement. "Do not leave that house," she said and hung up.

Slamming her car door, Callie strode toward the station, her phone buzzing in her pocket. Zel.

"Did you know she was going to do that?" he asked.

"No, Zel, I didn't." Already hyped up on too much coffee, she gritted her teeth and climbed the stairs to the third floor. With Zel out and Hendo and Chang working the break-ins, they were shorthanded and that was before adding in the need for a twenty-four-hour-a-day detail. Every inch of her skin grew hot as though all the anger and frustration were heating her from the inside out.

"Alright. Calm down, Cal, I didn't mean anything by it. From what you've told me, the girl is reckless enough to blurt something out, but I thought she might have warned you or something."

"She didn't."

"A helluva hot mess as Marcie would say."

She almost smiled, her gaze drawn to the empty chair behind his desk. She missed him. "When are you coming back?"

"Doctors want me to come in later today. If I pass, I'll be cleared for work."

"Well, I gotta say, tomorrow can't get here soon enough."

"Good to know you miss me, Partner."

They spoke for a few more minutes about the podcast and the promised episode. She had a list of people to talk to before then—including Lynnleigh again. "But first, I need to brief the Chief. He's called me three times since the episode aired."

"Ouch. Can't say I'm sorry to be out another day then."

"Yeah, thanks for that."

She pushed away from her desk when Hendo's name popped up on her phone, giving her another reason to delay the chewing out she knew was coming.

"Listen," she said, "I wanted to ask you to send me another picture of that box. I feel like I've seen it before, but I can't figure out where."

"Yeah, I'll send you pics of everything. We're here now. Angie's with us."

"Angie's there?" Callie asked. Why would an old box warrant a call to forensics? She didn't have to wait long for Hendo to explain.

"The box wasn't the only thing stashed between the walls. Found a sweatshirt and sweatpants. Both black. No labels or insignias. Maybe large or extra large."

She switched her phone to her other shoulder and sifted through the pile of folders on her desk. "I feel like there's something you're not telling me."

"Yeah, well, that's why Angie's here. The thing is, the sweatshirt has something dried all over it, something really dark. There are flakes of it inside the box, too."

"Flakes of what?"

"Blood most likely. A lot of it by the looks of it. The clothes were probably soaked when they were dropped in there."

"Blood. Are you sure?"

"Pretty sure. Angie thinks it is. Could be animal blood, but then why stash the sweatsuit? Wouldn't you just throw it away?"

"What did the owner say?"

"Doesn't know anything. He's lived here three years, but Angie says this looks like it might have been there a while."

This made sense with the owner calling Hendo after finding the box. "Where are you on the list of previous owners?"

"There's been a few, but also a bunch of renters. We're starting with Mr. Braun and working our way back. Going to be hard to know how far back to go without knowing how long the sweatsuit's been there."

"Can Angie tell you that?"

"Depends how degraded the blood is. There's also a lot of dust and drywall and other stuff on the sweatshirt now. And some mouse droppings. But she's going to type it, find out whatever she can. This whole thing stinks to high heaven, if you know what I mean."

She did. There could be a logical explanation or at least one that didn't scream felony, but she didn't think so any more than Hendo did. "Good luck. Looks like you've got yourself a murder case."

Chapter Thirty-Eight

Now

Gordon knocked on the door of the pretty brick colonial and peered back at the street behind him. He didn't have to see the faces in the windows to know there were eyes on him watching his every move. The houses were sizeable with postcard-pretty yards and SUVs in the driveways, but that didn't make the owners any less nosy than in smaller, less affluent areas. No. In his experience, the kind of people who lived in places like this kept their eyes open. Some guarded their homes and possessions like Roman treasures, but others were guarding something more precious—their status and place in the neighborhood hierarchy. He'd been in Hampstead long enough to know where the Coxes ranked on that ladder.

Barton Cox wasn't king. That honor most likely belonged to the owner of the plant. The president of the college. The mayor might have some status, and a few others, but Barton was up there. He owned a successful business, one that many of the residents in this part of the state relied on. He hadn't allowed his brush with tragedy to bring him down. If anything, he'd thrown himself into work after the murders, but a man climbing the ladder can't afford to do it alone. He'd remarried. Cindy Cox. A single mom to two young girls after her husband decided married life didn't suit him, and fatherhood even less. There was a quick courtship and an even quicker wedding. Two broken hearts made whole again. Or so the story went. Gordon had heard several versions during his interviews.

"Poor Barton. Can you imagine? Your wife, the love of your life, is murdered by your best friend? You stand by him because you can't believe it, but a jury tells you you're wrong. You hold your head up, and then the good lord sends you Cindy. That first husband of hers was a snake in the grass if there ever was one, but the girls take after their mother, of course. Pillars of the community, you know. Cindy Cox chairs the annual fundraiser for the school, and Barton does pro bono work for the animal shelter. Lucky he didn't leave town after what happened. Wouldn't blame him, really. His mother told me once that she had to talk him into staying that first year. Said it was hard to be here with all the reminders of Tina. Then he met Cindy, and things got better. I heard he wanted to move to Raleigh for a while because he was expanding the offices there, but Cindy wasn't having any part of moving the girls. Don't blame her." She clucked her tongue. "Such a nice family, too. Would have been a terrible loss."

But this was a small town after all, and not all gossip was so kind.

"Cindy drove that young Billy away. Pushing him to work harder and climb the ladder. I heard her say that once. 'Why can't you be someone?' What does that even mean? Anyway, she got her someone with Barton, didn't she? Jumped right up the Hampstead ladder to look down at the rest of us. Not saying she doesn't volunteer and all that, but she makes sure to let you know she volunteers because she's too important to actually work. Her momma worked at the old plant, you know. Her daddy, too, but you'd never know it to see Cindy now."

Gordon knew sour grapes when he heard it. Hell, he'd probably spewed similar words about someone in his circle, but he also recognized there were kernels of truth buried in both stories. Even so, it wasn't the gossip about Cindy that interested him so much as that about Barton and his late wife. The more time he spent in Hampstead, the more folks' guards came down and the more he learned.

"Barton was like a puppy dog around Tina, worshiped the ground she walked on. At least that's how it seemed. Not so sure she felt the same way. Truth is, I was kinda surprised she married him. I mean, he's done well, has the big house and fancy car and all that, but she had the shine. I don't know what it was about her, but people loved her, you know. She made friends wherever she went. Homecoming Queen, but in the nicest way. Grateful because of all the loss she'd been through after her daddy's accident. Lisa was her rock, but maybe Barton was too. Anyway, she was always the life of the party. Barton didn't even like parties, but he went. Following her around, like I said. I thought they'd be over after high school. To tell you the truth, I think she did, too. They were apart for a little while, and I lost track of her. She kind of disappeared, and then the next thing you know, she's married to Barton." The woman shook her head. "They say still waters run deep, right. That had to be it."

Gordon had heard so many stories about the Coxes, both the old and new versions, that they sometimes blended together in his mind. Standing on the doorstep of the Cox home now, he mentally rehearsed his script one more time. This was for Lynnleigh. He raised his hand and knocked again.

The woman who came to the door matched her profile picture if a little older and less airbrushed. She knew him in an instant.

"No can do," she said and started to close the door.

He jammed his foot into the doorway. "Please, Mrs. Cox. We don't have to record anything. Everything can be off the record, even. But I really need to talk to you. For your husband's sake."

One hand flew to her hip, and she lifted her chin. "Oh, please. You reporters will say anything. My husband warned me about people like you."

Although her words screamed 'get out,' her body moved back a bit. She didn't shove the door harder. She didn't reach for her phone. He'd been right about her. Barton Cox had been stonewalling him since the day Gordon had visited the man's office, but Cindy Cox knew him by sight, and she might not mind him as much as she claimed. In fact, she might even want her fifteen minutes. He took in the curve-hugging jeans, low-cut top, eyelashes that couldn't possibly be real, and diamond studs as large as his pinky fingernail. She liked being seen. The more he thought about it, the more he was sure he was right.

"Did you hear my podcast with Lynnleigh Lawson? Do you know about

CHAPTER THIRTY-EIGHT

Harry not being her father?"

Her hand dropped from her side, and she stepped closer, like an involuntary reaction to the news. "I did. I mean, I don't support what you're doing here, but everyone was talking about it, and since it involves my husband, I had no choice." She licked her lips. "That poor girl."

"Right. Can I come in?"

Those lashes flicked open as she scanned the quiet street behind him. Reaching out, she grabbed his arm and pulled him in, slamming the door closed a second later. "People around her talk." Her hands went back to her hips. "You have five minutes. No recording and off the record."

Thirty minutes later, he climbed in his car, his heart thumping hard in his chest. Cindy's words echoed in his brain. "Everyone thought Tina Cox was such an angel. Well, let me tell you, she wasn't. I'm not saying that because I'm jealous of a dead woman. I'm not." Gordon stopped short of pointing out that her repeated denial didn't strengthen her case. "I used to work up at the college before I married Barton. Did you know that?"

"Did you work in the same department as Tina?"

"No, but I saw her a few times and…" She stopped suddenly, holding a finger to her lips. "I shouldn't."

Perhaps she shouldn't, but it was clear to Gordon that this woman wanted nothing more than to spill the beans on her husband's first wife, whatever those were.

"I have to be honest with you. Tina Cox is kind of a saint in this town. And she's dead so…"

Gordon had been sure she'd been about to say something more. "But no one can be that perfect," he said. "The thing is, I need to know the real truth if I'm going to figure out who wanted to kill Lisa and Tina. I need to know if anyone had a problem with Tina. I need to know about her flaws. I need to know about the true state of her marriage."

"Well, Barton doesn't talk about that."

"But you do know something. And it could be the very thing that helps me to find who did this."

It was all the push she needed.

"Well," she said, pushing her hair off her shoulders. "There was this one time on campus. Tina didn't know I saw her. She was getting in a car that stopped to pick her up. I thought it was odd the way she looked around before she got in. So, I walked that way the next day when I took my lunch break, and it happened again. Same car. Same everything. Except the man reached over and touched the back of her neck, rubbing it. I swear she scooted closer, had her hand in his lap."

Gordon had stilled, his pulse quickening. "And?"

"And let's just say the man in the car wasn't Barton."

Gordon almost leaped out of his seat. He'd only been guessing when he'd theorized with Detective Forde, but could it be true? Byron and Tina? He heard the old dean's words in his head. *I believe Tina and Byron became friends. He was broken up about her death, of course, as we all were.*

Picking up speed on the main road, he reminded himself to slow down. If he assumed everything he'd heard was true, he still didn't know how it was relevant to the murders. Tina's murder was almost kind. Would a jealous husband be kind? Possibly, but that didn't make sense either. Besides, Barton Cox had been taking care of his sick mother during the murders. Maybe a spurned lover? And was this why Lisa was upset with Tina? Was this what they were fighting over when Patty Handler saw them at the fundraiser? He rubbed his hand across the back of his neck, an ache creeping upward. He didn't have any facts, only assumptions. And those didn't explain Lisa's murder at all. Maybe if Byron Marks would return his calls, but his office insisted he wouldn't be available for any interviews at all. That only convinced Gordon he was on the right track.

Still rubbing his neck, he considered taking his microphone up to the hospital and planting himself in the parking lot right outside those big glass doors. The Dean had to go inside sometime, didn't he? Gordon would have a minute at most before he was asked to leave, but he knew how to back away when necessary. He didn't expect Marks to answer, but you never knew. He'd gotten lucky before. He'd get right to the point, ask the man if it was true he was having an affair with Tina Cox. He could ask if Byron's wife, Amanda Marks, knew. He could ask… His hand stilled, dropping from his neck. Amanda Marks. One of the women who caused Tina to jump out of her chair with wet hair and run out the back door of the salon.

The ache in his head eased, and his lips turned up in a smile. If Byron Marks wasn't available for an interview, maybe the former Mrs. Marks was.

Chapter Thirty-Nine

Now

All people carried secrets. Callie knew this, and yet, she was continually surprised by the depths people went to in order to hide them. Sometimes, the secret is so deeply buried and so much time has passed that it's genuinely forgotten. Until it isn't. Lisa Lawson had a secret like that. A child with a man that wasn't her husband. She'd told no one. Or at least no one who would admit they knew. Not Harry's brother. Not Patty Handler. Not even Callie's mother. And yet, once the shock had worn off, these same people weren't surprised.

Patty Handler had wasted no time calling Callie after the podcast.

"I didn't know about Lynnleigh, but it makes sense in a way. I remember talking with Lisa and Tina about kids once after they got married. They weren't in a hurry. Harry, for sure, because he knew he'd be gone so much with the Army and would be no help, but not Lisa either. She had a job and was taking classes at night. I swear it was right after that we heard she was pregnant."

"What about the rest of it?" Callie asked. "I know this was a long time ago, but do you remember her coming home that weekend? After she'd moved away?" She'd shared Lynnleigh's conversation with the Army wife who claimed Lisa wasn't in a good way after a weekend at home.

Patty hedged. "I'm not one hundred percent sure it was that weekend, but I think so. Or at least I remember her coming home, and something went wrong."

"Tell me about it."

"With Lisa coming home for the weekend, Tina decided to plan a big girls' night out. I remember we all dressed up, had dinner, and went over to the tavern. There was a band that night and lots of dancing. Tina was the craziest, like always, but I did think she was drinking a little fast. I asked her if things were fine at home, and she laughed. 'Yep, Pats, that about sums it up. Fine.'"

"So, Tina was drunk?"

"We all were—even Lisa, although I could have sworn she'd been drinking Coke."

"That was unusual for her?"

"She drank, but not much. Lisa had a careful way about her. The way she dressed and what she said. How much she drank. She was like that even back in high school. If you didn't know her, she could seem a little standoffish, but she wasn't. Some of the boys called her stuck-up, all except Harry. There was this one guy who used to whistle at her in gym class, and whenever Harry wasn't around, he would be on her like white on rice. Maybe he had a crush on her, or maybe he just couldn't stand thinking she thought she was better than he was. She didn't know how to say she didn't because the idea never even occurred to her."

"Let me guess," Callie said, her fingers wrapping tighter around the phone. "Anthony Battle?"

"Yeah. Creep. That night, he kept trying to dance with her and break into our group. She told him she was married, but he just laughed and said he didn't see any husband around. He even followed her to the bathroom. I remember a bunch of us telling him to get lost."

"Did he?"

"I think so. I didn't see him after that. We stayed another hour, maybe. We thought we were so smart not to drive, and it wasn't that late. Maybe eleven? Anyway, Lisa's parents lived the closest. We split up at Front Street, everyone going their separate ways, promising each other we'd meet the next morning for brunch."

Callie felt the rush of blood in her ears. Young women walking alone at night. It shouldn't matter, but even in Hampstead, it did.

When Patty spoke again, her voice broke a little. "Lisa didn't come to brunch. I didn't see her again for a long time. She was six months pregnant, maybe seven by then. In spite of that, she looked thinner than before, was quieter.

"She never spoke of that night?"

"No. Once, at our tenth reunion, someone brought it up, and what fun it was. I remember how white she looked before she left the room."

There was nothing more to learn, and Callie hung up. Lisa had a secret, but so did Tina. Was her pregnancy her secret, or was it something else? What had Ben said? Avery spoke with Byron Marks alone. Why did he do that? Byron and Tina knew each other, and Gordon claimed Byron had been dodging him for days. It was one of the reasons she'd moved him up on her list. And now, the new Dean had finally agreed to come in with his lawyer. On the phone, he'd admitted he and Tina were friends. Was that all? Why all the secrecy? An incoming text shook her from her thoughts, making her jump.

Gordon: *Got a solid tip on Amber Wall. She's Amber Anderson now, and she's in Topeka. Sending you her number.*

Callie pumped her fist once. Gordon's play had worked. She knew that in light of everything Patty had told her about Lisa, she should go see Lynnleigh right now, but she couldn't. Not until she spoke to Amber Anderson about Battle's alibi. She had her finger at the ready when the phone in her hand buzzed again and Hendo's name flashed on the screen.

"Cal? I'm over at Angie's office with the sweatshirt and box from the Braun house. Confirmed it was blood."

"Well, I guess that's confirmation the break-in wasn't about cheap vases and used laptops. Good work."

"That's not why I called, Cal."

Something in the way he spoke made her body go still.

"Angie's gonna send you the preliminary report on the material." She heard the sound of an inhale and exhale. "Are you sitting down?"

Callie told him she was.

"Good, you're gonna need to 'cause this is some crazy shit."

"What is it?" The words came out harsher than she'd intended, but every fiber of her being was on edge now.

"Angie's still working on getting prints off the box, but she got a hit on the blood right away. DNA matched one victim in the system for sure. Most likely a second. Still waiting on that one." He cleared his throat. "But the thing is, the first match…it's Lisa Lawson, Cal. That sweatshirt is covered in Lisa Lawson's blood."

Callie felt her breath leave her body. A sweatshirt covered in Lisa's blood. It couldn't be. How? "Are you sure?"

"Have you ever known Angie to make a mistake?"

Her mind reeled. In no scenario had she seen them finding the clothes worn by Lisa and Tina's killer. It was the only new physical evidence in the case outside of the video in fifteen years. The sweatshirt and pants could all be tied to the double murder. And the box. "Oh, my God," she said, scrambling to her feet and pulling open files. "That's it."

"What?"

She tossed picture after picture aside until she found it, the same internet photo introduced into evidence by Brock Avery. She knew she'd seen that box before. "It's the knife. The box for the knife."

"There's no knife, Cal."

She knew it was too much to hope for. "He took it. That's why he broke into the house."

"Could be. Either way, we've still got the box and sweatsuit."

"How degraded is the blood?"

"Pretty bad in some spots. But Angie said she had enough good samples to make a positive identification for Lisa Lawson."

"How positive?"

"The sweatshirt is one hundred percent."

The sweatshirt. She remembered what Hendo had said about it. A dark hooded sweatshirt, the kind that could be purchased anywhere. No identifying marks or tags. Popular size. She spun around, zeroing in on the photo of the man who'd claimed Harry Lawson had been buying candy at the Stop 'n Gas and not in D.C. at a grocer's conference. A man wearing a black hoodie. Anthony Battle.

Chapter Forty

Now

Jeremy paced the floor in front of the motel room door, swearing under his breath. "I don't like it, Gordon."

"Neither do I," the podcaster said, even as he threw a microphone into his backpack.

"Let me come with you."

"You can't. I made a deal."

Steps slowing, Jeremy frowned. "Did she agree?"

"Yes," he said. A part of him wished she hadn't, but she did, as he'd known she would. Lynnleigh would do anything to find out the truth about her father. That it would be on his show might not be the way she would pick, but that was the way it had to be.

He pulled off his shirt and rifled through the drawer for a clean one. Pulling it over his head, he thought about the promises he'd made to get this interview, nothing short of selling his soul to the devil. The acid in his stomach burned. He'd promised to hold off telling the sponsors. He'd promised no cops. Just him and Lynnleigh.

It occurred to him that if he'd kept his mouth shut and said no right from the beginning, Lynnleigh couldn't have said yes. But he hadn't. There was the podcast, but it was more than that. He was a coward. She'd hate him with every fiber of her being if he denied her this, and he didn't think he could handle that. She meant too much to him. The man had made promises, too.

That was another thing Gordon was afraid of. What if he changed his mind, or worse, what if he told Lynnleigh something she couldn't live with?

A hand on his arm shook him from his thoughts.

"Gordon, I've been calling your name for like ten minutes." Jeremy stood close, worry lines etched into his face.

His eyes darted to the digital clock that sat on the night table. He let out a sigh of relief. Not ten minutes. Maybe five. He took a breath. He needed to go soon. "What is it?"

"I want you to text me as soon as you get there."

"I will. We'll be fine, Jeremy, but if I haven't texted you again after a half hour, call Detective Forde." He returned to zipping up his backpack and slinging it over his shoulder.

"You don't even know if you can trust this guy. The whole thing is weird."

The crack in his friend's voice made Gordon look up. "You're right. I don't trust him." He didn't know why he said that. He didn't have any real reason to feel that way. He just did. Probably because he was scared, the same as right after his brother died, when his father's grief had turned to hurled accusations and flying fists. No one in the family talked about that night, but Gordon had never been able to shake the feeling that his father wouldn't have reacted the same way if the situation had been different, if it had been Gordon who'd died in the car wreck instead of Max. How many times had his parents asked why Max got distracted? What had Gordon done? He couldn't tell them the truth when he didn't know. Max had been off that night. Gordon thought maybe he'd taken something. He'd been depressed since his girlfriend had moved away and wasted no time meeting someone else. When he'd tried to say he thought Max was sad, his father had flipped. It had been terrifying in the moment. The truth was, a part of him had never stopped being afraid. He avoided fights. He avoided getting close. And look where it had landed him. He'd lost Lynnleigh because he'd been afraid. He knew all of this on some level, but it was a different fear that had driven him these last months and weeks. He'd never been good enough. He'd never been strong enough or tough enough or smart enough.

His brain told him that the therapist his last girlfriend had insisted on wasn't far off when he said, "Your father doesn't want to be proud of you, Gordon. He needs to have an outlet for his unresolved grief."

"So, you're saying there's no point in trying?"

"What I'm saying is that you should focus more on trying to be proud of yourself than worrying about your father's feelings."

It all sounded easy in theory. Less so when his father's voice echoed in his head at night like the owls that hooted in the tree at the corner of the motel's lot.

"How do I do that?" he'd asked the therapist, his voice small.

"One day at a time. You won't always get it right, but you need to forgive yourself when you fail and try again." The therapist had leaned forward, his elbows on his knees. "Trust your gut, Gordon."

Gordon swallowed his doubt and fear now. "I know this seems crazy, Jer, but I have to do it." As he looked at his oldest friend, he felt a wave of love. Jeremy, for all his own quirks and problems, had never let him down. He owed him the same. "Look, I have an idea."

For the next five minutes, he outlined a plan, one that might not make the most sense but felt right. Going with his gut, he told himself.

Jeremy bit his lip as he listened. "I don't know. It's risky. What if he makes a stink? The sponsors could pull out."

"They won't," he said, crossing his fingers behind his back. The guy might be yanking Gordon's chain and be full of shit, but he claimed to know about Lynnleigh's real father. He claimed to know some other stuff, too. "It'll be fine. Can you handle it on your end?"

"Please." His friend spread his hands, palms up. "Is there anything I can't do?"

"Thanks, Jeremy. And listen, if it makes you feel any better, I'll run it by Lynnleigh on the way. If she says no, we'll bail on recording or bail altogether."

"She won't."

Gordon didn't have to think about it. Jeremy was right. Lynnleigh didn't care about risk anymore. She'd already put herself in the glare of the headlights more than once. "Then you'd better wish us luck."

Chapter Forty-One

Now

"I saw Byron Marks was in this morning," the Captain said.

Callie heard the question in his voice. Still, she limited her answer to a single yes.

Jackson, though, wasn't satisfied. "He was a friend of Tina's."

She hesitated. "Captain, you know I can't—"

"It's okay," he said, that resigned tone back. "I get it. I shouldn't be asking."

Callie slowed the car at the stoplight. "I'm sorry."

"Don't be."

Another mile passed before he spoke again.

"I assume you've found Amber?"

Callie hesitated. Like the rest of the town, the captain had heard Gordon's request for any leads on Amber Wall. Living in Topeka, Amber was married now, with two children. She hadn't wanted to talk at first, calling her time with Anthony Battle a phase and one of her biggest regrets. She'd talked about her family, her old friends, even asked after Captain Jackson. Eventually, she'd given Callie what she wanted. The truth.

"Forget that," he said before she could decide what to say. "I told you I get it, and then I went and asked another question."

"It's okay."

"It's not, and we both know it." He shifted to face her. "We also both know Waters would lose his mind if he knew I was even here right now. Are you sure you want to do this?"

Callie half-turned her head toward him while keeping her eyes on the road. "There's no choice unless he wants to sit with Lynnleigh himself. There's that wreck over on Route 449 near the plant and the domestic at that house in Hartwood. That leaves you, Boss." She slowed at a corner before adding, "Hendo and Chang are working on getting a warrant. As soon as they have it, maybe we can end this, but Lynnleigh needs to know what's going on."

"Just not me."

"Captain…"

He waved a hand in the air. "Babysitting it is. Beats sitting at my desk, I guess."

Callie drove down Lynnleigh's street, rehearsing the words she might say in her head. She wasn't sure how Lynnleigh would react to the news about the sweatshirt or the box, but something told her Lynnleigh would appreciate nothing less than the hard truth. She'd give her that, then wait for the fallout. Because there would be fallout.

In the driveway, she looked up at the small house. A light burned in the living room, and she could just make out the shadow of the patrol officer's head through the drawn curtains. She pushed the car door open. "Okay, here we go."

If the young officer she'd seen through the window was surprised to see the captain or learn that he was the man's relief, he hid it well enough. "She went to bed almost an hour ago. Something about wanting to curl up and make it all go away."

Callie considered letting the girl sleep but changed her mind. Things were happening fast now. "I need to wake her up." Her gaze wandered to the darkened hallway. "But maybe I'll brew a pot of coffee first. It's going to be a long night."

"I'll do it," the officer volunteered.

Nodding, Callie moved down the hall, taking in the framed photographs of Harry and Lisa. There was Harry in his uniform before he left for the military. Lisa and Harry in their wedding gown and dress uniform. Holding Lynnleigh. She swallowed the lump in her throat. This was the only family this girl had ever known. Callie took several breaths and knocked. She waited and knocked again. When no answer came, she gripped the handle and turned. Locked.

She stepped back a moment, staring at the door. A presence behind her made her turn around. Jackson.

"Something wrong?"

"I don't know." She found the patrolman filling a thermos from the freshly brewed pot of steaming black coffee.

"What time did you say she went to bed?" Callie asked.

"An hour, maybe."

"She's not answering, and the door is locked."

"Sleeping pill?"

Aloud, Callie agreed it was possible, but that didn't sound like the girl she was getting to know. Why would Lynnleigh take something to knock her out when she'd thrown the hook, offering herself up as bait? She'd be waiting, alert.

Standing in front of the door again, Callie's eyes narrowed as though she could see through it with superhero vision. Raising her fist, she knocked harder, her knuckles cracking against the wood. Silence. A sick feeling rose from her belly to her throat, and she swung back toward Jackson.

"Break it down."

Chapter Forty-Two

Now

After climbing in the car, Lynnleigh had asked a question or two, but since then, nothing. She'd said little when Gordon explained the plan, giving her okay as Jeremy had predicted. More than anything, he ached to know what she was thinking, but he knew better than to push. Who wouldn't need time to process everything he'd told her? Cindy? Amanda? Byron? He'd cornered the young dean at the coffee shop Amanda said he'd always favored. That may have been the most surprising of all.

"Look," the man had said, "I'm remarried now. I want to do the right thing, but I have to think about my family, about my position here at the hospital."

"That's why I'm here, Dean Marks. If you talk to me first, you can be the owner of your story, so to speak. You can tell it your way."

The man had started to stand, shaking his head. "I already talked to that detective, and my lawyer didn't even want me to do that."

"Well, there you go. You're listening to a lawyer who doesn't understand the court of public opinion. A lawyer will only tell you no comment. Whether you answer my questions or not, that won't stop people from talking."

"Talking about what. I haven't done anything."

"You had a relationship with Tina Cox, didn't you?" The man had frozen. "And you were one of the last people to see her alive."

Ashen-faced, he'd shrunk away from the podcaster. "H-How did you know that?"

Gordon hadn't been sure until that moment, and yet, he'd had reason to suspect. Barton went to his mother's every Saturday at ten, and Tina didn't have a hair appointment until twelve-thirty, and still, she was late. That, along with the pregnancy rumors and Tina's quick departure after Amanda arrived at the hairdresser's, told him something wasn't above board. "I know Tina Cox was pregnant, and the baby was yours, which would have made your life pretty difficult. You were married and—"

"Wait." His eyes had widened. "I don't know about any baby. If Tina was pregnant, she didn't say. Besides, I had a vasectomy after my last child with Amanda. You can look that up."

"Those aren't a hundred percent. Everybody knows that." Gordon had lifted one shoulder. "And you left town within days after Tina's murder—the woman you were having an affair with."

"You're twisting things." He'd lurched to his feet, his chair falling backward. Heads had turned to watch the dean jab his finger in Gordon's face. "I left because I took a new position with Mercy General."

"One that you might not have gotten if you'd been in the middle of a messy divorce."

Byron reddened. "We're done here," he said, spit flying from his mouth.

"I talked to your wife," Gordon said. "Your ex-wife. Amanda."

Again, Byron stopped in his tracks, chewing the inside of his cheek. "She hates me. Even after all this time. She'd say anything to hurt me."

Gordon didn't doubt it, but he wasn't about to give this guy a break. "Like I said, you can tell me your story, or you can let others do it for you. It's coming out either way."

He'd thought Lynnleigh might have a comment or response after he'd told her everything the man confessed, but there'd been none other than a thank you. He'd wanted her to be prepared. He understood, but he was still disappointed.

In the silence, he flipped on the radio, spun the dial, found nothing, and shut it off again. A handful of cars rushed past them in the other direction, and they drove on, the already sparse traffic beginning to thin.

"Are we almost there?" she asked, and then half laughed at herself. "That's what kids say on road trips, right? Over and over again until their parents swear they're going crazy."

He grinned with her, relieved that she seemed to have crawled out of whatever funk she'd been in since she'd slid into the passenger seat. "Yeah. My sister would do that. She'd keep asking until my brother Max would start telling knock-knock jokes just to shut her up. That would turn into silly songs, and next thing you know, we were wherever we were going."

She shifted toward him, a glint in her eye.

"What?" he asked.

"That's one of the first times I've heard you talk about your family and smile."

"Oh." He gripped the wheel with both hands. "You might be right. Maybe that's a good thing?"

"Can't be a bad thing."

"Right."

They passed a sign telling them they'd crossed the line into a neighboring county.

"Why are we meeting here again?"

"He picked it." Now that Gordon thought about it, the man's reasons had been vague. "Neutral, I guess."

"But a drive-in? It's weird."

"He probably doesn't want to be seen with us," he said.

"You mean he doesn't want to be seen with me?" She jerked her head toward the window, hiding her face. He wanted to tell her that wasn't true, but he wouldn't lie to her. He had no more idea than she did. Next to him, Lynnleigh tapped on her phone. "There's no movie tonight." She leaned closer to the window, peering up at the night sky. "It'll be dark."

Her words made the hair on the back of his neck stand up. Even if a drive-in meant meeting in the car, he'd thought there would be other people there, all lined up in their cars facing the giant screen. He'd actually pondered this as a problem—a Jeremy problem if he were honest.

"I'm sure it'll be fine," he said now. His voice sounded high in his ear, so he said it once more with more conviction. "The plan will work." He shot her a look from under his lashes. She stared out the window again, her thumbnail in her mouth. Not for the first time, he wondered what he'd gotten them into. They passed a sign for a rest stop, an exit boasting a hotel, another featuring a gas station. Five more miles before they took the exit for another two-lane road, this one with fewer cars and even fewer lights. "We don't have to do this," he said. "I can say you couldn't get away. I can say—"

"No," she said, her voice sharp. "We're going to do this. I need to know what he knows."

He didn't flinch. She'd always been fearless. Not like him. His grip on the wheel tightened. It was on the tip of his tongue to ask her what exactly they would know, but she raised a finger as they passed a sign.

"Two miles."

He drove slowly, partly to avoid hitting a deer and partly to delay their arrival. The closer they got, the more the butterflies fluttered.

"I came here with my parents when I was little," she said, her voice soft now. "To this same drive-in."

"You did?"

"Yeah, a few times. They would hold these movie nights for kids with free popcorn, and we would come, just the three of us. My dad didn't like movies with guns or violence or anything like that, but he loved kids' movies. *Toy Story* was his favorite. He liked Buzz and Woody—I mean, who didn't?—but it was the other toys he really liked. Said they reminded him of growing up. Mr. Potato Head, the slinky, the soldiers. He gave me the Jessie doll one birthday."

"Is that where you first saw *Toy Story*, at this drive-in?"

She shook her head once. "I didn't see it the first time until it came on TV. My dad didn't really like regular movie theaters. He was okay with people as long as they weren't too close, and you know how tight those seats are." She paused, remembering. "That's why he always took the stairs instead of elevators. Most people do that to count steps, but he wanted the space."

Gordon remembered he'd read something in the transcripts about Harry's selective claustrophobia. The prosecution had used it to discredit his claim that he'd been at a grocery conference. They were wrong.

"Anyway, the drive-in mostly showed second-run movies, the kind that had been out for a while. That's why kids' night didn't cost much." She inhaled suddenly. "There it is."

Even in the dark of the night, it was hard to miss the giant billboard announcing the drive-in. Behind the sign, the giant lot sat dark, only a single floodlight marking the location of the snack bar.

He wished he could keep driving, keep her talking, keep her safe, but he knew she wouldn't turn back now. He had no one to blame but himself. He'd set this meeting in motion.

At the entrance, he came to a stop. A heavy metal barrier blocked the pavement that led to the drive-in's lot. He got out, looked around, and slid back inside the car. "It's locked."

Her head rotated back in his direction, her eyes larger than ever in the dim light. "He's here," she said and pointed at the dark car parked near the trees. "It's not far. We can walk from here."

Even being five minutes from the car seemed too far to Gordon, but he said nothing. Instead, he reached into the inside pocket of the light jacket he wore and pulled out a phone. After punching a couple of buttons, he waited, then began to talk. "Jeremy, if you can hear me, send me the text." Less than five seconds later, they heard the buzz of a phone. He checked the text and, with a grim expression, nodded at Lynnleigh. "I guess this is it."

Leaving his headlights shining, Gordon got out and hurried to Lynnleigh's side. Wordless, they slipped by the metal bar. In his mind, he set the scene for his listeners. The air, crisp for this time of year, smelled of dirt and the lingering scent of oil and butter. Overhead, the dark sky pressed down on them, vast and starless. Gravel crunched under their feet. He strained to see the shadow of the snack bar under the light. Long and rectangular in shape, the building's glass door and front windows glowed where the single light shone. If anyone lurked in another window, Gordon wouldn't know; the rest of the building was shrouded in darkness.

"Where is he?" Lynnleigh whispered.

The pair slowed. "Do you have your phone?"

A moment later, she raised her hand, shining the small light on the ground in front of them. Lynnleigh started to walk forward again, but his arm shot out in front of her.

"Wait." He scanned the darkness but saw nothing. Cupping his hands around his mouth, he called out, "We're here." An owl hooted from somewhere in the distance. "We saw your car. Where are you?"

The sound of footsteps in the quiet made Gordon whip around. Next to him, Lynnleigh gasped. He saw him then, the round-shouldered figure of a man stepping forward into the light, a long-barreled pistol in his hand.

"Right here."

Chapter Forty-Three

Now

"**H**oly crap," the young officer said for the fifth, maybe sixth time. "She said she was going to bed. I knew it was early, but I figured she just wanted to be alone, you know."

Although Callie wanted to shake the kid, she knew it wasn't really his fault. In a perfect world, she would have had someone watching the back of the house, but small-town budgets didn't come with a line item earmarked for unlimited surveillance. Instead, she said, "Okay, tell me again exactly who she talked to and what she said tonight."

He ran a hand over his tightly cropped curls. "Sure, but there wasn't anything weird that I could tell. She got a few texts and one call. She didn't act like it was private, didn't even leave the room. I mean, she mostly just kind of sat there and listened."

"You didn't think that was odd?"

"She said it was a sales call and laughed about it, saying that normally she would hang up, but at least it was a distraction from the boredom of sitting in her house. She even said that to whoever called. 'I'm housebound, so I'm probably not the right customer unless you have a magic pill to change that.' Or something like that. Thought that was pretty clever, actually, and figured I could use that one next time someone tries to sell me a leaf blower or another car warranty."

"Okay, so the call ended, and she did what? Watched TV?"

"Well, no. She stayed on the phone a little longer and went to bed about a half hour later. The news was on before that, but I don't think she was really watching."

"Wait, she stayed on the phone? For how long?"

Red suffused the young man's skin, spreading all the way to his scalp. "I don't know. Another couple of minutes, maybe. Five at the most."

Callie bit back on the scream threatening to erupt from every pore. "I need to know every word she said."

When he was finished talking, she stared at her notebook, dissecting the words Lynnleigh had said on her "sales call." *Possibly. How? When?* It didn't take a rocket scientist to deduce the call didn't come from a salesman. Callie had a pretty good idea who did call, though. She tapped on her phone. The call went straight to voicemail. "Goddammit."

Callie found Jackson outside on the phone with Chang.

"Get her picture out to all the locals and start canvassing the area," the captain said. Hanging up, he faced Callie. "Well?"

"I think she's with the podcaster." He arched a brow. "He's not answering his phone. I need to go over there."

"I'm going with you."

She knew she should protest, but she didn't have the will. And there was no reason for him to stay at Lynnleigh's now. In the car, she pressed the gas and shook her head. "I shouldn't have trusted him. I thought we both wanted to keep her safe."

"Don't jump to conclusions, Forde. If she's with him, he's her friend, right? There's no reason to assume anything's happened to her."

"Maybe," Callie said, unable to shake a bad feeling she couldn't explain.

The tires on the city-issued sedan squealed as she pulled into the motel lot. Jumping from the car, she ran toward the room, Jackson right behind her. Light peeked from under the drawn curtains, and she stopped short. Gordon's car wasn't parked out front, but the voices inside made her turn around again. She pressed her ear to the door and drew back after only a few seconds.

"It sounds like Gordon. He's in there." She shouted his name and slammed her fist against the door. The voices droned on inside. "Gordon." Louder this time, the veins of her neck bulging. "Open up. It's Detective Forde."

The inside lock clicked, and the door swung open to reveal not Gordon but Jeremy, a finger to his lips. He grabbed her by the arm with his other hand and pulled her inside. "Wow, you got here fast," he said in an urgent whisper.

"Where's Gordon?" She wasn't yelling anymore, but she didn't whisper either.

The producer tapped his lips with his finger again. His odd behavior made her glad Jackson was right behind her. Jeremy pointed at a phone sitting on a table next to a microphone and a laptop.

Her gaze shifted from him back to the phone when Gordon's voice came over the line.

"You said you'd tell us about Lynnleigh's father if we came, and we did. We're here, ready to listen. Y-you don't need that…that thing."

"After you give me your phones."

Jeremy visibly tensed, his body leaning toward the equipment on the table.

"Why?" Gordon asked.

"Insurance. No recording."

A new voice. Lynnleigh's. "I promise, whatever you say, I won't tell anyone."

Callie's heart sank. She'd been right. Lynnleigh was with the podcaster, but it was small comfort. This was worse than she'd even imagined. So much worse.

"Then giving me your phones won't matter. Don't worry. You'll get them back before you leave." His voice shifted from wheedling to demanding when there was no response. "Now, or else."

Or else what? Callie wondered.

"Okay, okay," Lynnleigh said. "Here."

"Now you." A moment passed. "Stop stalling."

"Gordon, just give it to him," Lynnleigh said. "It's the only way. I need to know what he knows."

"I don't like it."

Neither did Callie.

"It's non-negotiable."

"Please, Gordon. You'll have your story."

"Yes, Gordon, you'll have your story," the man mimicked. Faint rustling noises could be heard over the line. "Good man." Something clattered to the ground, followed by the sound of cracking.

"Hey," Gordon shouted. "You broke those. You promised you'd give them back."

Callie frowned. If the phones were broken, how were they still hearing this? Next to Callie, Jeremy relaxed. She gestured at the voices and mouthed the word "how." Grinning, he whispered, "Gordon's got a second phone in his pocket. He figured no one would guess he had a backup. We're live."

Live? "As in broadcasting?"

"Yep."

It was all Callie could do not to scream. If only she'd gotten to Lynnleigh first. Neither of them knew what they were doing, and it had been reckless and naïve to assume this man wasn't dangerous.

"So, you'll get new ones," the man said. "Did you tell anyone where you were going?"

It was Lynnleigh who answered. "No."

"You weren't followed?"

"Do you see anyone else here?"

The man grunted. "Smartass like your mother, I see. Thought she was better than everyone, didn't she?"

"What? No, she didn't—"

"Not now, Lynnleigh," Gordon said, cutting her off.

"Listen to your boyfriend, Lynnleigh. Not now."

"You said you'd tell me the truth if Gordon brought me here," Lynnleigh said between shaky breaths. "I'm here in good faith. To talk. But I'd feel a little better if you'd put down that gun."

Jackson's hand landed hard on Callie's shoulder, the only thing that kept her from crying out. Catching her breath, she yanked Jeremy into the corner of the room. "You knew he had a gun?"

The young man's brow creased. "Yes. Didn't you get my text? I thought that's why you were here."

She pulled her phone from her pocket, and there it was.

Across the room, the man's voice chided the pair. "And I feel better having it, so I don't think so."

Chill bumps rose on Callie's arms. She looked back at Jeremy. "Where?"

He didn't hesitate, his face pale now. "A drive-in. I'm not sure where, but I wrote down the name."

"I know it," she said. Callie hadn't been there in a few years—not since Ben—but she knew they didn't run movies on weeknights. She pictured the big screen in her mind. It sat at the back of three acres, surrounded on three sides by woods. A parking lot and snack bar were nearer the front but hidden from the road by a thicket of shrubs and trees. Cars traveling past wouldn't even notice the darkened site. In a quick motion, she gestured toward the door. Jackson, seeing the look on her face, stepped outside.

"Thank you," she said to Jeremy. He nodded once, his eyes never leaving the phone on the table. The voice of Gordon sounded as they rushed outside.

"You said you would tell Lynnleigh the truth about her father. You owe her that at least."

In the car, Callie found the app to stream the podcast. As she started the engine, the man's voice spilled out of her phone. "You really are persistent, aren't you? Good at cornering people and getting them to tell you things. It's a shame this will be your last big hurrah."

Loud gasps echoed over the phone, and Callie pressed her foot to the floor. Throwing on the siren, she turned up the volume on her phone. On the screen, she saw a number ticking upward. Listeners. Fifty more. A hundred more. Within minutes, the number climbed by the thousands, no sign of slowing down. Next to her, Jackson was on his own phone.

"Please," Lynnleigh was saying, "I don't care what you do to me, but let Gordon go. I'm the only reason he's here. It's my fault." She half-sobbed. "I just wanted to know. Everything with my mother. With Harry. All of it. Please."

A brief silence followed. In the car, Callie held her breath, every muscle in her body tensed.

The man's answer was soft, different from the voice that had demanded phones and brandished a gun. "It wasn't my fault, Lynnleigh. I want you to know that. After all, I'm not a monster."

Chapter Forty-Four

Now

"I'm sorry," the man said. "We haven't started off on the right foot, have we? I didn't want to hurt anybody. I didn't. If only she hadn't gone and gotten pregnant."

Gordon sensed rather than saw the way Lynnleigh hung on the man's every word. She was so desperate to know. He understood, but something about this man's quick mood shifts scared him—more than the gun aimed in their direction. He forced himself to slow his breathing. He needed to think.

"You didn't know about the baby," Lynnleigh said.

"Not at first. She didn't tell me, did she?" The man couldn't disguise his bitterness. "I guess she wouldn't, but nothing happened like she said it did. She didn't want to talk to me, would barely even acknowledge me."

"Wh-what did she say happened?"

"Lies." His voice hardened. "She was a liar, you know. Stuck up, too. She wouldn't admit it out loud, but deep down, she was. I was never good enough for the likes of her or her friends. Bitches, both of them." The man spat on the ground, and next to him, Lynnleigh flinched.

Gordon reached for her trembling hand. He needed to divert the man's attention somehow, keep his focus away from Lynnleigh. He needed to stall. "Why live in Hampstead? Why not leave and go somewhere else?" Gordon asked.

The man's eyes landed on him then, shining in the darkness, and Gordon's entire body shuddered at the deadness in that gaze.

"This town is like a sickness," the older man said. "Keeps drawing you back. You can't ever really leave—even when you try." He let out a sigh. "It's her fault. All of it was her fault …" his words faded.

Moving closer to Lynnleigh, Gordon frowned. He was having a hard time following what the man was talking about. Aloud, he asked, "Why did you hate Harry?"

In the dim light, the man's face took on a ghostly quality. "What makes you think I did?"

"You framed him for the murders, didn't you?" Gordon said, surprising himself. He hadn't even suspected it until the moment he said it.

"Shows how much you know. He did that all by himself. He was famous for his temper, his paranoia. It was only a matter of time before he ended up behind bars anyway."

Yanking her hand from Gordon's, Lynnleigh took a step forward, her eyes flashing. "He was twice the man you are. How dare you?"

The man's jaw tightened. "I've tried to be nice."

"You call this being nice? You say Harry's going to jail was his own fault? He was innocent. And my mother was a bitch?"

"I said they were both bitches. Both of them." She sucked in a hard breath. "You said you wanted the truth. I'm giving it to you." He took one step forward and then another. Gordon could see the man's upper body now, his shoulders, his outstretched arm. "If you don't like it, that's just too damn bad."

Gordon couldn't take his eyes off the gun, looming large in the man's hand, bobbing up and down with each word. He swallowed, his mouth suddenly dry. "What are you going to do?"

"Shut up," the man hissed. "I'm not talking to you now. I'm talking to her."

Gordon slid close to Lynnleigh again, his heart jackhammering under his shirt.

The man clucked his tongue. "Getting a little more than you bargained for, aren't you?" He waved the gun in Lynnleigh's face. "The truth isn't pretty.

Are you sure you still want that?"

"Yes." Lynnleigh sounded small and tentative, but she lifted her eyes to his, refusing to be cowed. "I'm sure."

"Good," the man said with a gleeful nod. "Listen up then, because I've got a helluva story to tell."

Gordon cringed, more afraid for Lynnleigh than ever. The man was enjoying himself too much.

"Your mother didn't want you. It was Harry who changed her mind, convinced her not to get rid of you. Let's just say she had one drink too many at the Tavern one night, and one thing led to another. Of course, being married, she didn't want word to get out, wanted to forget the whole thing, but there you go."

Lynnleigh's hand floated to her heart. "Wh-what?"

"Don't listen to him, Lynnleigh."

"You heard me," the man said, shooting Gordon a dark look. "You said yourself Harry wasn't your father. I don't know what you expected. Where'd you think you came from? Some sweet adoption. Hell, no. Your mother sure as hell kept the truth quiet, didn't she? Not a whisper, which is saying something in a town like Hampstead. But Harry, he knew. If I had to guess, he regretted that one. Why would a man want another man's bastard?" He cocked his head, watching Lynnleigh closely. "Want me to keep going?"

She swayed on her feet, her hands grabbing at empty air. "I-I..."

"Lynnleigh," Gordon half-shouted, half-screamed. Her legs seemed to give out beneath her, and he leapt forward, but he was too late. Her body, suddenly limp, hit the hard ground with a thump.

Chapter Forty-Five

Now

Callie stomped on the gas, her guttural growl drowning out the live podcast.

Jackson placed his hand on her arm. "Forde, keep your head on straight."

Her mouth clamped shut, and she lowered her head. She breathed in and out. In and out. The captain sat back again. From her phone, they both heard the whisper of voices.

"Lynnleigh, wake up." It was Gordon. "Wake up."

"What's the matter with her?" asked the man, his tone more curious than concerned.

"Are you kidding me? She fainted. You freaked her out, and it's hot as hell out here, and she fainted. What did you expect?"

"She asked for it, didn't she? People always say they want the truth, but that's a lie. They never really do."

A low moan sounded over his words.

"Are you hurt?" Gordon asked.

"I don't think so."

The words sounded weak, but she was alive, and Callie exhaled.

Next to Callie, Jackson said, "We're not far now. Turn the siren off."

He was right. Alerting the man to their presence might do more harm than good. Along with the sudden quiet, the absence of the siren brought an instant calm. Callie's muscles loosened and her pulse slowed. The girl had fainted. That was all.

Gordon helped Lynnleigh to her feet. "Look, you've had your fun. Let us go."

"What's the rush? We're just getting started."

"Lynnleigh needs to lie down. Let us both go, and I promise, we won't say anything about being here or you. We—"

"No."

Callie's head jerked back, hitting the headrest. The vehemence in that one word was like a sucker punch, stealing her breath. She felt Jackson's eyes on her, understood his surprise. It wasn't the man who'd drawn a hard line in the sand. It was Lynnleigh.

"I'm not going anywhere until you tell me why you killed my mother and Aunt Tina. You did, didn't you?" Her clipped tone left no room for question. "This isn't just about Harry or my father. I need to know why you would do such a horrible thing, how you could let Harry go to prison for you."

"Better him than me."

"Is this some kind of game to you?" Lynnleigh's words vibrated with outrage.

"No game. I'll tell you what you want to know, but I don't like your attitude. You need to understand."

"Fine," she said, "I'll try," Lynnleigh paused, "to understand. Like you said."

The way the girl said "to understand", Callie imagined her fingers raised and bent, miming air quotes. The tiniest smile tugged at her lips. The girl had spirit.

"Good," the man said with a grunt.

Time seemed to slow in that moment as Lynnleigh and Gordon, Callie and Jackson, and all the streaming listeners waited for the man to tell his story.

"I loved her," he said, finally. "We'd known each other since grade school. Well, I knew her. I'm not sure she noticed me for the longest time. I'd see her downtown sometimes and try to stand near enough to hear what she was saying. Sometimes I could. Sometimes not. She was never alone. The two of them were always together. Lisa and Tina. Tina and Lisa. Even back then. Like a package. In high school, I started to get a reputation. Not really the good kind, but it did make me stand out, and for the first time, she knew who I was, not that she wanted anything to do with me."

As they neared the sign to turn off, Callie switched off the headlights and slowed the car to a crawl. She pulled onto the shoulder behind Gordon's car.

"The lot is locked," Jackson said.

Callie had expected as much. Searching behind them, she spied a second car parked several yards back, halfway into the trees.

"Did you tell her how you felt?" Lynnleigh asked, some of her anger eclipsed by something even more powerful—curiosity.

"Not at first. I asked her out. She turned me down. Many times. But you know that, don't you?"

Callie climbed out of the car, careful not to make a noise, unsure how far beyond the entrance they were. Drawing her gun, she stuck her head back inside the car. "I'm going in."

"You need backup," Jackson said, already getting out of the car.

"No. You're not even supposed to be here."

"Forde, you can't go in there without backup. The man has a gun."

"Hendo and Chang are right behind us."

"Right behind us isn't here."

From Callie's phone came the sound of Lynnleigh's voice. "What did she ever do to you? What did either of them ever do to you? You didn't have to…"

"I did." Steps echoed through the phone. "I did have to, Lynnleigh. Just like I have to now."

Sirens wailed then, still distant, but close enough to present a problem. Callie's heart jumped to her throat, but before she could say a word, Jackson had his phone to his ear, already barking orders. The sirens turned away, and seconds later, the night went silent again. When no gunshot followed, Callie's body sagged in relief.

"When Hendo and Chang get here, tell them to come around the back side." She squared her shoulders then and checked her vest. "I'm going in the front." In the light of the dash, she saw Jackson shake his head. "That's an order, Captain." She took one step. "Please." Without waiting for a response, she closed the door with a quiet click. Gun in hand, her pulse steady under the heavy vest, she slid past the parking lot barrier to enter the drive-in lot. Callie was in.

Chapter Forty-Six

Sweat coated Gordon's skin, and Lynnleigh's palm felt slick in his hand. Every time he looked down the barrel of that gun, he couldn't catch his breath. He cursed the oppressive heat, cursed the man, but more than that, he cursed his dumb pride. He could say he didn't know why he'd agreed to this, but he did. He'd wanted to be the big man on campus. Solve the crime. Worse, he'd wanted something even more selfish. He'd wanted to be the hero. To be the one to give Lynnleigh peace, but there was nothing peaceful about this man or the gun in his hand.

Suddenly, the man's head whipped around. Gordon and Lynnleigh followed his line of sight. Were those sirens? But no sooner had a tiny seed of hope bloomed before it died again. The sirens turned away, fading along with any chance of being rescued. No one was coming. Not the cops. Not Detective Forde. Maybe the phone in his pocket wasn't working. Maybe Jeremy didn't know the danger they were in. He glanced back at the man. While the quiet after the sirens had left Gordon jumpy and unsettled, the man seemed to visibly relax.

"Time to end this little party," he said, his lips turning up in that weird, Joker-like smile.

Lynnleigh let out a little cry, and Gordon squeezed her hand. This was his fault. He knew it. He had to do something. Anything. Swallowing his fear—or at least banishing it long enough to form words—he stepped toward the man. "So, that's it? You got rejected? That's your reason for killing them both?"

"I told you to shut up." The man waved the gun in his direction again.

Gordon raised his eyes from the gun to the man's face, angry now. "Don't talk to me like that."

The man blinked before his face broke. Peals of laughter echoed in the night. "You're brave, are you?" he managed to sputter between guffaws. "That's good."

Gordon stiffened. He leaned his head back toward Lynnleigh's. "You need to run."

She hesitated only a moment before whispering back. "Not without you."

The man's smile dipped. "No one's going anywhere." Gordon stepped in front of Lynnleigh, putting himself between them. Licking his lips, the man grinned again. "Not before I've gotten to the good part."

Behind Gordon, Lynnleigh sucked in a breath.

"What do you think your mother said to me when she saw me standing in her living room with Harry's knife?"

"I-I don't know."

"Guess."

Gordon looked over his shoulder to see her shaking her head, mouth moving, but no sound coming out.

"She said she doesn't know," he said. "Can't you see how hard this is for her?"

"Shut up. Shut up. Shut up." He lunged at Gordon then, swinging the gun, catching him across the nose. The sharp crack of breaking bone echoed across the empty lot. Gordon rocked backward, his vision blurring. Something wet and warm dripped over his mouth and chin. He blinked hard but could only make out shadows.

"Gordon? Are you okay?"

Lynnleigh's voice seemed to come from somewhere far away. Unsteady on his feet, he listed, his knees buckling under him.

"Gordon?" He tried to answer, but words wouldn't form. Gravel scattered as she jumped to her feet. "You've hurt him."

"He should have stayed out of it. He's even more stupid than I thought. Couldn't take a hint. Practically ran my car off the road following him."

"What are you talking about?"

"None of this would be happening if you'd left well enough alone. I tried to warn you."

"Warn me?" Her hands flew to her mouth. "Oh, my God. Was that you? The bomb in my mailbox?"

"It wasn't supposed to hurt anyone. I only wanted to make everyone pay attention and cancel that stupid podcast. Things could have gone back to normal."

"But Detective Forde? She would have—"

"She would have what? She would have found nothing. Whatever trail there was is as cold as Frosty the Snowman. Their focus would have shifted to crimes they could solve, not fifteen-year-old mistakes."

"My father was innocent."

"You think that matters? The cops want to forget about what they did to him as much as the rest of this town. Even if they did come sniffing around, I had insurance for that. Your father isn't the only patsy in this town. He wasn't even my first choice, but like I said, he buried himself. How was I to know he didn't have a good alibi?"

Gordon's lashes fluttered, closed again. The voices floated over his head like clouds he couldn't quite reach.

"He was your best friend."

"I stood by him, didn't I? No one can say Barton Cox wasn't a solid guy. I never said a word against him, but make no mistake, Harry Lawson didn't have any friends left by then," Barton said. "That's what happens when you're paranoid. No one can stand to be around you. That's what's so ironic about this whole thing. The idea that he would kill Lisa is ludicrous, but everyone believed it. No one could imagine I would hurt Tina. Not beautiful, perfect Tina. I'd loved her my whole life. Everyone knew it."

Gordon opened one eye. Above him, Lynnleigh lifted her palms. "Why?" she asked, voice strangled.

"I told you. She got pregnant. I could forgive the affair. That asshole wasn't going to leave his wife. She said he loved her, but even she suspected I was right. Unlike Harry, I had no interest in raising another man's child. I wanted her to get rid of it. She would have, I think, if it weren't for your mother. She stuck her nose in. Tina was going to keep the baby. Said she was leaving me, didn't love me anymore, and wasn't sure she ever had. Lisa put that in her head. I know she did." The pitch of Barton's voice rose higher the more he talked. Gordon wiggled his fingers, his eyes fully open now. "I told her she couldn't raise a baby alone. What would people say? She laughed at me. Laughed. Said she had Lisa to help her. She'd be fine. Lisa. Lisa. Lisa. I was sick of your mother's interference in our life. She was my wife. Mine!"

"You're insane." Lynnleigh's feet shuffled backward.

"Says the girl who came to a drive-in without a clue."

"They'll find us. They'll know it was you."

Gordon stifled a groan. He had to do something. And then he remembered the phone in his pocket.

"I don't think so," Cox said. "They'll be looking at Anthony Battle after they find the nasty messages he's been leaving on the podcast's website. A search of his shed will put the nail in his coffin when they find my gun and your father's knife."

"Th-the knife? You have it?"

"Thought it was gone, didn't you? Should've been, but Lisa didn't make it easy. It all took longer than I thought, and I couldn't have my mother waking up and noticing I was gone. I had no idea how long those pills would keep her knocked out."

"But where? How?"

"I stashed everything at a housing site I'd been part of. It was easy to drop everything in, left to rot. It would still be there today if it weren't for that damned video. It's insurance now. This will all be over soon."

Gordon found his pocket. If he could get the phone, he'd dial 911.

"You can't."

Gordon's fingers touched glass.

"Who's going to stop me?"

A branch snapped and cracked, and Lynnleigh gasped.

"I am."

Chapter Forty-Seven

Now

"Detective Forde," Cox drawled in the same moment he grabbed Lynnleigh around the neck and pulled her close, the barrel of his gun pressed into her temple. His glasses glinted in the dim light, eyes searching behind her. Without letting go of Lynnleigh, he half-turned, looking over his shoulder to the trees before zeroing in on the snack bar. His gaze returning to the detective, he clucked his tongue. "Playing the Lone Ranger today?"

Callie said nothing.

"Suit yourself. I wasn't expecting you, but no matter. I can kill two—no three—birds with one stone."

Her eyes flicked from him to the still form of Gordon lying on the ground. "Do you really want to kill a cop, Mr. Cox? You know how that will go for you, don't you? There will be a nationwide manhunt. Is that what you want?"

He laughed then, the corners of his lips drawn wide, his smile more sinister than joyful. "What manhunt? Lynnleigh will shoot you right before she turns the gun on herself. No one will be looking for me. No one but the press. They'll come to me as the last survivor of the Hampstead tragedy, but I'll do what I always do. Say nothing. The press, as much as they don't want to admit it, eat that shit up. Barton Cox, stoic, loyal, long-suffering. It's a beautiful thing." He lifted his chin, all smiles gone. "Lynnleigh's been depressed. Everyone knows that. They'll write about how Lynnleigh blamed you and her friend, how she was depressed, how she couldn't go on. There won't be any manhunt."

"Sounds like you've got it all planned out."

"I've always been able to think on my feet, Detective."

"You're a smart man." Callie didn't wait for him to respond. "Does your wife know where you are right now, Mr. Cox?"

It wasn't much of a play, but she wasn't ready to show her hand yet.

He snorted. "My wife doesn't care if I'm on the moon as long as her bank account is high enough and she can be queen of Hampstead. She's not complicated, Detective. Not like Tina."

"You loved Tina."

"She was my wife."

"But you killed her."

"I don't need to explain myself to you. I thought we already established that."

"No, you don't, but let me guess anyway." She needed to keep him talking long enough for Hendo and Chang to take him down, long enough to keep them alive. "Tina was pregnant. She was having an affair with Byron Marks."

The thin smile he wore slipped. "Well, haven't you been a busy little bee?" He cocked his head to one shoulder. "How did you find us, Detective? Did Gordon tell you?"

"No."

"Lynnleigh?"

"No, again."

He snorted then, the sound reminding her of an angry horse swatting away flies. "So, you followed them. I should have figured they'd be too stupid to know. But you, I might have underestimated you, Detective Forde."

"I didn't follow anyone."

He stared a moment as though struggling to make sense of her words before deciding it didn't matter. "Lay your gun down," he said. "Over there by the sidewalk."

"I can't do that."

His eyes glittered like marbles behind his glasses, and his arm tightened over Lynnleigh's chest. He took a step back, dragging her with him. "You can be the first to go then."

"You wanted Tina to have an abortion, didn't you?"

He blinked.

"But she wouldn't do it, would she? You blamed Lisa, convinced she was the reason. You'd always resented their relationship, resented that Tina loved Lisa more than she loved you. You were jealous of Lisa, weren't you?"

"That's not true."

"Isn't it? The truth is, Lisa didn't talk Tina out of anything. Tina wanted a baby, and Lisa supported her the way she always did. The only thing she insisted on was that Tina tell the father. She thought he deserved to know."

"Please. The way Lisa told Lynnleigh's real father?"

Callie ignored him. "They fought about it at the fundraiser. That's what Patty Handler saw that night. Tina hated that Lisa was upset with her, but they could never stay mad at each other for long. Tina had made another decision, though. She was going to leave you, wasn't she?"

Barton's lips parted. "How do you...?" He gave a shake of his head. "Enough." He took another step back from Callie.

"How do I know? Everyone knows."

The gun at the girl's temple slipped. "You're lying."

"You murdered Lisa because you thought she convinced Tina to keep the baby," she said, mind racing. Where were Hendo and Chang? She needed them here. Now.

"Lisa did convince her. She knew how much Tina wanted a baby, and she knew about the abortion Tina'd had when I went away to college. She didn't even tell the guy, because why? He'd dumped her before she even knew about the baby. I was the one she could count on. I came back. I was the one who was always there for her."

Some of the pieces clicked into place for Callie then. Not quite a knight in shining armor, but he'd come armed with compassion and worship. That must have looked good to a girl who'd had her heart broken.

"She deserved better than him. She deserved someone who understood how special she was, who would take care of her, who would always look out for her."

"Like you?"

"Yes. She was always mine. Is still mine."

The depths of the man's obsession with Tina hadn't waned. He'd hidden it well enough when he was younger, but now, Callie could see the cracks. It was time to find out what the truth might do. "Byron Marks wasn't the father of Tina's baby."

His lips parted ever so briefly before slamming shut again. "Bullshit. We'd tried for years."

Callie shrugged. "I've read the autopsy report. Lisa insisted Tina tell you, even though she was going to leave you."

His forehead creased. "That's a lie."

"If you say so." Callie lowered her head enough to scan the woods from under her lashes. Had that shadow moved? She needed to keep him talking a little longer. "How long had you planned to kill Lisa?"

His lips twisted into a sneer. "First the lies and now this. You think this was about Lisa? It was never about her. That was the bonus. It was about Tina. Everything was always about Tina. She needed to be punished. All I'd done for her. Everything I put up with, and she was going to leave me? I was never going to let that happen. And then it came to me. I could get rid of Lisa and punish Tina at the same time."

"Oh, my God," Lynnleigh breathed, tears streaming down her face.

"I made her watch," he said, his face distorted in memory. "That was her punishment. To watch every single time Lisa bled, to hear every single time Lisa screamed and know it was her fault, all her fault. She should have been grateful."

Lynnleigh cried out, the sound strangled in her throat, but Barton only laughed.

"She begged me to stop. I knew she would. She cried the way she always did. Made all kinds of promises, but it was too late for that." His voice dropped lower, reliving the moment. "I couldn't let her leave me and have another man's baby. She had to be stopped. Not that I wanted it to come to that. You understand, don't you? She gave me no choice."

Swallowing the bile that rose up in her throat, Callie forced a nod. Back was the man who wanted understanding and forgiveness, and for a brief moment, he was Barton Cox again, mild-mannered accountant, devoted husband, community leader. She wondered when Tina had discovered the dark side of Barton's obsession. Was it after five years? Ten? Did she make excuses for him? Did she feel guilty about his love for her? Did she suspect it wasn't love, but something else, something deadly?

"She gave you no choice," she repeated.

A shadow slid down the outer wall of the snack bar and slowed, halting. Hendo or Chang—she didn't know which—had taken up position. A quick glance and she confirmed that a second detective had materialized in the trees. She sucked in the night air, taking a deep breath. She wasn't alone now, but Barton Cox would not be an easy man to take down. Unpredictable under the best of circumstances, he might snap at any sudden movement. The last thing she needed was a shootout in the dark with a hostage. Before she could execute a plan, Gordon groaned and pushed himself up on one elbow.

"Detective Forde was right," he said, his words slurred and thick through his broken nose. Breath ragged, he struggled to sit up. "Everyone knows what you did—or they will soon."

"God, will he ever shut up?" Cox asked with a growl.

Under Barton's arm, Lynnleigh whimpered, and Callie's unease turned to dread. There was no more time to wait. She widened her stance, her body tensing.

"On the podcast," Gordon said. He'd managed to sit all the way up by then. The skin of his cheeks looked ghostly in the light, and blood covered the lower half of his face. "The one on now. You and me and Lynnleigh. We're live."

Barton blinked once, his voice incredulous. "That's not possible."

"On my phone."

"I took your phones. Smashed them."

"Not all of them."

Callie's heart thudded under her vest. "Don't move, Mr. Cox."

He either didn't hear or didn't care, his focus on the younger man.

"You're surrounded," she said. In the next second, Hendo and Chang stepped out of the darkness, their own guns drawn.

His head jerked up then. Anger flashed, and before she could react, he pressed the girl's body to his, blocking any shot from their vantage points. "Back up," he said, "or I'll shoot her." He dug the barrel into the soft skin at Lynnleigh's hairline.

"Everyone can hear you. You're on now," Gordon said, raising his own voice. "Live. We're live," he said again. Callie understood what he was doing, desperately trying to drag Barton's attention away from the girl and the detectives, keep the man concentrated on him and him alone. It was brave, and she watched helplessly as the podcaster lifted his arm and waved the second phone in the air, the screen coming to life in his hand. "Say hello to my listeners."

Callie saw the way the truth dawned on the man, the way the shock made his features go slack, his glasses slipping down his nose.

Her finger tightened over the trigger, and she advanced one foot, two. Following her lead, Hendo and Chang moved in tandem with her, closing the circle around him.

Gordon kept talking—to his listeners now—struggling to enunciate through his broken nose. "As you've all heard—"

Barton's shriek ripped through the air, the sound more animal than human, and Callie shivered in spite of the sweat dripping into her eyes. Hendo and Chang froze, too stunned to move. From somewhere came the sound of sirens closing in, drowning out his cries. The girl, trembling from head to toe, openly sobbed now. Nostrils flaring, Barton seemed to notice Callie creeping forward for the first time and bared his teeth.

"Back off," Barton half-screamed. "I could shoot any one of you right now," he said. "Take you all down with me. And before you run your mouth about how there's three against one, you don't have to tell me I'd be dead before I could take a step, because I will have taken one of you with me. That makes me the winner." He hurled the threats like lasers, hot with fury.

Callie calculated the distance between them. Still not close enough to tackle him before he could get off a shot.

"Not you, Detective," Cox was saying. "You get to be the one who lives. There's something poetic about the idea of you having to raise a glass in memory of one of these idiots."

His gaze landed on Hendo then. "I remember you. You came around after Harry was arrested. Drove me to the station to be interviewed yet again. Kept telling me how sorry you were. My wife. My best friend. Poor Barton Cox. Everyone said it. You were just like all the others. Too stupid to know what was right in front of you."

"We all made mistakes," said a new voice from the trees. "Me more than the others."

Behind his glasses, Barton's eyes grew wide. "Captain Jackson, come to clean up your mess?"

The captain ignored the question. "It's over, Barton."

"It's over when I say it's over."

Jackson's steps crunched over the ground, his shape still shrouded in semi-darkness. "I can shoot you right now."

"In the back?"

"Why not? My career's already over. You made sure of that. It would be poetic, right, just like you said." Callie's heart rose up in her throat. She'd never heard Jackson talk that way before. It was true the Chief had banished Jackson and made noises about pushing him out. That would kill him, but this went deeper than that. He'd failed to bring Lisa and Tina's killer to justice. How far would he go to assuage that guilt now?

"You're a changed man, are you? That's not the detective I remember."

Jackson ignored the jab. "Last chance. Put your gun on the ground and your hands in the air."

Straining to see in the dark, Callie caught a glimpse of Jackson stepping out from between two large trunks. Near enough to register the three guns trained on Barton and the single one buried in Lynnleigh's hair. The captain's face hardened.

Callie still had no shot. The girl remained trapped against Barton, her body blocking even a headshot. Hendo and Chang would need to move to have an angle that didn't endanger Lynnleigh. The sound of her sobs had subsided. She no longer swayed on her feet, and her arms, limp moments earlier, were stiff with anger, fear, or maybe both now.

"Don't come any closer," Barton said. "I'll kill her. You know I will."

Captain Jackson's steps came to a halt. "You'll be dead, too."

"I'm dead either way." His laugh was joyless, a clipped barking sound. "If I can take the last Lawson with me, so much the better. Either I kill her, or you do when you shoot me."

Lynnleigh's light eyes darkened, and her fingers curled one by one, hands balling into fists.

"I've got nothing to lose, do I?" asked Barton.

Callie felt sick to her stomach. If there had ever been any chance of him giving himself up, it was gone now. He'd kill Lynnleigh before he'd let them take him.

Sirens and tires screeched at the entrance to the drive-in. Doors slammed.

"Tell them to back off."

Callie's gaze flicked to Hendo, and she nodded. He raised his radio, giving the orders.

Barton shuffled to his right, further from the reach of the single light over the snack bar, keeping Lynnleigh close. Jackson moved with him, like a shadow, keeping his distance. Barton muttered under his breath, the words too low for Callie to make out.

Locking eyes with Callie, Lynnleigh's chin tilted upward ever so slightly. Callie drew in a breath. She knew that look. It wasn't much different than the one in Mrs. Holcomb's classroom, challenging Callie to break through her shell. Whatever fight the girl possessed might have been dimmed for a little while, but it hadn't been extinguished yet.

Giving Lynnleigh a brief nod, Callie stammered out the first thing that came into her head. "Let Lynnleigh go, and we can take that into consideration, figure something out."

"Too late."

"You don't know that. You've been under a lot of stress, haven't you?"

Behind Barton, Jackson tiptoed lightly. "If you let her go, that will count in your favor. Maybe the prosecutor will show some leniency. It has to count for something, right, and—"

The man's grip loosened for less than one second, no more than a fraction, but it was enough. Lynnleigh's head, which had crept forward ever so slightly, now swung back with such force, the crack of bone on bone sent a shiver up Callie's spine. Barton stumbled backward, his hand flying to his face. Lynnleigh shot forward, tripping and falling to the ground. The single blast tore through the night, sending Callie reeling. Hendo and Chang charged in to find Lynnleigh scrambling backward to Gordon, his blood pooling on the ground.

Howling like a wounded animal, Barton advanced. Catching herself, Callie brought her gun around, taking aim, but another shot sounded first, followed by the sound of nothing at all.

Chapter Forty-Eight

Now

Callie looked up from her phone and smiled. "Welcome back to the land of the living," she said. Gordon hadn't gotten his color back, and he was still connected to too many blinking machines, but he was awake. That was something.

He blinked, his gaze moving from her to the IV, to the fluorescent lights, and to the huge whiteboard on the wall.

"Lynnleigh?" he croaked, brow crinkling.

"She's fine. She just went home to change her clothes."

His eyes closed again, and he took a deep breath, the air whistling through his nose. When he opened them again, he asked, "She's coming back?"

Callie nodded. "She should be back in a half hour, or so. Until then, you're stuck with me."

"It could be worse," he said, the words coming out in fits and starts, lips twitching.

She burst out laughing. When she caught her breath, she lifted the cup Lynnleigh had filled for him. He drank eagerly. "I think I'm supposed to tell someone you're awake," she said.

He reached a hand out to touch her arm. "Not yet. Tell me what happened after…after I was shot."

She hesitated, thinking about Lynnleigh's bravery and the way the girl had driven Barton back, risking her own life to give them a chance. In the chaos, Barton had panicked. Falling backward, he'd pressed he trigger. No one would ever know for sure if he meant to hit Gordon, but she suspected it was random. The young man would survive, his injuries critical but not fatal. He'd lost a lot of blood, though, and his face looked like he'd been hit with a two-by-four. Still, with rest and physical therapy, he'd be fine.

"Barton was shot."

"How?"

She told him about Captain Jackson and how he'd somehow gotten a shot off before anyone else, dropping Cox in less time than it took to snap her fingers. He listened without interrupting, biting his lip once or twice. When she finished, he frowned.

"Will he make it?"

Again, she hesitated. Barton Cox had murdered two women. He'd let his friend die in prison for his crimes. He'd shot Gordon and would have killed Lynnleigh given the chance. Many believed only death was good enough for the man who had once been the recipient of an entire town's sympathy and admiration. They'd put him on a pedestal, and they blamed him for it. But Captain Jackson wasn't one of those men. He'd shot Barton in his right shoulder, the impact causing his arm to go limp. Within a minute, he'd been surrounded and placed under arrest.

At the hospital, Barton had tried to stab himself with a pen he'd swiped from a nurse. After that, he'd been sedated and strapped down until he could be transferred to prison, shoulder wrapped and arm in a sling. Cindy had filed for divorce without visiting her husband one time.

Chief Waters had nearly blown a gasket that Captain Jackson was on the scene, much less fired his gun. If he didn't suspect mutiny, he might have fired the captain on the spot. As it was, he invoked a suspension, but already he was backtracking. He needed Jackson, and he knew it. But none of that was for Gordon's ears.

"He will," she told him now.

"Was that true—what you said about the baby—that it was Barton's?"

"Well, no one thought to test until later, but yes. I think their relationship had fallen apart, and whatever happened between them in those last months and years had been hard on Tina. When he didn't believe her about the baby, that only confirmed for her that she'd made the right decision about leaving him. It never occurred to him that he might be killing his own baby in spite of everything. How could she be leaving him if that were true?" She offered a smile, changing the subject. "Anyway, you and your podcast made the nightly news," she told him. "You went viral."

"Huh." He gestured for more water. "Guess you weren't too happy about that."

"I'm still not, if I'm being honest. I don't know what you were thinking, putting yourself and Lynnleigh in danger for everyone to hear. What if it had gone wrong—which it almost did?"

He blanched but stopped short of an actual apology. "I could have done things differently, but all's well that ends well, right?"

"No, Gordon. Barton Cox is going to stand trial, and finding a jury that hasn't heard your podcast or seen a post about it is going to be next to impossible. Do you understand that?"

"But he confessed. Jeremy was supposed to cut the feed after he confessed and contact you if anything went wrong."

"He did."

"Good." Gordon sank deeper into his pillow. "It's over then. Case closed. That might not have happened if we didn't set up that live event."

She squirmed, regretting starting this conversation at all. Maybe she liked him better asleep. Clearly, his ego hadn't suffered any injury. "Gordon, if I were you, I'd rethink—"

"Thank you," he said, cutting her off. "You saved my life and Lynnleigh's. If you hadn't shown up, I don't know what would have happened."

She studied him a moment. "How did you know it was Barton?" She didn't tell him about the warrant they'd been seeking after learning from Byron that Tina had become afraid of Barton or that they'd found bloody clothes that would have been tied back to him in time. From there, it wasn't hard to figure out he'd given his mother a little extra sleeping aid on the day of the murders.

"I didn't. Not really. I'd interviewed dozens of people by then and read every file too many times to count. I thought maybe if I confronted Byron Marks, he'd tell me Tina had threatened him or something, but all I really learned was that he didn't know about any baby. I started to think what real motive did he have? If not Byron, who would want Lisa and Tina dead?" He paused to sip again. "Then I remembered what you said at that press conference, how you needed to consider the murders from a variety of angles and perspectives, including motive and opportunity. I'd been to see Cindy. She gave me an earful, and that got me thinking, too. She'd spent her entire marriage competing with the memory of a dead woman." He shook his head once. "That's when I realized Barton hadn't moved on. Not really. Lynnleigh didn't want to believe it at first, but then she started thinking about how he'd never really reached out to her, never really seemed like he cared. And then she remembered how much time Tina had been spending at their house before she was killed, not so much that she'd moved in, but more than normal. And so, I contacted him about being on the podcast. He balked at first, and then he said he knew something about Lynnleigh's real father." Gordon's eyes filled with tears. "He said he'd talk to me if it was both of us, so he could tell her the truth. I almost got her killed, didn't I?" His head rolled from side to side against the pillow. "It was stupid, I know. You saved us both. Thank you."

Momentarily speechless, Callie didn't know what to say. Once again, the kid had surprised her. "It's like that bullet made you nicer and smarter."

He half-laughed and grabbed at his side, the pain making him wince. "I'm not sure everyone would agree with you." He lifted a shoulder. "But you know what, that's okay."

She was about to ask him what he meant but thought better of it. Instead, she said, "Happy to have worked with you, Gordon Little, but let's not do it again, okay?"

A grin split his face. "Wait, can you say that first part again? About being happy to have worked with me?"

"Absolutely not," she said with a laugh. "And if you tell anyone I said it, I'll deny it."

His hands came up in mock defense. "Yes, ma'am. Guess I'll have to find a new partner on my next case."

Callie didn't understand the podcasting business or the phenomenon of true crime addiction, but she did understand human nature. There would always be people who slowed down at car wrecks or set their recorders for shows like *Dateline* and *48 Hours*. They wanted to bear witness, as long as it wasn't happening to them. Gordon let them see with their ears, let them follow along with him, let them try to think like investigators. And he was good.

"Guess you will. I'm happy for you." This was the truth at least. Callie was saved from saying more when Lynnleigh slipped through the door, eyes lighting up when she saw Gordon awake. The girl had barely left his side since he'd been brought in. Jeremy, too, had taken up residence in the room more often than not. She remembered her conversation with Lynnleigh from earlier.

"Did Anthony Battle assault my mother?"

Callie had been expecting the question, but she wished she had a better answer. "If he did, she never filed a complaint."

"Did you bring him in? Did you ask him?"

She'd looked the girl in the eye. "He says he didn't touch her."

"He's done it before. Assaulted women. Just because he wasn't charged doesn't mean he didn't do it." Callie said nothing. Lynnleigh snorted and looked away. "There are DNA tests."

"There are," the detective said. She considered saying more, but changed her mind, unsure if it would do more harm than good. Anthony Battle had lied about seeing Harry that day. She couldn't say why exactly, although she had a few guesses. Even now, he refused to budge from his story that he'd made a mistake. But Amber had told the truth all those years ago. He'd been with her during the murders. He'd achieved minor hero status during that trial, but he'd fallen quickly after. Even before that, he was a drunk with a bad temper, flitting from odd job to odd job. Amber had stopped short of saying he'd hit her, but she'd said enough for Callie to understand that Anthony Battle didn't think much of women. Never had and never would. No one would accuse him of being father material.

"I loved my parents," Lynnleigh had said finally. "And they loved me. Maybe Harry wasn't my biological father, but he chose me, he chose to be my dad." She looked up at Callie. "You know, there was never a single day I didn't feel loved. Not one."

"That's a lucky thing to be able to say."

"It is, isn't it?" A single tear trailed down her cheek, and she wiped it away. "I think maybe I've already had the best parents I could have." With that, she'd left to shower and change clothes.

Lynnleigh rushed to Gordon's bedside now. "You're awake."

Callie stood up. "That's what I said." Grabbing her hat, she gave Lynnleigh the chair and nodded at Gordon. "I'll let the nurse know," she said, well aware she probably should have done so the minute Gordon came to.

"No need to rush about it," the young man said, blushing through a flurry of kisses.

Letting the door swing closed behind her, Callie felt her own lips turn up into a grin. Maybe she'd take her time after all.

Acknowledgments

Life gets in the way sometimes. We're busy. Things happen. Sometimes good things and sometimes bad. Either way, they can stop us in our tracks. Like everyone, it's happened to me. During the writing of this book, I found myself on that roller coaster, often distracted, and frequently short on time. Bringing this story to life turned out to be a series of sprints (stops and starts and feverish writing sessions) instead of the normal marathon (long but steady). As most authors will tell you, there's no right or wrong writing process—there's *your* process. For the first time, my process was a little topsy turvy. In the end though, that makes *The Murderer's Girl* a survivor and for that, this book will always be close to my heart.

Whenever I finish a book, I always begin tallying a mental list of everyone I need to thank. I do my best to include everyone, but if I've left someone out, please know that it wasn't intentional.

First, thank you to all the people who put together and work on true crime podcasts. Confession: I do listen to true crime podcasts (I am a crime fiction writer after all). I have some favorites and some I like less. I don't listen all the time, but if the host makes the story compelling, I'll stick around. Out of this love for a good true crime podcast, Gordon Little was born.

The words that introduce you to Gordon (and his love of chicken wings) flowed onto the page without much work. I could see him and hear him in my mind. No, he's not based on any one podcaster, but his eagerness to prove himself in an increasingly competitive business could probably describe many real life podcasters.

Podcasts come in all shapes and sizes. There are heavily sponsored podcasts with big name hosts and smaller podcasts recorded in closets with inexpensive microphones purchased at a local Wal-Mart. Gordon is a little of both. He is still amateur enough to second guess himself but persistent enough to keep trying.

Within these pages, I've tried to strike a balance between the podcast and the police investigation. According to my research, how police departments interact with private citizen podcasts can vary depending on a number of factors, most importantly, how active the investigation might be. In *The Murderer's Girl*, Callie inherits what's essentially a cold case but is reclassified as fully active. It's the perfect set up for a true crime podcast!

I'm often asked at writing conferences about setting which leads to a discussion of the small town setting in this Callie Forde series. Hampstead, Virginia is fictional, a product of my imagination. None of the streets are real or the plant or the college. However, the nearby towns of Charlottesville and Richmond are. I wanted to create an enclave that pulled from some of my favorite things in several small college towns in Virginia (we have several). I hope you love Hampstead as much as I do.

As I said earlier, my writing process with this book included a lot of quick writing sprints. Thankfully, my good writing friend, Kris Kisska, and I meet on a regular basis for this very purpose. It's amazing how many words a writer can get onto the page when they turn off their phone and turn on a timer. Thank you, Kris.

Many people believe that after an author finishes writing and types those two little words, THE END, the book is done. We wish! In truth, it's only after the first draft is finished that a lot of the real writing gets done. Characters are fleshed out, plot lines are tightened, and scenes are trimmed or expanded. For me, that stage of writing is just as satisfying as the discovery of the story itself. But it also helps to have early readers to look at those pages with a clear eye. I've shared this before, but I'll say it again, the two I go to first are my daughter, Cameron Murphy, and my sister, Donna McGrath. Their feedback is always objective and insightful. Also, if those two can't be honest with me, no one can! Another early reader was Sue Pfeffer. Thank you, Cameron, Donna, and Sue.

Book clubs are the best, and I'm lucky to have visited many, but I'm even luckier that my own book club has chosen two of my books as our picks.

Authors love getting to talk about their books, but it's even more special when it's with friends. Thank you so much.

Mystery writers are a truly supportive and generous community. I am so thankful. I won't name names here because, frankly, I'm afraid I'll leave someone out but I think you know who you are. However, in a more general sense, I am grateful for all my author friends in my local chapter of Sisters in Crime and in RVA. You are the best! Thank you to my wider circle of author friends who have blurbed for me, promoted a post, or shared my books. I hope I can always do the same for you. Thank you to the authors I raise a glass with, sit on panels with, and share war stories with. I always come home inspired by all of you and look forward to the next time. Thank you.

Of course, I don't know what I would do without my extended Murphy and Larsen families. They never fail to ask about my books, order my books, and share my books. The same is true for my family of friends. From Ginger, Virginia, Ann, Anne, and Martha to Dodi, Tracey, and Becky, to Brooke, Marcia, Karen, Cheryl, and Mary to Karen and Jen, and Shelley and Karen, and Kate, Beth, Maria, Lisa, and Beverley, and so many more, thank you!

A HUGE thank you to all my newsletter subscribers and the readers who seek me out at conferences and book festivals. Whether it's sending me a sweet email or finding me to sign a copy of my book, it makes my day each and every time! Thank you.

Thank you to the incredible team at Level Best Books. Thank you to Deb Well for all you do. Thank you to my amazing editor Shawn Reilly Simmons who gives her best so that our books can be their best. Thank you!

Thank you to my son, Thomas Murphy, for the design of the front cover. It was my hope that the Callie Forde books would feature dramatic and eye-catching covers and his original artwork does just that. Thank you so much.

Thank you to my agent, Rebecca Scherer, for her enduring support through this author journey and may it continue for many years to come.

Thank you to my late husband, David, for sending the bluebirds and the occasional hawk. I feel you every time. And finally, thank you to my children,

Cameron, Thomas, Luke, and Meredith for being you. I am the luckiest
mom ever.

About the Author

The first thing K.L. Murphy wrote was a modified screenplay of a 1970s TV show. She and her siblings performed that show for their own built-in audience (mom and dad) to rave reviews (again, mom and dad!). Later, she moved on to high school journalism before graduating from college and taking a detour into finance and banking. Once she began writing again and focusing on fiction, the process felt like coming home.

K.L. Murphy is the author of *Last Girl Missing* (Book 1 in the Detective Callie Forde series) and the forthcoming *The Great Forgotten* (November 2025) as well as the award-nominated *Her Sister's Death,* a January 2023 Once Upon a Book Club Pick. Of *Her Sister's Death, Publishers Weekly* said, "Murphy keeps the tension high..." and "readers will eagerly turn the pages" and *Library Journal* called the book "[A] riveting tale..."

In addition, she is the author of the Detective Cancini Mystery Series featuring *A Guilty Mind, Stay of Execution*, and *The Last Sin*. Her short stories have appeared in several anthologies and she co-edited *Crime in the Old Dominion*. K.L. makes her home in Richmond, VA, where she loves spending time with her family, friends, and two amazing dogs.

AUTHOR WEBSITE:

https://kellielarsenmurphy.com/

SOCIAL MEDIA HANDLES:
https://www.instagram.com/k.l._murphy/
https://www.facebook.com/klmurphyauthor/

Also by K.L. Murphy

Last Girl Missing (Level Best Books)

Her Sister's Death (CamCat Books)

The Last Sin (HarperCollins/Witness Impulse)

Stay of Execution (HarperCollins/Witness Impulse)

A Guilty Mind (HarperCollins/Witness Impulse)

Short Stories in *Deadly Southern Charm, Murder by the Glass, First Comes Love Then Comes Murder, Friend of the Devil: Crime Fiction Inspired by the Songs of the Grateful Dead, and Crime in the Old Dominion* (co-editor)